THE MINOTAUR

A GODS AND MYTHS NOVEL

SOPHIE ASH

CONTENT WARNING

This book contains graphic violence and gory death scenes.

Our main characters enjoy primal play, dirty talk, and other sexual acts intended for adults.

Chapter 7 contains an attempted sexual assault by a minor character.

Themes present in this book include: sexual assault, abuse of power by a corrupt government, classism, exploitation, and loss of family/community.

1

ARIADNE

"Ariadne Saavas." A guttural voice called my name through the door, followed by four heavy knocks. "This is the MSP. We need you to come with us."

Mom and I exchanged confused glances across the table. Her brows knitted together, the lines in her forehead deepening. Before either of us had a chance to speak, the pounding came again.

"Ariadne Saavas. This is the MSP. We need you to come with us." The officer's tone didn't shift a fraction the second time. He sounded almost robotic.

The third set of knocks followed right after, and this time, I jolted up from the kitchen table and scrambled for the door, which buckled pathetically under the weight of the shifter's fist.

"Ari, don't!" my mother hissed at me under her breath. Fear shone brightly in her eyes, her arthritic hands clasping together on the tabletop.

I hesitated a foot away from the door, looking at her to see if she had any other ideas. But no, she was just as frightened of what stood behind that door as I was and wanted to delay the inevitable.

When the MinoTek Shifter Police came knocking, you always answered.

"If you don't open this door, we will be forced to come in and remove you from the premises," called the voice from the other side. And I knew he would make good on that promise. I'd seen it happen to others.

I slid open the deadbolt and pulled the doorknob—no fancy panels or pressurized sliding doors for us—to greet the massive shifter on the other side.

His face looked like that of a normal man, a boy really, around eighteen years old or early twenties. His low, guttural growl that called my name did not match his young, clean-shaven baby face. Neither did his body, which was the biggest clue that this man was no ordinary human. He stood at least seven feet tall and was absolutely hulked out with muscles that didn't look real.

"Ariadne Saavas." He repeated my name in that flat, robotic tone before holding his hand out, palm up.

My heart sped up at the thought of him yanking me over the threshold like I was a piece of string, never to return or see my mom again. But no, he wouldn't do that. As downtrodden as we were, the City-State of MinoTek had protocols in place.

Kidnappings never happened, and never by the shifter police. Crime was practically nonexistent in MinoTek. I had nothing to fear. This was just a routine neighborhood check.

Still, my hand shook as I extended it toward the massive police officer. He took my wrist, turning the inside up with a hand the size of a dinner plate, and scanned the ID chip in my wrist with the handheld scanner in his other hand.

When the red laser light turned green and the scanner

chirped at the confirmation of my identity, he released my hand and returned the scanner to his belt.

"I need you to come with me," he said in that same flat tone.

My throat went dry, and I swallowed to bring back some moisture. Beyond him in the courtyard of our apartment complex was another officer standing next to a MSP squad car. The car he assumedly wanted me to get into.

"Can I ask what this is regarding?" I asked in a small voice, bringing my forearm protectively to my chest.

"Your presence is required at the capitol. I don't have the clearance to say any more."

I looked over my shoulder at my mom, who had started to get up from the table. "No, Mom. It's okay." I extended a hand in her direction and forced out a smile. She couldn't take her arthritis medication for another hour, and her knees would be painful if she stood and walked around too much.

"Well, what do they want?" She blinked at the man in our doorway, eyes narrowed and suspicious.

"They want me to go with them for...something." My gaze returned to the officer. "Listen, can we do this another time? I'm my mother's only caregiver. She depends on me to—"

"No. Your presence is required now." The officer's face flickered with some emotion breaking through his robotic stoicism. "If you do not come willingly, we will be forced to physically remove you."

Everyone knew about the shifters' inhuman strength. There were photos of them lifting cars to apprehend suspects and shoving grown men into their squad cars like kittens into cages. The last thing I wanted was to be handled in such a way, but I also couldn't leave Mom alone.

"How long will this take?" I asked. "I need to be back within a few hours."

"I don't have the clearance to say. You must come with us now."

My mind swirled with confusion. What did the MSP want with *me*? Mom and I did everything MinoTek demanded of us. We never stepped out of line. Except, well...

My thoughts drifted to the pamphlets on the kitchen table, a publication titled *The Black Papers*. We'd been reading them before the knock came at the door. MinoTek frowned upon criticism of the state and radical opinions, but *everyone* read those articles. They were distributed freely, stuck in the crack of our door every week, and the only entertaining thing available to read, honestly.

The shifter stepped forward at my hesitance, the sudden invasion of space forcing me to step back. His guttural voice morphed into a low, canine growl. I barely heard Mom's gasp over the sound as his face changed. The officer's baby face was gone, replaced by that of a snarling wolf with gray fur and long, white teeth.

"This is the last time I will ask you, Ariadne Saavas. Come with us to the capitol, or I will be forced to remove you."

I'd never heard a shifter speak through his animal form before, but those snarling wolf jaws were enough to force my compliance without the repeated command.

"I'm coming," I choked out through my parched throat, heart racing. "I'll go. I just...just need a minute."

The wolf shifted away, and the baby-faced officer returned. "You have sixty seconds." He turned, ducking under the door frame to wait outside.

Once he was gone, our meager, one-bedroom apartment felt massive.

"What do they want?" my mom repeated, leaning heavily on the edge of the table as I got my shoes on.

"I don't know. It has to be some mistake." I forced an eye roll, trying to put on a brave face so she wouldn't worry. "You know, another stupid glitch in the system."

Mom pressed her lips together, seemingly unconvinced. "I hope that's all it is. Fucking high-tech cities."

I chuckled while pulling on a sweater. It wasn't the first time she grumbled about technology running an entire city-state. I lost count of how many stories she told me of the cities and towns she'd traveled through when she was young. Some had populations of only a few thousand people, and no one had ID chips. Back then, they carried ID cards in their wallets, if they had them at all. She'd said rich and poor shared the same roads and even went to the same markets for supplies.

"Don't let the wolf hear you say that," I said with fake cheer as I hugged her. "I'll be right back, but if I'm not home by eight, take one pill, okay?"

Mom clung tightly to my forearm with a grip that had to be painful for her as she stared at me intently. "You better come back tonight, daughter. Do you hear me?"

"Yes, Mom." I returned her squeeze, forcing a smile through the dread in my chest. "This all has to be a mistake. I'll be back before you know it."

* * *

IF I HAD BLINKED, I WOULD HAVE MISSED THE ENTRY INTO UPPER MinoTek from the southern slums where I lived.

Crumbling, centuries-old buildings and roads filled with potholes gave way to sleek, glassy structures without a blemish in sight. Bright LED streetlights zipped past the MSP squad car as we drove by. The roads were smooth and looked freshly washed, glossy and reflecting the bright lights. Apartment buildings stretched up toward the darkening sky, all straight lines and perfectly symmetrical windows on every side.

I couldn't believe it was the same city. This side of MinoTek felt like a different planet. Before now, I'd only seen it on the flatscreen programs and in printed magazines. The Upper Side was touted to us as a dream, a goal to achieve. If we just worked a little bit longer, a little bit harder, we'd soon find ourselves living the Upper MinoTek lifestyle.

A familiar resentment bubbled up from where I'd shoved it down the last time. I'd lived in the slums my whole life, scraping by with my mom, and everyone I knew did the same. We worked ourselves to the bone with so little to show for it, and why? Where was the fabled bridge from poverty to riches? For us and countless others, living on the upper side of the city was nothing more than fantasy.

I didn't even care about being rich. I just didn't want to choose between Mom's arthritis medication or dinner on the table. I wanted to live in a place that didn't get roof leaks every monsoon season. From what I saw in the back of that squad car, there was no bridge. Just our world and theirs, no overlaps.

According to *The Black Papers* pamphlets, lots of people in the slums were sick of our conditions. The anonymous journalists wrote about corruption among the MinoTek authorities. They said Prime Minister Minos and his father did this on purpose—created a society where the poor never crawled their way out of the slums, and the rich became obscenely wealthy, practically gods.

I didn't know what to believe. I didn't know crap about politics or economics, but I wanted to believe in the genuine goodness of people. My neighbors and I had helped each other countless times. We shared resources and cooked community meals so no one would starve. The older folks watched young children while their parents had to work. Everyone shared tools to fix our broken-down apartments, because the property managers were utterly useless.

Surely it wasn't that unusual to just be good to others.

Right before the shifter cop came to my door, I had been reading a *Black Papers* article about a doctor who had mysteriously disappeared. The journalist claimed that the doctor had been undermining MinoTek authorities, possibly tampering with or removing people's ID chips in the name of autonomy and privacy. The official story put out by MinoTek media was that the doctor had retired and moved. Unofficially, the *Black Papers'* writer believed the doctor had been sent to die in the labyrinth.

That story was fresh in my mind as the shifter parked the car in front of a huge building with columns lining the front. The wolf's partner, another large, baby-faced man, opened my door and allowed me to exit the car by myself but took my arms and placed handcuffs on my wrists faster than I could blink.

"What—what is this?" I jerked away on instinct, but the shifter clasped a meaty hand around my arm to hold me in place. "Am I being arrested for something?"

"No," he said, not even looking at me. His gaze was straight ahead on the building entrance. "Just standard procedure. Move."

The other one took my opposite arm, and together, they escorted me toward the imposing structure of glass and polished marble. I could barely keep up with their strides and practically jogged so that my feet wouldn't drag.

We entered a massive lobby with a desk and receptionist at the far end, but the men bypassed it, heading for a set of elevators. I kept staring at the receptionist, a woman with long, manicured nails typing on a slim keyboard, hoping she would look up and see that I was in distress, but she never did.

As if I didn't feel enough like a prisoner, being shoved into a small, metal box with two massive shifters certainly sealed the deal.

I'm not going home tonight, am I?

Shaky, panicked breaths followed that thought, made louder by the dead-silent elevator. The two cops hardly seemed to breathe at all, standing like statues on either side of me. Meanwhile, my cuffs rattled from the trembling in my limbs. I wracked my brain for *anything* I might have done that would get me arrested. And I came up with nothing.

"Courtroom Nine," announced the soft AI voice before the elevator glided open. My two statues returned to life and proceeded to guide me down a short walkway to a set of secure doors.

The wolf held up his wrist to the scanner. With a soft beep, the door slid open, and they guided me through to a room where six people were already waiting.

An elderly man in black judge's robes sat at the far end of the room, elevated above everyone else. He was typing something on a slim keyboard and didn't even glance up as I walked in. Everyone else, three men and three women sitting to the left side of the room, regarded me curiously as I was led to a small table directly in front of the judge.

"Ariadne Saavas?" the judge asked in a droll tone, still typing and looking at the screen.

"Um, yes." I forced a swallow and a deep breath. "Sir, I believe there may have been a mistake—"

"Do not speak unless spoken to, girl." Only then did the judge make eye contact with me, giving me a distasteful sneer from his elevated position. "Your name is Ariadne Saavas, yes or no?"

"Y-yes." I tried to stiffen to halt my trembling, but that only seemed to make it worse.

To my left, the people who I could only assume were the jury, began typing on their own handheld keypads.

"Miss Saavas, do you know why you're here this evening?"

"No, sir." I craned my neck to look up at the judge. "I have no idea, I—"

"You're on trial for being in possession of illegal materials," he continued drolly.

"*What?!* Sir, I apologize, but that can't—"

"What did I say about not speaking unless spoken to?"

"But, Your Honor, I—"

The judge slammed his gavel down, the percussion of wood echoing harshly throughout the small courtroom. "One more unsolicited word out of you, and I'll double the length of your sentence. Am I understood?"

My teeth sank into my lower lip, eyes burning angry tears at the sheer unfairness of it all. The judge was an elderly man, his hands looking slightly arthritic as he tapped on the slim keyboard in front of him. I'd bet a year's salary he didn't have to worry about affording his medication. Mom and I had to scrimp and save and ration her dosage just to keep her pain at a manageable level.

"Do you recognize this, Miss Saavas?"

A projected image flickered onto a screen behind the judge. It was a photo of one of the *Black Papers*, just like the one I'd been reading at my kitchen table when the cops showed up.

"Um, yes, sir. But I don't understand—"

"It's a simple yes or no question, Miss. No need to elaborate."

The image disappeared and the judge resumed typing. "Have you ever read material such as that which I just showed you?"

"I mean, they're passed out everywhere for free—"

"Again, it's a yes or no question. Please answer it honestly. Lying to a judge will add to your sentence."

I didn't know what my sentence was for my alleged crime, but I forced myself to breathe deeply, trying to gather strength. "Yes, I've read those pamphlets before."

"And are you aware that the possession or consumption of any literature not sanctioned by the City-State of MinoTek is illegal within the boundaries of the city-state?"

I swallowed and tried for another deep breath to calm my rising panic. "Respectfully, Your Honor, I don't understand why I'm being singled out. Like I said, they're passed out for free. Everyone reads—"

He struck down the gavel again, the blow feeling like a punch to the gut. "Just answer the fucking question! Or I *will* hold you in contempt."

I was full-on shaking from head to toe now, the hope of returning home quickly sinking like a dead weight. How the fuck was this trial legal? I didn't have a lawyer or anyone to advocate for me. I was only trying to defend myself, and this judge was treating me like some unruly criminal.

Because you were born on the wrong side of the city, that's why.

"Yes," I said, my voice small and defeated. "I'm aware."

"Good. So your plea is guilty." His tone and the tapping of his keyboard was damn near cheerful.

I remained silent, not wanting to test his ire any more, when he hit the final key with a flourish.

"Ariadne Saavas, you are sentenced to three months in the labyrinth for consumption of media against the state."

"What?" I barely had time to process before the two massive

shifters took hold of my arms and started dragging me away. "No, *please!*" I struggled with all my might, but it was no use against the two hulking cops. "Please, Your Honor! My mother is not well, and she depends on me! I can't leave her alone! I'll serve my sentence, but not in the labyrinth, *please—*"

"Get her out of my courtroom." The judge sighed and rubbed his temples before glancing at his watch. "Let's get this next trial over with." He had just sentenced me to my death over reading a pamphlet and couldn't care less.

All I could think about was Mom as the cops dragged me away. Not that they would care, but my heart broke with a new realization.

They had given us both death sentences today.

2

ZERUHN

"What's got you so excited, Lago?"

The jackalope zoomed around my sleeping cave like he was having the time of his life. He practically bounced off the stone walls, twisting his body in midair in the way rabbit-like creatures expressed happiness. The large moth wings on his back helped him to stay airborne for a few extra seconds on each jump.

Those wings were of little use for anything else, as were the antlers on his head. Like me, he was a lab-created freak. An experiment that went awry because some scientist was bored.

Maybe that was why we became friends. He was certainly better company than anyone else that ended up in this forsaken hellhole.

Lago zoomed toward me and jumped again. This time, one of his antlers knocked into my left horn.

"Careful, little friend," I chuckled, reaching to pet one of his long ears. "Don't want you to get caught and snap your neck. Who would I talk to then?"

It was then that I heard the familiar, subtle hum of machinery, and I perked up, leaning forward in my sitting position.

"They're bringing another one so soon," I mused, petting down Lago's back. "You think this one will be a challenge for once? It's been so boring lately."

The jackalope looked at me, then scratched the base of his antlers with his foot.

"Yeah, you're right. Probably not." I rose to full height and stretched, careful to angle my head so my horns wouldn't scrape the cave ceiling. "Should we see what showed up anyway?"

Lago was already ahead of me, hopping down the rocky path like a sure-footed mountain goat. I only knew what a mountain goat was because of a discarded magazine that had drifted into the labyrinth through the small river that coursed through here. All I knew of the outside world was what people dumped over the edge of the waterfall and what the team of scientists taught me in the lab.

That and whatever I learned from the simpering prey that was brought to me.

Even though it was often the same, I enjoyed seeing my prey from a high vantage point for the first time, where they couldn't see me. They knew I was in here, otherwise they wouldn't cry and beg to be released.

It was foolish, really, and mildly irritating that they were so predictable. If they all really knew of me, they'd know escaping the labyrinth was fruitless.

Some of them seemed resigned to their fate and didn't put up much of a fight at all. I commended their acceptance of the situation, but those people made for the most boring prey.

I reached my hiding spot, hidden in the shadows of the surrounding boulders. Night was falling, and it wasn't like I had to try hard. My heart jumped with excitement as the panel changed colors on the wall below, shifting from red to green. The door slid open with a hiss, and a smile pulled at my lips at the sounds of a struggle. *Good. This one's a fighter.*

"I need to contact my mother! Please, she'll suffer without my help! Why won't you listen?!"

A woman, I realized with delight. Her emotion-filled voice sent a dull pulse through my cock. It had been a long time since I'd hunted a woman. Even longer since I'd fucked one, and this one already made such beautiful sounds.

She was dwarfed between the two shifters dragging her in, all arms and legs as she thrashed and kicked to get free. Her struggle had no effect, of course, but her spirit was admirable.

"Listen, please! I'll cooperate! I'll serve my sentence. But I *need* to reach my mother! She's the only family I have...stop! Where are you going?"

The shifters deposited her several feet away from the door, returning to the exit without another word. The woman got up to run after them, a common mistake.

You're going to regret that, doe eyes, I thought.

Like clockwork, the shifters spun to face her with their taser guns ready. The woman either didn't see or was too determined, but she crashed into them with the full force of her body. They caught her easily between them and jammed their stun guns into her ribs. Her cries were those of shock and pain, slight body convulsing with the current of electricity running through her.

She slumped to the ground when they released her and lie unmoving as they left. The door slid closed and the panel turned to red again. I leaned over from my lookout spot, eager to get a clear look at my new prey.

This woman had long, black hair and medium-brown skin, well-kissed by the sun. Her round doe eyes were a dark gray, like a violent storm, or maybe that was just a reflection of her mood upon being thrown into the labyrinth.

She was thin, with small breasts, high angular cheeks, and pronounced hip bones and collarbones. Hm, that wouldn't do. My prey needed some nutrition, some fuel to give her stamina in order to have a fighting chance against me.

She'd never win, but I wanted to enjoy hunting this creature. I liked that storm in her eyes and the scrappy way she fought against those shifters. Right then, she didn't move at all, but lie flat on her back with only her chest moving in ragged breaths.

I eased further back into the shadows, excitement making my tail swish behind me. "What do you think, Lago?" I whispered. "Should we introduce ourselves or let her settle in for her first night?"

The jackalope's nose twitched, and he thumped a leg on the ground. I grinned in response. No wonder he was zooming around so much earlier. He was just as excited to meet her as I was.

"Let's go, then."

I let the shift take over, giving in to the persistent itch always present under my skin. My body transformed, growing a full foot taller and packing on muscle as my feet turned into hooves. My human legs morphed in shape and size until they were the rear legs of a bull, covering me in short, dense fur from the waist down.

Thanks to my existence as a failed shifter prototype, my arms and torso remained fully human. My full shift completed with the transformation of my head, my skull and horns growing heavier, longer, and my facial features stretching out into the form of a bull.

My hooves crashed down over the rocky terrain, and I inhaled great huffs of breath through my wide nostrils. Oh, this woman smelled *sweet*. I wondered if she tasted like the ripe fruit that grew on the trees near the top of the labyrinth. She would be a prize worth hunting, I already knew it.

Lago raced out ahead of me on the path to her. He always liked to catch our prey off-guard before they saw me. No one expected a jackalope with bright, colorful moth wings to be in the company of the labyrinth's monster.

I could smell the woman's fear tainting her sweet natural scent and heard her increasingly fast breaths and heartbeats as I approached. There was no need to be quiet now, she knew what was coming.

This woman was about to see what only the dead knew of.

The face of the minotaur.

3

ARIADNE

The pain from the stun gun left my body quickly, though I'd lost all motivation to move from the floor.

I was really here, in the fucking labyrinth. The prison I would never leave. I'd never see Mom again. All for reading a stupid pamphlet.

My best hope was that the neighbors would look after her, but it wasn't the same. They weren't family. She'd get worried about me, which would exacerbate her painful symptoms and make her medication run out faster. If only I could just talk to her, maybe tell her to burn all those fucking pamphlets so they wouldn't target her next.

I closed my eyes, not even wanting to gauge my surroundings. I thought I caught glimpses of skeletons when the shifters dragged me in here, and now I didn't want to find out if that was true.

If it was, then there was no hope. None at all. I wasn't ready to release that last thread of hope of seeing Mom again. Not yet.

If those piles of bones really were human remains, then the

minotaur was not only real but was just as horrifying as the stories made him out to be.

He was made into some kind of boogeyman in the slums, a scary bedtime story for children. *Pick up your shoes or the shifters will throw you in the labyrinth with the minotaur, and you'll be eaten!*

Our neighbors told variations of it to their children all the time with laughter in their voices. How else were we to cope when friends and neighbors disappeared with no rhyme or reason, if not with morbid humor?

I couldn't bring myself to laugh about it now. Maybe if I survived the night, but my only focus was figuring out a way to contact my mother. It had to be past eight in the evening now. She would definitely be wondering about me.

The cold quickly set in and pulled my thoughts toward finding warmth. I drew my arms and legs up close, shivering as I turned onto my side on the cold, rocky ground. From what I could gather so far, the labyrinth was some kind of cave. With how cool the air was, it had to be at least partially underground. It had been warm and humid outside only an hour ago.

Lying in a fetal position and shivering through my thin clothes did nothing to keep me warm, so I cracked my eyes open despite my steadfast reluctance.

And found myself face-to-face with a human skull grinning back at me.

"Shit!" I sat up and scooted on my butt away from the partial skeleton that had once been a *person*, only to run into another pile of bones that looked suspiciously like ribs. "Fuck!"

My heart jammed up into my throat, beating furiously like it was trying to escape my body. As my vision adjusted to darkness, I saw them everywhere. Bones were arranged in small piles, as were various articles of clothing. A man's jacket hung on the edge of a rock and I remembered how badly I was shivering. But fuck, I couldn't just take a dead man's jacket!

Somehow I heard soft steps on the rocky terrain over my furious heartbeat and panicked breaths, and jerked my head towards the sound. "Who's there?"

I didn't know why I bothered asking. It was clearly the minotaur, come to put me out of my misery and add to his creepy bone collection. Too bad that my clothes were threadbare and probably wouldn't fit him.

But instead of a hulking, murderous beast approaching, it was a...rabbit? Or a hare? I never could remember the difference. It resembled a wild rabbit, with long ears and legs, and a slender body covered in grayish-brown fur. I sat frozen, watching it hop curiously closer to me, because this was no ordinary rabbit.

This creature had a set of deer antlers on its head and large green moth wings on its back. Its head seemed to droop forward slightly like the antlers were heavy, and the wings didn't seem to do much except flap lazily.

"What...the hell are you, little guy?"

The rabbit paused a few feet away from me and lifted to stand on its hind legs, nose twitching. Could it understand me? Was it somebody's pet? Or was *this* the big, bad minotaur everyone was afraid of?

My gaze slid around to the piles of bones surrounding us. Surely a rabbit creature, even one with antlers and wings, couldn't have killed all these people, right?

The rabbit lowered its forelegs to the ground and hopped over to the jacket hanging on the rock. It took the garment down with its teeth and a shake of its head and promptly hopped back to me.

"What are you...Oh, no."

The creature hopped over to me and stood on its hind legs again with the jacket in its mouth.

"Look, you're sweet, little guy. But I can't. It's some dead man's jacket."

A cold, howling breeze made me shiver even harder, and the rabbit's ears flicked as if to say, *I can't believe you, lady.* It hopped even closer and dropped the jacket over my feet. Already my resolve was withering. The dead didn't need to keep warm, but my teeth started to clack from shivering so hard.

Just for tonight, I thought. *I need to live through the night and then figure out what I'm gonna do.*

I crouched slowly to pick up the jacket, watching the rabbit to make sure it wouldn't bite me or stab me with one of those antlers. The strange animal stared at me in return, its fluffy moth wings flapping a bit faster once I stood with the jacket in my hands.

I'd barely had time to put my arm through a sleeve when another noise made me freeze—the footsteps of a much bigger animal. My muscles unlocked just enough for me to whip around, and I wished I hadn't.

He was *enormous.* At least eight feet tall, maybe nine if I included the horns stretched up to the ceiling. The massive head of a bull snorted and growled angrily, tossing around on his neck like he couldn't wait to gore me with those brutal horns. His torso was that of a man's, shirtless and riddled with muscles like the shifter police seemed to be. Several long scars cut across his body, like trophies on display.

What I thought was a pair of brown pants were actually legs covered in short, brown fur. They ended in hooves as large as plates, and a long, slender tail cut aggressively through the air behind him.

I wanted to cry, scream, run for my life, maybe even piss

myself, but I couldn't will myself to move or even breathe. The minotaur was real, and he was more terrifying than I'd ever imagined.

So much for lasting a single night here.

His nostrils flared with a great huff of breath, oversized human fists clenching at his sides as he approached me. It was so jarring to see, distinctly human and animal features all coexisting on the same body. Did he have the brain of a bull too? Or was there human intelligence in that animal head?

I was so busy staring in fascination at the strangeness of him that I realized too late that I needed to *run* if I wanted the slim chance of surviving. The minotaur's stride was so long, and he was mere feet away. Those horns would skewer me in seconds if I didn't run *now*.

Damn my shocked, terrified body for not working. I could only stumble back a few steps on jelly legs and couldn't seem to tear my eyes from him. The minotaur grinned—so eerie to see a human expression on a bull's face—as he continued toward me.

When my back hit a rocky wall, that was the moment I closed my eyes. I wanted my last thought to be of my mom before I died, not how horrifically and painfully this beast was going to kill me. My legs gave out, and I began sliding to the ground, eyes squeezing tightly shut even when a massive hand pinned my shoulder against the rock to hold me in place.

"Open your eyes, prey. Look at the one who hunts you."

Part of me was oddly fascinated by how clearly he spoke with a bull's mouth. If I wasn't seconds away from bleeding to death, I might have taken a peek. But more than anything, I just wanted this over quickly. The sooner it happened, the faster my mom would find out, and the sooner she could find someone else to help her. I just closed my eyes tighter, bracing myself for the pain.

But the minotaur would not be deterred and let out an aggravated huff. "Open your eyes, or I will peel your eyelids back myself."

Oh, for fuck's sake. Why?

I allowed light in slowly at first, then my eyes widened the moment I could focus. And then I blinked several times, unable to believe what was in front of me.

The minotaur was...a man?

He still had horns, a tarnished golden color, curving up from his forehead. But his face was human now. Normal, if even handsome. Russet brown hair covered his head in thick waves, and the soft beard coating his jaw was the same color. His eyes were the same dark gold as his horns. A scar cut just underneath his left eye, and there was another on his forehead.

A risky glance downward showed there was indeed a pair of pants on his human legs. The pants sat low on his narrow hips, probably to accommodate the tail still slashing around behind him. He was still ridiculously muscled and tall, but his proportions seemed more human-like now.

When I brought my gaze back up to his, those golden eyes were feral. He truly was a predator, no matter how human he looked.

"You're in shock and overrun by fear now," he stated matter-of-factly. "I can't wait until it wears off and your survival instincts kick in."

My mind raced with questions, with pleas and begs for him to not do this, but I could only stare up at him dumbly, a rabbit in the jaws of a wolf.

"I can't wait to see how badly you want to live," the minotaur continued. "I hope you fight me as hard as you did those shifters who brought you in." Excitement flashed in his strange eyes as he smirked. "You better not disappoint me by making it easy."

So he saw the moment they dragged me in, watched me from the shadows like some creep. A shiver ran up my spine from the thought of him watching my every move. And it sounded like he wanted to do more of that, watching me. But to what end?

"You're...you're not going to kill me?" I asked in a shaky whisper.

He threw his head back and laughed, a sound just as unhinged as it was pleasant to listen to. "Oh, no, sweet prey. No, I want you healthy and strong. Do you know why?"

The minotaur then leaned down, his face inching closer to mine. I tried to squirm away but his massive palm against my shoulder held me fast. I could smell him this close and had the crazy thought that he didn't smell terrible. Even nice, in fact.

It was looking like he might kiss me, or bite me, maybe. I couldn't decide which was worse, but he brought his lips to my ear instead, and whispered a haunting promise.

"Only then will I delight in hunting you."

4

ARIADNE

That first night was the worst of my life. It was so dark and unbearably cold. I didn't sleep at all, but just curled up on the ground, huddled under the jacket and shivering. Every noise startled me, making me gasp and search the darkness that my eyes never seemed to adjust to. And with the constant wind rushing through the labyrinth, there were always noises.

The only light came from a long, winding opening in the cavern's ceiling. It looked so impossibly far away, like the top of a skyscraper in Upper MinoTek. Not that the sky was anything great to look at. There were no stars, no moon. I'd never seen an actual starry sky in my life, only in pictures. I only saw the familiar reddish-gray color of the city's light pollution, which did nothing to penetrate the eerie darkness here in the labyrinth.

This darkness was just as unsettling as the faraway cave ceiling. Someone always had lights on in the slums. It was how we looked out for each other.

When daylight eventually filtered in through that distant

cave opening, exhaustion had finally caught up to me. But I still couldn't let myself sleep.

I rolled up to sitting, groaning at the aches and stiffness in my body, then looked around for a clearer idea of my surroundings. I didn't know what I expected, but it wasn't plants.

Yeah, plants. Mossy and fern-like greenery grew in rocky crevices everywhere. One tall stretch of rock wall had green vines running up its surface.

The rocks themselves were all a mish-mash of things, with no clear pattern. I brushed away some sand and dirt on the ground to find stone tiles, clearly cut and laid in a pattern by human hands. The tiled floor veered to the right, where stone archways created corridors that led deeper into the labyrinth. That area also had brick walls, some broken down and crumbling, others still standing tall.

The other side of the labyrinth was, for a lack of better term, wilder. These rock formations were only shaped by natural processes over millions of years. They were craggy and rough, creating cliffs, caverns, and their own maze of tunnels within this massive space. My neck ached as my gaze went higher and higher, searching for the tops of the highest formations. Would it be possible to climb one and escape through the hole in the ceiling?

Spurred by this hopeful idea, I got to my feet and started walking. The picked-clean skeletons didn't deter me, nor did the knowledge that the minotaur was in here somewhere. I would climb and claw my way out if I had to.

The impossibility of such a task became clear within an hour of scoping out the rocks, however. My shoes slipped in every groove as I tried to climb, and what little hand-holds I found cut painfully through my palms. With every attempt, I only got a few feet off the ground.

I was already sore and exhausted. The labyrinth was already beating me up just by existing.

My last climbing attempt ended with me landing hard on my butt. My palms stung so badly, it brought tears to my eyes and a whimper to my throat. The skin of my hands was tender, torn and bloody.

Somewhere else then, I thought. *Maybe not right here, but there has to be a way up.*

There wouldn't be so many skeletons if there was a way, a cruel part of my brain answered. *The minotaur himself wouldn't be trapped here if there was a way out.*

I couldn't let that thought defeat me. I had struggled every single day of my life. I could escape some stupid cave.

Once my erratic breathing slowed to normal, I became aware of a distant sound. It was a constant, steady background noise that I hadn't noticed before. When I realized it was running water, only then did I notice how parched my throat was. It had been hours since I had anything to eat or drink, and my body headed toward that sound on autopilot.

Maybe I should have been more careful, moved more quietly, and stayed vigilant in case the minotaur decided that now was a good time to hunt me. But nothing filled my head besides easing my bone-dry throat and calming this gnawing emptiness in my stomach. Water first. Survival first. Then I would figure out how to escape.

I was almost too desperate for a drink to notice the beauty of the stream, idyllic and tranquil with plants growing along the edges. If this wasn't the same prison where dozens, if not hundreds of people had met their deaths, it would have been a pretty place for a picnic.

I fell to my knees on a grassy bank and dunked my hands in the rushing water. The icy temperature immediately soothed the ache of my sore palms. I cupped my hands and brought them to my mouth, sucking down the chilly water with all the finesse of a large dog drinking from a bowl.

Over and over, I dunked my hands and drank deeply, until I was too full to take another sip. My stomach stuck out, round and sloshy with liquid. Fatigue hit me hard then, and I could barely keep my eyes open as I sat back. This area of the stream ran directly under the opening in the ceiling, and I was in a small patch of sunlight. Instead of feeling cold like before, I was almost pleasantly warm.

And I was so, so tired.

Just for a minute, I thought as I leaned to one side. *I just need to rest for a minute...*

My head hit the soft grass, and I was out like a light.

I WAS WOKEN UP BY MY STOMACH'S VIOLENT PROTESTING. BEFORE I'd even opened my eyes, I felt the pressing need to vomit. My stomach cramped and heaved, forcing out all of the water I drank.

I threw up in the grass I'd just been lying in, clutching my stomach as I coughed and gasped for air. My stomach immediately seized again, sending another painful cramp all the way up until I vomited again.

It wouldn't stop.

Again and again, my body heaved, but there was nothing left. I coughed up saliva and bile while my throat burned. I was drenched in sweat, now even more exhausted and thirsty than before.

Once it finally seemed to pass, I reached a shaky hand

toward the stream for a drink. The moment I felt droplets on my tongue, my body responded violently again.

It's bad. The water's bad. I knew this logically, but fuck, I was *so* thirsty. My throat was on fire, and I needed to get this taste out of my mouth.

After multiple stops and starts because I couldn't stop gagging, I managed to gargle some water without swallowing it. It didn't help much, but was better than nothing.

I moved to a dry patch of grass alongside the stream and just laid down. Hot tears pricked at my eyes, which just made me feel even more pathetic. I was starving, sick, dehydrated, and my stupid body wanted to deplete me of even more water.

I didn't want to die like this. But I couldn't escape, couldn't drink the water, and would soon be too weak to do much else.

I didn't seem to have any other choice.

* * *

I COULDN'T REMEMBER FALLING ASLEEP, BUT I MUST HAVE. I WOKE up to my stomach growling with hunger, my throat painfully dry. And something smelled absolutely amazing.

My swollen eyes cracked open to the sight of a plate next to my face.

A plate full of food.

I sat up like a shot, staring down at what couldn't be real. Two small birds, plucked and cooked to perfection with golden-brown, crispy skin. They sat atop a bed of some kind of fluffy, pale grain. A serving of cooked vegetables also sat on the edge of the plate, still steaming. Everything smelled like butter and spices.

My stomach's growl could be heard up to the sky, and I was absolutely salivating. But I couldn't bring myself to touch the food. There was only one person who could have left it, and he, at some point, wanted me dead. The memory of being violently sick was still fresh. What was to stop him from poisoning the food to torture me even more?

I stared at the plate of food long enough to eventually notice a piece of paper folded and tucked under the edge of the plate. Curiosity got the better of me, and I grabbed it. Tucked inside were a handful of round, gray tablets. Puzzled, I unfolded the paper to find a note written in a messy, childlike scrawl.

Eat and drink without fear, doe eyes. Let the tablets dissolve in water for thirty minutes before drinking. Look to your left. The first one should be ready by the time you awaken.

Sure enough, there was a large metal thermos next to the stream a few feet away. If the note was supposed to put me at ease, it only made me more anxious. I looked all around me, as if I could catch a glimpse of him. This place was his home, his territory. And as he had made abundantly clear, I was his prey.

The minotaur had come up next to me. He could have killed me in my sleep but left me a plate of food and water purification tablets instead? Also, he was apparently literate, which begged even more questions. The legends always painted the minotaur as more beast than man. But even if he could shift to mostly human, how did he learn to write?

Regardless of that, the gesture of leaving food, along with the note, almost seemed kind, and I had to remind myself that it was actually cruel. He said that he wanted to hunt me. That he wanted me healthy and strong so it wouldn't be too easy for him.

I went back to staring at the food. I'd just be playing into his game if I ate it. If I stayed weak and starving, I wouldn't be good hunting for him.

But then I wouldn't be strong enough to attempt escape either.

Another hunger pang ripped through my stomach, and I could feel my resolve waning. *Alright, I'll eat,* I decided. *I just can't let him catch me.*

When my brain had enough fuel to think past survival, I'd figure out the next step.

I scooted toward the thermos of water and swirled it around to dissolve the remaining crumbs of the tablet at the bottom. Then I tilted it up and drank a careful mouthful, fighting every instinct to drain the whole thing.

My self-control could only last so long though, and I tore into the plate of food like it was the last meal I would ever eat.

5

ARIADNE

Food continued to mysteriously appear over the next several days.

It wasn't like I stayed in the same spot near the stream either. Every day, I explored the labyrinth extensively in search of an escape route. I frequently got lost and stumbled upon some new area every time I went walking. What I would've given for a ball of string or something to help me create a trail.

No matter where I laid my head down to sleep, a steaming plate of food and freshly purified water waited for me when I woke up. The food was usually some kind of grain, protein, and vegetables. A well-balanced meal, apparently portioned out for someone of my size because I always cleaned the plate.

Only the rich ate meals like this, from what I'd seen on our limited flatscreen stations. The thought was unnerving, considering I was literally in a prison. Our meals in the slums consisted of whatever we could afford or what the neighborhood had to share. Meat was rare, and it often couldn't be trusted to be fresh or uncontaminated. Our community meals were usually stews of some kind, with grains, hearty broth, and sometimes a few vegetables, if we were lucky. Before now, I couldn't remember ever truly feeling full.

Except for that first night, I never saw the minotaur. And I found myself continuously torn on whether to feel creeped out or comforted knowing he was constantly watching me. Even stalking me, one could say.

I'd never eaten so well in my life, but I knew that would only last so long. My time was limited, and I had to strike the balance of being strong enough to escape but not enough that he deemed me strong enough to hunt.

The other weird thing I noticed over those first few days? I was really fucking lonely.

I'd never been truly alone before. Mom was always with me or one of our neighbors. Members of our community always checked up on each other. People disappeared too often not to, and it wasn't like the shifter police ever carried out welfare checks or actually searched for the missing. So we had to take care of each other.

Never before had I gone days, or even a single day, without talking to someone. I almost wished the minotaur would start his hunt just so that I could have another person to interact with. Even his weird rabbit pet would be better than being completely on my own.

Sure, I had spotted a couple of other animals here. Mainly insects among the plants, as well as birds that flew in from the opening in the ceiling. Some had made nests along the cliff walls, and listening to their birdsong in the morning was nice. But I wasn't planning on being here long enough to tame a wild bird so that I could have a pet. It would just be nice to not feel completely alone.

One morning, I decided to walk through the area with the

man-made stone tunnels and floors. I'd likely get lost and not find my way out, but what else was new?

The arched doorways were high and ancient-looking. I walked into one massive room that could probably fit my whole apartment building inside. The ceiling stretched almost as tall as the main labyrinth but with no opening to the sky. Some glass in the windows remained, some with different colors and images with people on them. Beyond the windows was just more rock and cavern, so I wondered what the point of them was.

I continued wandering the halls, turning left and right at random. At one point, I heard a sound and tried to follow it. Like the stream, it was a constant background noise, echoing off the stone floors and ceilings. My footsteps hurried. If this was another stream, another water source, maybe I could follow it outside.

My wandering took me to another room, smaller than the first one but still large enough to make me pause. A tiled pool of water took up the entire room, with only a border around the edge wide enough for a couple of people to walk side-by-side.

A steady trickle of water poured into the pool from a stone fish sculpture. Its mouth hung open where the water steadily poured out. I approached the stone figure cautiously, equally bewildered and impressed. Where was the water coming from? There were no more streams that I could see. The fish seemed to be carved out of the wall it was jumping from. Was there a water supply behind this wall?

When I approached to look further, I noticed something else. A few woven baskets lined the walls, all filled with different objects. One had folded towels. Another had bottles of soaps, oils, and lotions. All luxurious and tiny—every bottle was smaller than the length of my hand. The third basket had toothbrushes—all individually wrapped and with various dental office names on them, like they had been samples to give out.

Seeing all the products at once made me instantly aware of how filthy I was. I hadn't washed since the day I was brought here, which had to have been nearly a week ago. I had thought about bathing in the stream, but it felt too open and exposed, especially knowing the minotaur was always watching.

But in here...

I chewed my lip as I walked around the border of the pool, running my hand along the stone wall. There were no windows here, only two open doorways on opposite sides of the pool, the one I came from and the one across from me. If I was quick and made sure to keep an eye on those doorways, maybe a bath wouldn't be so bad?

And if the minotaur did appear, what would I do then?

"Fuckin' drown myself," I muttered.

I warred with myself for several more minutes, passing my gaze over the doors, the pool, and the baskets.

"Okay, fine. Fuck it," I decided, quickly flinging off my borrowed jacket and the rest of my clothes. Scrubbing and rinsing myself would take five minutes tops. The sooner I got it over with, the better I would feel.

Once down to my birthday suit, I grabbed a towel and a body wash at random, then carefully slid into the pool. A gasp left my mouth at first, and then a sigh. The stream had been icy, but this temperature was *much* nicer. Not quite hot bath water, but close to the tepid, lukewarm temperature that I was used to in the slums. Right then, it felt absolutely heavenly.

I scrubbed all the important bits, then dunked fully underwater to rinse. My soapy water slowly traveled through a grate just under the lip of the pool. Once again, I wondered where the water came from and where it went.

More questions filled my head as I hurriedly unwrapped a toothbrush and gave my mouth a good scrub. Did the minotaur use these items? Was this *his* personal bathing pool? I thought back to when he'd leaned in so close to me on the first night. I had expected him to smell like a barn animal at best, but he had actually smelled pleasantly clean.

"Last thing you should be thinking about, Ari," I muttered after spitting. "Talking to myself is probably going to be a regular occurrence now," I added.

I toweled off, then pulled my clothes back on, feeling better than I had in days. "Feeling like a new woman," I said, stretching my arms over my head. "Maybe tomorrow I'll follow the wild stream and see if it leads anywhere outsi—"

Something grabbed my upper arm from behind and held it in a crushing grip. I froze while my heart jumped wildly in my chest. A warm, clean scent, faintly musky, filled my nostrils, and I knew it could only be one person.

How the fuck did the minotaur sneak up on me without making a sound?

While my heart beat frantically and every muscle in my body locked with fear, he seemed incredibly calm. I felt his body's heat at my back, radiating low and constant. His grip on my arm was relaxed for how strong it was. This predator had his prey exactly where he wanted it, and did not fear its escape.

The next thing I felt was the warmth of his breath on my ear and then his lips grazing the shell of it. I heard the amusement in his voice when he spoke.

"Run, doe eyes."

Even though I knew the command was a taunt, knew it was exactly what he wanted, that word flipped a switch in my brain.

And I ran.

Thankfully, I had just put my shoes on before he showed up,

because it would suck to run over stone floors on bare feet. Just like when I entered, I zigged and zagged through the tunnels with no rhyme or reason. For all I knew, I'd run in a complete circle and end up back in the bathing room.

The thought only spurred me to run faster, pumping my arms and willing my legs to go as fast as they could. I stole one glance behind me and didn't see the minotaur, but I was nowhere near ready to claim a victory.

Fuck, my chest was already burning and a cramp stabbed in my side. I wasn't an endurance athlete by any means, and I couldn't keep this up much longer.

That's exactly what he wanted, I realized. *For you to deplete your energy so he could finish you off easily. Prepare to become Random Skeleton #384.*

The thought gave me an extra burst of energy as I made another sharp left turn. Maybe I wasn't in the best shape, but being desperate to live certainly was a great motivator.

I nearly sobbed with relief when I spotted a tunnel leading outside to the main area of the labyrinth. Without thinking, I sprinted that way, my speed and momentum too great to stop when a massive figure dropped down out of nowhere, blocking the exit.

The minotaur huffed, grunting with amusement when I crashed into him. He was so solid that I bounced off his torso, landing on my butt in front of him. For some reason, I looked up toward his face, and I screamed.

He was partially shifted again, with his bull's head and lower body. There must have been a ledge he was sitting on just outside the entrance, because he ducked to step into the tunnel, and his brutally long horns scraped the edges of the arched doorway.

A hoofed foot stepped closer to me, and then another. That

was what got me scrambling to my feet and running in the opposite direction—back into the maze of tunnels. But most of my energy was already depleted, and my wheezing breaths betrayed the defeat I felt.

Who was I kidding, though? Even if I'd made it out of this area, the entire labyrinth was his domain.

Still, I kept running. Slower and clumsier this time, and even now, the minotaur was out of sight. The whole thing was a fucking cat-and-mouse game to him.

I ended up in the first large room again and decided I'd climb out a window. The rock wall on the other side made it too narrow for him to wait for me out there. And if he was behind me, he was too damn big to follow me through the window.

Once again, freedom felt so close. I ran to one window where most of the colored glass was missing. The stone ledge was thick enough for me to sit on, and it gave me a nice, tall platform to get my feet underneath me. I ducked my head under and through the opening, reaching to press my palm against the rock on the other side. It was only a few feet away. I could definitely fit in the gap, while the minotaur couldn't.

I had just gotten one foot out of the window when a hand closed around the ankle of my other foot. I screamed and flailed, kicking in pure terror. But the minotaur only wrapped a tree trunk-sized arm around my thighs and plucked me from the window like I was a disobedient pet.

He said nothing as he placed me on the floor, while I desperately babbled and pleaded for my life. My eyes shut because I didn't want to face this. I probably made no sense as I sobbed and hyperventilated. I tried to explain about my mom, about the fact that I was innocent and unjustly put in here. I just said whatever came to my racing mind, because I knew it was the end.

The minotaur said nothing. He just held me in place with two massive hands on my shoulders, his great huffs of breath ruffling my hair.

When I ran out of things to say, I felt the weight of a finger tracing my cheekbone and the side of my face. I was so exhausted, so defeated, I couldn't even bring myself to pull away.

"Look at me, prey," the beast commanded.

My eyes cracked open and spilled fresh tears. The minotaur had shifted back to his human form. Even though his horns were smaller in this form, they still curved toward the ceiling like brutal weapons.

His expression was...odd.

His brow furrowed, as if concerned or confused. Eyes the color of tarnished gold searched my face as if trying to understand the reason for my tears and heartbreak.

After a few moments, he appeared to reach a decision. "I want only one thing from you, doe eyes."

My life, clearly.

But then he stepped in closer, to the point where he spread his legs on either side of mine. He leaned down, those terrifying horns inching increasingly closer to my face. His bare torso nearly brushed against mine, and his body heat flickered out to me like a bonfire.

Oh no. He doesn't mean...oh, please, no.

I had assumed, perhaps naively, that the minotaur's only desire was to kill. Never did I imagine he'd have *other* desires.

"What?" I squeaked out after a long pause.

His eyes flicked down to my lips before meeting my gaze again. "Your name."

My brain screeched to a halt. "My...name?"

"Yes. Tell me your name, and I will release you." A hungry smile pulled at his lips. "To hunt you another day."

Part of me wished to beg him to end me now. I couldn't do this again, not *another* hunt. I'd rather give it all up than be toyed with like this again.

It was only thinking of my mom that made me pause. Living another day meant another chance to see her. Another chance to escape. A slim chance, obviously. But if I died now, that chance would be gone.

So I pulled in a shaky breath and said with all the bravery I could muster, "Ariadne."

The minotaur did the absolute last thing I expected and pressed a firm kiss to my mouth.

That made my eyes go wide, and I froze again, too stunned to react. My head spun with thoughts, however. Most of them wondered why and the rest were utter shock and disbelief that this was happening. A couple thoughts like, *His beard and lips are much softer than I imagined*, did cross my mind.

He pulled away, straightening to his full height again. "Thank you, Ariadne." As he turned to leave, he threw me a smirk over his shoulder that looked suspiciously close to flirtatious. "Until I catch you again."

6

———

ZERUHN

riadne. Her name was Ariadne.

Movement in my peripheral vision pulled my thoughts from my pretty little prey.

"Stay here, Lago," I growled. It was the fourth time I had to tell him to stay put. "We're not seeing Ariadne today."

The jackalope stared at me, nose twitching furiously as he thumped a foot in irritation. He'd been curious about her ever since she came here, and he kept trying to hop further away from me for a closer look at her.

I couldn't blame him. The doe-eyed prisoner intrigued me immensely, especially since the hunt yesterday. She'd been on my mind constantly since then, like the lingering pain from a fight that stuck around long after. My instincts were trying to tell me something, not that I could always trust those.

I was artificially made, pieced together from human and animal DNA alike. There was nothing natural about me, nothing *right* about me. Even as a shifter, I was a dud. A proto- type that didn't work as intended. So it only made sense to assume my instincts were just as faulty as the rest of me.

I didn't trust why my brain seemed stuck on Ariadne. And I didn't trust *her* either. That was why I didn't want Lago getting too close to her unless I was nearby.

"What if she throws rocks at you like the last one did?" I asked him. "Or tries to hunt you for food like the one before that?"

The jackalope only yawned, then hopped away to rub his antlers against the wall of my sleeping cave. I returned to staring at the ceiling, reclining on my makeshift bed, patched together with discarded blankets and clothes.

This morning, I made food for Ariadne, left it next to her while she slept, and then watched her, as usual. She seemed more hesitant to eat and left most of it on the plate, which concerned me.

And it bothered me that it concerned me.

I thought back to yesterday during the hunt. Seeing fear in the face of my prey used to excite me. Their babbling and begging was once amusing. But in recent years? It had become dreadfully boring. Every single prisoner—man, woman, human, or shifter, was exactly the same.

On the surface, Ariadne was no different.

But she didn't *feel* the same.

I rubbed my chest, the spot where her effect on me seemed especially concentrated. Her fear during the hunt hadn't been enjoyable, or even boring, for me. Her tears and expression of utter defeat made me...uncomfortable.

I wanted it to stop. I wanted her fierce expression that she had given those shifter guards when she tried to run through them. I wanted the storm in her eyes, a bit of which returned when she told me her name.

"Ariadne." Her name made my mouth do interesting things. It increased that ever-present sensation in my chest.

She did something to my instincts that sent me completely off-kilter. It meant nothing, but it was aggravating how much this threw me. Even the way I left food was different. I gave her complete meals every single morning and before she woke up, because I didn't want to frighten her. With other prisoners, I was much more sporadic, and I certainly didn't care about frightening them.

My thoughts wandered to right before I initiated the hunt, and a groan left my mouth. She'd been in my bathing pool, and the sight of her had hardened me unlike any other woman I'd ever seen.

How the water and soap had sluiced off her skin, molding to her shape. What surprised me most was the utter pleasure I felt, not just at the sight of her unclothed body, but also that she was not as thin as her first day here. Because I had been feeding her.

Why? *Why* did that fill me with such immense satisfaction, more than anything else?

I let my head thump back on the floor, releasing an aggravated sigh. My hands twitched at my sides to palm my cock, which had thickened *again* at the thought of her.

If I just killed her like I had every other prisoner here, none of this would be bothering me.

But...I didn't want to do that either.

That was another unnerving thought. I *actively* didn't want to kill Ariadne. In fact, I would prevent her death if such a situation arose.

I wanted to keep her. With me.

I rubbed my forehead, releasing another sigh. The lab that created me had been defunct for twenty years. Otherwise, I'd ask the scientists to recalibrate my instincts, because all of these thoughts were annoying.

The closure of that lab was why I was here, rather than still enclosed in a cold, sterile room. As fucked up as my creation and existence was, I was glad for the open space and the scenery. The lab gave me phobias of restraints and enclosed spaces. It was why I preferred staying in a cave rather than the ruins of the chapel down in the main valley. Too many walls. Too low ceilings.

Lago stopped rubbing his antlers on the wall and cocked his head toward the cave entrance. He hopped closer to the opening and stood on his hind legs, ears straight and alert.

"What is it?" I crossed my feet at the ankles. "Or are you trying to fake me out to see Ariadne again?"

Every muscle in his body went rigid, his rabbit instincts on high alert for a predator. After a few moments, he hopped to me and pulled aggressively on my pant leg.

"What?" I demanded, swatting him away. "They wouldn't send another prisoner in, not so soon."

I ate my words a few seconds later when I heard the subtle hum of machinery. There were several pressurized doors in the outside tunnel that always led prisoners to the labyrinth. That hum could only be those series of doors.

"Fuck!" I shot to my feet, barely taking notice of my horns scraping the cave ceiling. Together, Lago and I bolted to my lookout point.

This...panic and unease were strange feelings for me too. It wasn't unheard of for the labyrinth to hold more than one prisoner at once. Unusual, but not uncommon.

But right then, I didn't want to share this place with anyone but Ariadne.

We got to our hiding spot just as the final pressurized door slid open. Two shifters held a struggling human man between them. He was bigger and stronger than Ariadne but still no match for my fellow lab-created freaks who dragged him to his doom.

Even so, while I had admired Ariadne's fight, this man's wriggling only looked pathetic in my eyes.

"You didn't give me a fair trial!" he shouted. "Call and ask her! She *wanted* me! You'll see, I'm innocent!"

The shifters ignored him like always and dropped him unceremoniously in the dirt. Much like Ariadne had, he noticed my collections of bones I'd placed at the entrance. The hiss of the door closing pulled him from his momentary shock, and he scrambled for the exit.

"Wait, stop! You can't leave me in here!" He pounded at the reinforced steel door until it became clear that no one would come for him. While shaking his fist and catching his breath, he slowly turned around to face his fate.

My lip curled with distaste at the sight of him. I knew immediately he would be just like all the others. Boring and maybe a nuisance, at best. I couldn't wait to get rid of him.

"Um, hello?"

The hesitant, feminine voice had me clenching my fists and suppressing a growl, while the man's eyebrows drew up, his face relaxing with clear relief. No! Why the fuck was Ariadne here?

"H-h-hello?" the man answered. "Is someone there?"

Ariadne peeked out from behind a rock and smiled—*smiled!* —at this pathetic waste of air. She would smile at him but not me?

That thought made me so irrationally angry.

The man smiled back and gave a small wave, to which Ariadne returned. "It sure is nice to see a friendly face," he said.

"Sure is nice to see a human one," she replied.

What? I do have a human face! I wanted to yell. Just not

human enough, as my horns and eye color constantly reminded me.

"Did you, um, want some food?" Ariadne gestured to her half-eaten plate next to the stream a short walk away.

I suppressed another growl of frustration. *Do not offer him food! I made that for you!*

"That would be great, actually. Thank you." The man continued to smile at her, and I wanted to remove it permanently. Along with his entire head from his neck. "I'm Rich, by the way."

"Ariadne." She gave her name to him so freely, while I had to hunt and catch her for it. Besides being a fellow human, what did *he* do to earn her name?

They walked together toward the stream, and my rage was moments away from boiling over.

I had just watched my prey walk into the den of another predator.

ARIADNE

Rich was a middle-aged man. His clothes were worn and threadbare like mine, but I didn't recognize him from my neighborhood. He must have been in another area of the slums then. I sat back and watched him polish off the remaining food left for me by the minotaur. When he finished, I handed him the tumbler of purified water, which he gulped down greedily.

"Thanks." Rich wiped his mouth on his sleeve and belched. "Damn, I guess being thrown in prison really works up an appetite, huh?"

I offered a polite smile. "I guess so. What were you tried for?"

He rolled his eyes. "Some bullshit petty theft charge. You?"

"Yeah, something like that."

"So when did you get tossed in here?" He drained the rest of the water.

"About a week ago." I held my hand out. "Here, I can refill that."

"A whole week?" Rich's eyebrows lifted. "You're tellin' me you haven't run into the minotaur in that time?"

"Um." I bit the inside of my cheek as I dunked the thermos in the stream. "Not directly, no. I've heard noises and stuff, though." I couldn't explain why I chose to lie. While it was comforting to have human company, I didn't know anything about Rich. He could very well be guilty of what he was tried for, if he was even telling the truth about the crime.

And it was hard to ignore that some part of me felt oddly protective of the minotaur. I didn't want to share that he'd been leaving me food or that he'd hunted me and let me go after I gave him my name.

Or that he kissed me.

Yeah, that part still threw me for a loop. I definitely wanted to get a better feel for Rich before divulging any of what had happened since I got here.

"So, it's just you and me, huh?" Rich smiled at me and, instead of feeling comforted, my gut clenched with unease. "I always thought those stories about the minotaur were bullshit."

"Well, I would still remain alert," I said. "Like I said, I've heard noises. There's lots of hiding spots. The minotaur could just be waiting to make a move." *He is definitely watching us right now.*

"I'll protect you if you get scared." Rich leaned toward me, still smiling in that unsettling way, and I leaned away in a move that I hoped wasn't too obvious.

"I've been able to manage so far." I cocked my head. "You know, considering the circumstances and all."

"Right, and that's good. Something definitely took out those sad sacks all piled up near the entrance." He jerked his chin toward the skeletons, and I gave a tight-lipped nod in agreement.

* * *

I spent the rest of the day taking Rich on a tour of what I knew of the labyrinth, which was primarily the open main area where the stream cut through. He seemed keen on exploring the man-made area with stone floors and tunnels, but I made excuses for not going in there. For some reason, the thought of being alone with him in the bathing pool made me vastly uncomfortable.

The minotaur never showed up, and I almost wished he would. It was a nagging feeling I couldn't explain. The little time we'd spent in each other's company mainly consisted of me being terrified and running for my life, and yet I almost preferred his company to Rich's.

Something about Rich just nagged at me in a way I couldn't explain. Even when I wasn't looking at him, I could feel his stare on me, like dirt on my skin that I wanted to wash off. His smile never became any less off-putting, and he always seemed to stand too close to me. Everything about his presence just made me deeply uncomfortable.

Considering the only other man in here literally wanted to hunt me down, I didn't know which was truly the lesser evil.

As night fell, it only got worse.

"We should sleep close to each other," Rich suggested. "Watch each other's backs. Maybe share body heat if it gets too cold."

He said it so nonchalantly, I could almost believe he didn't have nefarious intentions behind it. But I felt his gaze burning into the side of my face, ogling the hell out of me while I pretended not to hear him.

"What did you say you were tried for again?" I asked, washing my hands distractedly in the stream.

"Huh? That's a hell of a left turn." Rich chuckled. "I thought we were figuring out sleep."

"Humor me." I looked at him, finding his eyes already glued to my face again. "I just forgot, that's all."

"Vandalism," he huffed. "I tagged one of them ritzy uptown buildings."

"Oh, right." I tried to make my smile look sheepish while my teeth were actually grinding in my jaw. "So, I think we should actually sleep in shifts."

"Shifts?"

"Yeah, one person stays awake for a few hours while the other sleeps. Then we switch." I wiped my hands on my pants to dry them. "I can take first watch. You must be exhausted after the day you've had—"

"Nonsense!" Rich cut a hand through the air. "You've shown me around, shared your food and water with me. You rest first. I insist."

"Oh no, I really don't mind. I've gotten used to this place. But for you, the stress and adrenaline must be—"

"Exactly." He cut me off again. "I'm not going to sleep a wink anyway. And besides," his eyes raked over my body, "no offense, but I can probably fight off a minotaur better than you can."

I swallowed. My whole being was screaming at me that this was a bad idea. I did not want to sleep while he was awake. But I wanted us to sleep near each other even less.

"Okay," I forced my mouth to say. "There's a little cave further up this way that blocks most of the wind, so I like to sleep there. It's just big enough for one person to lie down, so we can take turns guarding the entrance."

That probably wasn't a clear enough hint that I didn't want him anywhere near me while I slept, because Rich smiled broadly. "Excellent. Lead the way."

I trudged in that direction, my feet feeling heavier with each step closer to my private sleeping area. I scanned the surrounding rock pillars as I did, looking for a set of golden horns, but saw none.

"Hm, that cave is small," Rich said when we reached our destination. He sounded disappointed.

"Yeah. It only really fits one person, like I said. But it's good protection from the wind. That boulder there is a good lookout point." I pointed at the rock a good ten feet away. "When you get tired, you can come wake me up, and I'll take over."

"Sounds good." He took his sweet time meandering toward the rock. "Sleep tight."

"Thanks." Eager for some space from him, I went to squeeze into the cave and nestled into my small pile of stolen clothing from the skeletons. Physically, I was exhausted, but my mind wouldn't stop racing.

The minotaur likely knew Rich was here. What did that mean for Rich? For me? Would he hunt us both in the same manner? Somehow I doubted it. Rich's days were likely numbered, but so were mine. I felt a stab of guilt at being so unnerved by him. He was likely the last human I'd have contact with.

No, I'm escaping, the stubborn part of my brain said. *Tomorrow, we'll look harder at where the stream flows in and out. A second pair of eyes will help, and then I'll get back to Mom.*

Satisfied with that thought, I drifted off to sleep sooner than I expected.

* * *

I woke up to what sounded like rain at first. A steady, constant...something. When I went to rub my eyes, a moaning sound made me freeze. And then I heard loud, heavy breaths.

Oh, fuck. Oh no, don't tell me...

That sound wasn't rain but a man jerking his cock.

Right next to me.

I was lying on my side, facing away from the cave entrance. I didn't dare turn over. It was hard enough to keep my breathing even and pretend I was still asleep. All my instincts were fucking right about this creep. No wonder he was squirrelly about what he was tried for.

Rich moaned again, muttering curses under his breath. My horror only mounted when I felt the probing touch of his fingers against my back. He paused, probably waiting to see if I'd move, then continued.

Don't fucking touch me, you sick bastard!

I didn't know what to do. My ability to process and form a plan stuttered down to nothing when his fingers reached over my side, heading for my breast.

What would he do if I flung his hand away and yelled at him to fuck off? Make excuses? Play it off? Or actually assault me?

I didn't know the answer. The safest option seemed to be to continue to pretend to be sleeping and wait for it to be over.

Then different sounds made my eyes snap open. The clapping of great, heavy hooves on stone and angry, snorting breaths.

Rich's hand pulled away from me immediately. "Holy fuck!" he cried out.

I rolled over to see a massive silhouette towering just outside of the cave. Steam escaped the wide nostrils of the bull's head. The minotaur's fists clenched at his sides, and every muscle in his body popped with an inhuman amount of mass. The long tail behind him was a blur from slashing around so angrily.

Rich stared at the minotaur in open-mouthed shock. His pants were open, and his dick now hung small and limp between his legs.

"I—look, I brought her for you!" He waved a shaking hand in my direction. "A sacrifice for you! As a tribute to y-your power and greatness."

I almost wanted to laugh at his ridiculous lie. Then I remember that he thought I'd never seen the minotaur before.

"S-such strength and prowess l-like yours should be honored. Do what you like with her. I-I just ask that you spare my life in return for this gift." Rich's whole body shook as he bowed his head, trying to look humble while throwing me under the bus.

The minotaur never spared a glance at me, though. His molten gaze remained fixed on the cowardly man with his pants still loose. Then he moved, striking with the speed of an experienced predator. The next thing I heard was the sickening crack of Rich's head against the lookout boulder.

Rich let out a pathetic whimper, his feet kicking at air because the minotaur held him up by the throat. I couldn't look away as the horned monster lifted Rich higher, his arm wrought with muscle and fully extended. Rich looked like a child in comparison to the massive creature clutching him in an iron grip.

Rich's face slowly turned purple while he pulled at the minotaur's hand around his neck with no effect. Then the minotaur opened his hand, jutting his head forward just as he dropped Rich.

I would never forget the sound of horns piercing a body for as long as I lived. I screamed, but it didn't erase the sound. Nothing ever would. Just as I would never forget the sight of it right before my eyes.

The minotaur's horns stuck out of Rich's back, covered in blood and viscera. I rolled out of my sleeping cave and promptly vomited all over the ground.

Even then, I couldn't tear my eyes away.

The minotaur reached up with both arms and plucked Rich from his horns as easily as removing a chicken from a roasting spit. He then shifted to his human form, blood and gore still dripping down his face, arms, and torso. With a sick splat, he slammed Rich against the rock again, holding him up by the throat. To my horror, Rich's eyes blinked slowly and his jaw worked up and down like he was trying to speak.

After being impaled on the minotaur's horns, he was still alive.

The minotaur leaned in close to the dying man's face, teeth bared and eyes blazing. "You do not touch what's mine."

He released the man's throat, and Rich fell to the ground in a crumpled, bloody heap. If he wasn't dead yet, it was only a matter of minutes. Only then did the minotaur look at me.

His eyes locked onto mine as he wiped Rich's blood from his face. That eerie gold color burned like it had been melted in a forge. Other than that, I couldn't read his expression at all, probably due to my own shock and the fact that his face was still covered in gore.

Just as quickly as the moment happened, it ended. The minotaur looked away to stare down at Rich, still bleeding out on the ground. He bent to grab the dying man's leg, then turned and left, dragging Rich's body along behind him.

8

———

ARIADNE

I couldn't sleep after that, let alone eat or drink, or fucking cope with reality, if I had to be perfectly honest. Every time I closed my eyes, I saw Rich's mangled, bloody body with the minotaur's horns protruding from his back. I felt almost as sick as when I first drank the water from the stream.

Daytime came, and the minotaur never returned. I couldn't even begin to guess where he went. Where did he take Rich? What did he do with the body? Oh God, was he a cannibal too?

My stomach lurched, and I started coughing. I had to get out of here. It all came back to that. I just witnessed one man get brutally murdered, and that was more than enough. It didn't matter that Rich was a gross pervert. Such a brutal death was uncalled for.

If it wasn't his execution my mind fixated on, it was the minotaur himself. I'd never seen him so angry before. When he was hunting me, he seemed almost playful. It was a game to him. Last night had a completely different feel to it. He didn't engage with Rich at all, except to kill him.

It was almost like he was being protective of me.

I snorted so hard, it started up my coughing again. "Yeah right, Ari."

The minotaur was just upset that he had to share his toy with someone else. That's all I was to anyone here, something to play with.

Well, I was done being a plaything. And I was going to get the fuck out.

With that determined thought, I left the cluster of rock formations which I'd deemed *my* cave and headed for the stream. Today, I'd follow it and see where it led. With luck, it would guide me out of here. All water had to go somewhere, right?

My stomach growled as I walked alongside the rushing water. The minotaur hadn't brought me food this morning. Maybe my belly didn't get the memo, but my head couldn't get past the sick image of the minotaur cooking up poor Rich for breakfast.

"Hehe. Poor Rich," I snickered. "I'm really fucking losing it, aren't I?"

I dipped the thermos in the stream and dropped a purification tablet in it. Water would have to do until I got to the outside.

My walk continued for roughly another half hour. I still couldn't wrap my head around how *big* the labyrinth was. It seemed like all the slums of MinoTek could fit inside with room to spare.

I hit a gentle downhill slope, and the sight ahead of me made my heart sink with despair.

The stream emptied into a small lake.

It was pretty, no doubt. Soft, green grass covered the ground, and there were actual trees here. More rock structures surrounded the lake, which was more of a pond, really, on the far side. The sun shone brightly, and I realized the opening in the cavern ceiling was wider here. It almost felt like I was outside in a valley between some rocky hills.

But not even the prettiest view changed the fact that I was still imprisoned here in the labyrinth with a monster.

"Fuck!" I wanted to throw my thermos of water, but again, that was what kept me alive. It just felt like another taunt from him. *He* provided the container and purity tablets, after all. Arrogant, murderous, probably-cannibalistic, horned asshole.

I spun around in a huff to start walking the other direction. Now that I knew where the stream emptied, it was time to figure out where the water came from.

And if *that* didn't lead to a way out...

"Don't think about that, just keep it moving," I said.

"...help..."

I thought I'd imagined the soft voice until I heard a pained groan right after.

"Hello?" I called, my heart racing as I spun toward the pond again. It definitely wasn't the minotaur, he couldn't fake that voice. Another human then?

"...over here...help, please..."

I headed directly toward the raspy, whispery voice, realizing just then how incredibly stupid I was being. Even if it wasn't the minotaur, it could be one of his games. My instinct was always to help when needed, and even if he didn't know it yet, it was a weakness he could exploit.

Just don't get too close, I decided, peeking around a boulder near the pond shore. That went out the window when I saw who the voice was coming from.

My eyes widened in recognition at the young man lying on

the ground. He was pale and drenched in sweat, wearing only a white T-shirt and a pair of boxer shorts. His head lifted weakly from the ground, eyes red and lips chapped. I saw the same recognition in his eyes.

It was the shifter police officer who'd taken me from my house.

His gaze went to my water jug, and his cracked lips parted. "...Please..."

Damn my bleeding, helpful fucking heart. I unscrewed the thermos and approached him slowly, but it wasn't necessary. Something was terribly wrong with him, and he couldn't hurt me if he tried.

His eyes closed, the purple veins in his eyelids stark against his pale skin. "...sorry about...just...so thirsty..."

"It's okay." I didn't know why I said that. Nothing was okay. Still, I knelt next to him and cupped my hand so he could drink from the container. The shifter seemed barely strong enough to swallow. He choked on more water than he drank.

"What happened to you?" I asked once he'd gotten a couple mouthfuls down.

He blinked and tears dripped from his eyes and down his nose. "...Dying..." He blinked again, like he was trying to focus on me. I noticed his eyes becoming milky. "...Sorry...for..."

"It's okay," I said again. "You were following orders, right? It seemed like you didn't have a choice."

The shifter's head shook weakly. "No...choice..."

I reached for his hand, feeling sorry for the man who'd dragged me from my home and thrown me in here. What a sick twist of irony.

I felt fur under my fingers, and when I looked down, saw that his large hand was tipped in black claws and morphing into a wolf's paw.

The shifter let out another pained groan, blood vessels bulging on his pale skin. "...Run," he rasped. "...Can't... control...it."

I dropped his hand and stood, just now noticing the foam building around his mouth and his teeth growing into long canines. Unable to look away, I started walking backwards, and my back promptly hit a wall.

A warm wall that breathed and was also groaning in pain. I spun around to find myself face-to-face with a gorilla. This shifter was also foaming at the mouth, his eyes bloodshot. Where the fuck did he come from?

As I was backing away from him, a low growl sounded behind me. I glanced over my shoulder to see a massive wolf licking the foamy saliva from its jaws, its hackles raised, making it look enormous.

Fuck, I was even stupider than I thought, getting caught between *two* shifters who looked ready to kill each other.

"Ariadne!"

I didn't know whether I was saved or even more screwed when the minotaur called my name. He climbed down from the tallest boulders, nimble as a billy goat, and glared at the two shifters when he hit the ground. He'd at least cleaned himself of Rich's blood, which was a relief to see.

"Get behind me," the minotaur barked.

Oh, so he was saving me then. I could handle that.

But when I ran, the wolf and gorilla tried to follow.

I heard the battle roars and for a split second saw a massive black-furred arm swinging toward me. I shut my eyes and dove for safety, but the blow never landed.

The next several minutes were dominated by the sounds of flesh being pummeled, roars of pain and aggression, bones cracking, and more brutality than I ever wanted to imagine. I kept my eyes shut and slammed my palms over my ears, staying like that until most of the sounds had died away.

When I dared to look, the wolf was lying dead in a heap of gray fur, his neck bent at an odd angle. The minotaur and gorilla circled each other warily, both spent and badly injured. Now in his bull-headed form, the minotaur's horns were coated in blood, and the gorilla clutched at a gaping wound on his side. The minotaur dragged a bloody hoof behind him, and he looked to have been bitten on his arms and torso several times. A large red bruise spanned nearly his entire right side.

The gorilla bared his teeth at his opponent, but the roar that followed was weak. When his hand moved over his wound, I could see some of his internal organs. The minotaur stamped his good hoof and bellowed, nostrils flaring, but he too sounded weak.

It was an endurance test now, both of them seeing who would be the last one standing.

The minotaur lowered his head, aiming his horns at the gorilla as he pitched forward.

"No!" I squeaked out, covering my mouth.

He'd fallen, landing hard on his forearms with little strength left to catch himself. The gorilla had fallen too but backwards to avoid those horns. And that was what defeated him.

They were on the shore of the pond, and the gorilla slipped on grass that had been slicked with blood. He fell into the water, and there was only a minute of struggle before the surface was calm again.

Everything was quiet, almost peaceful again. Birds chirped, and the water trickled. The minotaur's labored breathing was the only sign that anything was amiss. That and the body of the wolf, naturally.

The minotaur shifted back to his human form, which seemed to take a great deal of effort in the state he was in. His eyelids drooped heavily, those molten gold eyes locking onto mine just for a moment.

"Ariadne..." he whispered before losing consciousness.

9

———

ZERUHN

For a moment, I thought death might come for me after all. Blackness pulled me under like a great, dark wave, and I gave into its embrace with no resistance. A fight to the death between two shifters certainly wasn't the worst way to go. *Finally, this fucked up existence can end.*

But as soon as sweet nothingness overtook me, the aches and pains of my physical body pulled me back. I groaned, both with pain and frustration, as consciousness and sensation returned. *Another day, another death that isn't my own.*

My eyes cracked open slowly, expecting the harsh sun to be in my eyes like it always was when I woke up after a shifter fight. But this time, something hovered over me, blocking the light.

"Lago, get off," I croaked. It wouldn't be the first time he'd sat on my chest while I was unconscious.

Something tugged and itched at my side, and I went to swat at it blindly.

"Don't rip those out," someone chided me. "I just got you to stop bleeding."

I opened my eyes fully and blinked several times in disbelief.

It was Ariadne at my side, my doe-eyed prey. She was stitching together a wound on my stomach, just under my navel. Her brows drew together in concentration as she pulled a small bone needle and a length of thread through my flesh. The sight was oddly fascinating and grotesque, and it still couldn't keep my gaze away from her face.

"What are you doing?" I asked her after a moment of watching her work.

"Sewing you up, what does it look like?" Ariadne didn't sound pleased about the task. "So your guts don't litter the ground like those two." She jerked her head, indicating the bodies of the two shifters I'd killed. "Or like Rich," she added in a small voice. I could only imagine that Rich was the disgusting human man who'd whipped out his cock at the first opportunity.

"You're helping me." I wasn't usually so slow to figure things out, but this threw me for a loop. "Why?"

Ariadne shrugged, continuing steadfastly with her work. "Seemed wrong not to. It was too late to help any of the others."

"You would help *them*?" I almost laughed, but breathing and talking were painful enough. "The shifters would have ripped you apart and fought each other to the death over your corpse. And the human?" The memory of her talking and smiling at him so readily pulled a growl from my chest. "If you had wanted him to touch you, why did I smell your fear and disgust?"

"I *didn't* want him to! Just—" She cut herself off, apparently unwilling to argue.

"Then I did you a favor," I said through gritted teeth. "His attempts only would have gotten worse if he'd been allowed to live."

She glared at me, pausing with the needle hovering over me

like she wanted to stab me with it. "What did you do with his body?"

I blinked at her. Maybe I was dead, because this whole exchange was too strange to be reality. "What does it matter?"

"Did you eat him?"

I did bark out a laugh at that and promptly regretted it when the muscle spasm tugged painfully at the threads holding my wound together. "No. I don't eat humans. I buried him so he wouldn't stink up the place." She looked relieved for a moment until I added, "When his bones are picked clean, I'll add him to my collection at the entrance."

I didn't do that with *all* of the skeletons of the people I'd killed. Just the ones I liked the least.

Ariadne huffed out a breath through her nose, much like my bull head did when aggravated. It looked much cuter on her, though. "What was wrong with the shifters?" she asked next in a small voice. "Why did they act like that?"

My eyebrows went up in surprise. "You don't know? They were simply expired."

"Expired?" She frowned.

"At the end of their lifespan," I clarified. "Done. Finished. When shifters reach their end, they go rabid and crazed by violence. They will kill anything in their path until something else kills them."

"But." Ariadne's frown deepened. "The wolf looked so young as a human. Early twenties, maybe twenty-five at the most."

Poor thing. She truly didn't know. The cold, dead remnants of my heart actually ached a little for her.

"Twenty-three to twenty-five years is the typical lifespan of a shifter." *Except for this one,* I thought bitterly. "They're usually put out into the field at fifteen and serve the state for eight to ten years."

Ariadne's mouth fell open. "That's terrible! I mean, for humans that's *so* young!"

"Shifters aren't born. They're created," I said. "Most of them are clones."

"I knew that. I just never thought about it, I guess. I can't imagine being at the end of my life at twenty-five years old, that's insane."

"Scientists have never been able to extend their lifespan beyond that, not without compromising on other features," I explained. "The pre-programming, the human DNA spliced with animals', the massive amounts of testosterone for muscle mass and strength—all of it accelerates the wearing down of the body and the brain."

Ariadne looked at me with a shrewd expression, her eyes narrowing. "How do you know so much? And wait, aren't *you* a shifter?"

"Not a very good one." I chuckled before remembering how painful everything was. "If you really want to help me, get the first aid kit from my sleeping cave. Lago will show you the way." I jerked my chin at the jackalope munching on grass several yards away.

"First aid kit?" Ariadne looked between me and Lago, her hair making a shimmering dark wave as her head moved.

"You did a fine job of stitching me up." I looked down at her work. She'd closed up the worst of my wounds on my stomach, ribs, and forearm. "But I'm assuming you didn't use sterile tools, so I'll still die of infection without the items in that kit."

Ariadne scoffed as she got to her feet. "I understand how preventing infection works. Excuse me for finding it strange that *the minotaur* keeps a first aid kit."

She walked off, following after Lago, and I enjoyed the sight of her long legs until she was no longer in my view. I closed my eyes again while I waited for her to return, taking careful, measured breaths so as to not aggravate my wounds.

The strangeness of my having a first aid kit had nothing on the fact that my prey, a labyrinth prisoner, had stitched up my wounds. I was all but certain that Ariadne had saved my life.

Why?

I terrified her. She preferred the company of a perverted human over my own. I killed the pathetic man not only because he pleasured himself without her consent, but because my selfish, territorial instincts didn't want to share her with another. He would try to take her from me, to make her his. I couldn't allow that.

And I'd do it again.

I killed easily and often. But I'd never done it for those reasons. I'd never felt so possessive of a prisoner before. And it was only getting worse as time passed.

Women were rare in the labyrinth, but Ariadne wasn't the first. Some past prisoners had also witnessed me fight expired shifters before. They were all probably rooting for my death.

Putting them out to pasture, that was what the guards called dumping shifters in here. Sometimes they killed each other before I got to them. I always considered those kills a mercy, to be honest. Living with a rabid, deteriorating mind seemed like a special kind of torture. Another wolf, probably a clone of the one who'd just bitten me, had begged me to kill him last year.

I thought I'd seen it all. But absolutely no one who had been tossed in here had ever treated my injuries before. My head was still spinning around that when Lago and Ariadne returned. I gingerly sat up from my reclined position, took the kit from her, and started rummaging for the antiseptic spray.

"You're welcome," Ariadne grumbled irritably.

I paused. An unusual feeling, which I recognized as embarrassment, welled up in my chest. "Sorry. Thank you."

She then made a face, one I couldn't interpret. I could rattle off all kinds of molecular processes, but human expressions were difficult for me. I never spent enough time with someone to interpret their range of expressions and emotions.

"What?"

"Nothing." Her features smoothed out with a small shake of her head. "I didn't actually expect a thanks from you, I guess."

I wanted to study all her expressions in great detail, to trace her brow and her lips to really know the differences in what she was feeling. Everything she did, thought, felt, knew... I wanted to download it all and store it away like precious keepsakes.

"Why not?" I pressed. "I'm grateful to you for this." I held up the first aid kit. "And for the stitches too." I cocked my head, still watching her expression for any clues. "Although I'm not sure what compelled you to help."

"Yeah. Neither am I, to be honest." Ariadne smoothed her hair away from her face. "Anyway, you were going to tell me how you knew so much about shifters?" Now her head cocked, almost mimicking my expression. "You are one, aren't you? But you look older than twenty-five."

"Correct. I was released from intubation thirty-four years, eight months, and twenty-one days ago." I held back hisses of pain as I sprayed the antiseptic over my injuries. "But as you probably noticed, I can't fully shift into my animal form." I scratched at the base of my left horn. "And I keep some animal traits in my human form."

"I can see that." Ariadne's gaze lifted as she followed the length of my horns.

"I was one of the prototypes before MinoTek engineers adjusted the shifter blueprint to what they use today. So I wasn't pumped with the same amount of hormones and foreign DNA that the current lot has."

"So you can live longer but don't have the full shifting abilities," Ariadne observed. "Are there more like you?"

"There were. The scientists killed them all."

"What?" she gasped. "Why?"

"All the prototypes were defective in different ways. Weak immune systems. Under-developed brains and other organs. Some had terrible, painful deformities."

"That's awful." Ariadne brought a hand to her chest. "But they didn't kill you, obviously."

I couldn't help but smile at that. "They tried."

"And failed?"

"Ariadne." Fuck, I loved the way her name tasted in my mouth. "Haven't you noticed? They've been trying to kill me every single day that I've been alive."

10

———————

ARIADNE

The minotaur spoke so nonchalantly about death and killing. It was unnerving, to say the least.

And still I found myself eager to hear the warm depth of his voice, the cadence in which he spoke. He was far more chatty than I expected. I expected short, blunt sentences and brooding silence, but he talked about prototypes and genetic engineering like someone who had gone to school in Upper MinoTek.

"They threw me in here because all of the state's attempts to kill me had failed." He said it almost proudly, with a subtle lift of his chin. "No one else they've thrown in here has succeeded in killing me either, so in the labyrinth I remain." His molten gaze slid toward me. "Unless you become the one to do it, Ariadne."

I couldn't decide if the way he said my name sounded like a taunt or a caress. "Why would I kill you?"

"Why not? I can see and smell your fear." He looked away, golden horns cutting sharply through the air. "You humans always smell like fear."

"That doesn't mean I should kill you. Besides," I pushed my

hair back, annoyed by how flustered he made me, "you're injured. It wouldn't be a fair fight."

"Fair?" He barked out a laugh before grimacing with pain. "Does the human world really care about fairness?"

He had a point there, but I wasn't about to admit that to him.

"It wouldn't matter how you did it," he continued. "They'd sing your praises. Ariadne, the one who bested the minotaur! They might even let you out of here and parade you through the streets."

"And then they'd throw me back in here and I'd be alone, fighting for my life while they bring more prisoners and your corpse rots," I snapped. "So no, thanks. I have no plans of being all alone as the queen of the labyrinth."

The minotaur was quiet for a few moments, looking thoughtful. "It is difficult to spend most of your life completely alone. You're right about that."

Don't do it, I thought. *Don't start feeling sympathy for him.*

"Anyway," I sighed. "I'm not a killer, and I couldn't just leave you for dead either. It's wrong."

He laughed more softly this time, mindful of his wounds. "That's sweet of you, doe eyes. But also foolish."

"What makes you say that?" Defensiveness rose in my voice.

Those golden eyes slid toward me again. "This changes nothing. Tending to my wounds doesn't mean I won't resume hunting you when I recover."

"Oh, trust me," I huffed. "I didn't expect you to have a change of heart."

His eyes narrowed for a moment like he was insulted. "Then why *did* you help me?"

Because I was raised to help people in need. My mom would never let me hear the end of it if I didn't. Because no matter who you are or what you've done, I don't want you to suffer.

Instead of voicing all this, I shrugged. "It's just the right thing to do."

The minotaur huffed, gingerly shifting around to test his range of movement. "You have a strong sense of right and wrong, Ariadne."

"Somebody has to."

* * *

I HAD STITCHED THE MINOTAUR'S WOUNDS WITH A BONE NEEDLE that I found in my sleeping cave and an unraveled length of string from my shirt. But he still had a broken ankle, and I was lost on what to do about that.

So he set it himself, and then I had to help him wrap it. He gave no obvious signs of pain, aside from clenching his teeth and a few grunts here and there. It was clear that he'd set his own broken bones before and had likely stitched his own wounds, from what I could tell by his scars anyway.

For the second time, I tried to shove down the sympathy that rose for him. I couldn't imagine anything more lonely than tending to one's own wounds after being attacked, with no one else to care for you.

He's also killed people who were defenseless, I reminded myself. And now my mother was another person who was forced to fend for herself. She was the one I needed to worry about, not him.

"I can't walk on this," the minotaur grunted out after tightly wrapping his ankle. "You need to return to my cave and grab my crutches. They're leaning against the right wall."

Of course he would already have crutches, and be especially surly with a broken ankle, on top of all his other injuries.

His face softened just a fraction at my defiant look. "Please," he added in a gentler tone. "The faster I'm on crutches, the sooner you don't have to help me anymore."

"Fine." I rose to my feet. "I'll be right back."

I was pretty confident I knew the way from grabbing the first aid kit earlier, which was good for me since Lago chose to stay near the minotaur's side this time. When I looked over my shoulder, the creature had stretched out on its belly, relaxed and at ease next to the injured minotaur. I had just looked away when the minotaur gently petted the animal's back.

What a confusing person. How could someone so blood-thirsty show moments of warmth and kindness? He didn't know I was looking, so it couldn't have been for show. I hurried my footsteps, my curiosity now piqued. I had grabbed the first aid kit and ran before, but now I had some time to snoop.

The minotaur's sleeping cave was larger than the one I'd found for myself, cutting deeper into the rocky wall and with a taller ceiling. It was roughly the size of a small studio apartment, and he clearly made this space a home. I spotted the crutches immediately, and they were clearly factory-made—a lightweight metal with plastic components. Just like with the first aid kit, I wondered, how did he get these things?

I stood in the middle of his cave and turned in a slow circle, taking in all of the minotaur's belongings.

A crude bookshelf leaned against the far wall, and it was packed full of books. Many of them were fat and the pages rippled like they had been waterlogged and then dried. Moving closer to read the spines, I saw a chaotic mix of fiction and non-fiction. There were several books on scientific theories and even textbooks on engineering and physics. One shelf was entirely novels—titles I'd never heard of, like *Fahrenheit 451, To Kill a Mockingbird,* and *Animal Farm.*

Next to the books, another shelf held over a dozen flat panels and screens chaotically attached to wires. It looked like an unfinished project, like the minotaur took apart electronic devices just for the fun of it.

I scratched my head as I continued to look around. I knew he could read and write. He had more than a typical shifter's intelligence, which didn't seem to extend far beyond repeating orders and forcing people into compliance. But from the books and items here, plus how he spoke, it painted a picture of someone of much higher intelligence than the typical human too.

A memory flashed through my head from when I was around eight years old. I was in school, a single room with a moldy smell and water damage on the ceiling. The teacher used an ancient blackboard with chalk—nothing like the Upper MinoTek private schools with touchscreen tablets and AI teaching boards.

I was friends with a boy whose name escaped me, but all the teachers called him "gifted" and "genius". I didn't know what it meant at the time, but he was always bored because the school-work was too easy for him. He finished his assignments early, and then gave me hints for the answers.

One day, two MinoTek officials came to our classes. We were all starstruck by their sleek, clean suits without any stains or wrinkles. They talked to our teacher for a minute, and then took my friend out of class. He rolled his eyes as they led him away, because I guess this was normal for him. Adults often talked to him, he'd said. They asked him complex questions, as if trying to figure out how smart he really was.

I never saw him again after that day.

When I asked the teacher about him a few days later, she said he'd been placed in a different school better suited to his gifts. Again, that went right over my head as an eight-year-old.

But standing there, in the minotaur's cave eighteen years later, it made me wonder.

The minotaur wasn't shy about mentioning that he was lab-created. Was his intelligence a product of that as well? Or was it some kind of natural gift, like my friend who had been taken away?

And regardless of what the answer was, where did he get these books and things? Was he really a prisoner here like me, left to die?

The questions stewed in my head as I grabbed the crutches off the walls and made to leave the cave. Something else caught my eye, and I paused in the doorway to look closer. Next to his bed, which was a thin but clean mattress and several neat layers of blankets, was a photograph of a woman. Not a digital image, but a real photograph printed on paper. Even those of us in the slums rarely carried around physical photos anymore.

The image was unframed and sitting on a small side table. The woman was smiling radiantly, her joy shining through the dots of ink on the paper. She was dark-haired, maybe in her thirties, and wearing a dress.

She was also pregnant, supporting a third-trimester baby bump with one hand as she smiled at the camera. This woman, in this moment, had been absurdly happy. She'd probably laughed between smiling for the photo, the happiness just exuded from her.

I stared at that photo for an uncertain amount of time, just even more thoroughly confused by the minotaur and the mysteries surrounding him. Who was this woman? She was clearly important enough to put at his bedside so that he saw her every night.

More importantly, why did I care?

I hurried away with crutches, hoping my delay hadn't been noticed.

"Enjoy snooping through my things?" the minotaur huffed, reaching for the crutches as I approached.

So much for that.

"I wasn't *snooping,*" I protested, handing them to him. "I just...looked around a little."

"Did you see the dictionary on my bookshelf?" He secured the crutches under his armpits and pressed himself up. "You're welcome to look up the definition of snooping yourself."

I refused to take the bait and looked on warily as he got himself to standing. Using the crutches pulled at his stitched wounds, and he still seemed to have trouble taking deep breaths. The bruise taking up his whole right side was also darkening to a reddish-purple color.

"Do you need help?" I asked before I could think. He'd gotten to standing only to look ready to fall over again.

"No, I just—" He teetered to one side, and I rushed over to support his unbruised side.

"I got you." He was heavier than a sack of bricks, but with my help, the crutches, and his one good leg, the minotaur managed to keep standing.

He made a disgruntled noise. "Just to my cave, then, where I can rest."

"Magic word?" I couldn't help but smile. This situation was just bizarre and morbid, so why not go all in and ask for manners?

The minotaur clenched his teeth and growled, "Please."

I placed a hand on his waist and wrapped the other around his back, careful to avoid his injuries. It occurred to me then that I'd never seen him wear a shirt, and I wondered if he owned any.

His skin was warm to the touch, hard muscles flexing underneath as he moved. To his credit, he really did try to avoid putting too much of his weight on me. I wondered how much of it was his pride versus genuinely trying not to crush me under his bulk.

It was a slow, arduous walk to his cave. The sun had already moved across the chasm in the ceiling, and light in the labyrinth was fading. I hadn't realized the shifter fight and the aftermath had taken up most of the day.

"Do you have a name?" I asked when the mouth of the minotaur's cave came into view. Of all the things I wanted to know about him, starting with that seemed like the most obvious. Days had passed since he'd learned my name. It only seemed fair that I got his in return.

He moved away from me to lean against the rock wall leading into his cave. There he left his crutches before turning around on his good foot and easing down to his bed on the floor.

"It's Zeruhn," he said. "My name is Zeruhn."

"That's...unique," I mused. "Does it mean something?"

"Heh." A smile pulled at his lips. "Not really. I was Prototype number 0-9. One of the scientists combined them into the name Zeruhn because it sounded better than two numbers. More human, I guess."

"I see." I liked his name, but for some reason, I felt shy about telling him that.

An awkward silence followed. He was settled in at home, while I just stood outside of it. I cleared my throat. "Well, uh, goodnight, Zeruhn."

"Stop." His voice carried the edge of a growl. "You haven't eaten since yesterday." He jerked his chin toward the cave entrance. "There's water and a few birds in that cooler around the bend. I'll prepare them for us."

"I'll get them for you, but I—"

"Ariadne." Zeruhn's golden eyes heated. "You have only eaten what I provide you, and I will not have you starve. Get four birds and enough water for the two of us."

I hesitated for a moment longer, then turned to follow his instructions. Part of me wondered why I wasn't running as fast as I could to my own little cave but mostly, I was grateful to get a meal in my belly soon.

And as much as I hated to admit it, I was also glad to have someone to eat with and talk to.

The cooler turned out to be a solar-powered mini-fridge, the panels perfectly positioned to get as much sun as possible. Inside was a stainless canteen of water, already purified, if I had to guess, and several cuts of meat.

The birds were already plucked, gutted, and washed. If I didn't know any better, they looked just like the meat I sometimes picked up from the market back home, if not better. When I returned to Zeruhn, he had already set up a small camping stove with a pot of rice.

"Is that solar-powered too?" I asked, helping myself to the seat across from him.

"It is now." He took the meat from me and proceeded to rub it with spices. "It was a propane stove before, but I rigged it to become solar-powered when I ran out of gas."

"How did you learn how to do that? And where did you get all this stuff?" I gestured around the cave to the crutches, the books, and the various electronics everywhere.

"I'll tell you all my secrets, Ariadne." He set the birds on a small skillet on the stove. "For a price."

"A price?" My stomach turned. Of course he would want something. They always did.

"I'll let you name it." Wicked humor lit up his eyes. "So think carefully."

"Yeah, I'll be sure to let you know." I rubbed my forehead as the food cooked. The fatigue of the day finally caught up to me, and I was dying to eat and then sleep for a full day.

Zeruhn and I both ate ravenously, too occupied with stuffing our faces to talk much more. Once every morsel was gone, however, the part of me that insisted I should leave got increasingly louder.

But the cave was warm and comfortable. I felt my eyelids drooping from fatigue, and it would be so easy to just lay down...

"You can stay if you wish." Zeruhn said it so quietly, I almost didn't hear him. "I won't touch you. Or myself, for that matter." His lip curled with disgust, and I shuddered at the memory of Rich hovering over me.

Horns and shifting aside, I couldn't deny there was a huge difference in how each man came across to me. Rich had creeped me out from the start and certainly would have taken advantage of me. Zeruhn was clearly the more dangerous of the two. He was far more powerful, and he killed without hesitation.

And yet, it almost felt like he wasn't a danger to *me*, but only me.

He didn't set off the same gut feelings as Rich did. I believed him when he said he wouldn't touch me, but was that just me being foolish again?

"What about when you did it before?" I asked.

Zeruhn's eyes narrowed. "Did what before?"

"Touched me."

"And when did I do that?"

"You...*kissed* me." It was jarring to say aloud, like voicing the words cemented them into reality. "After the bathing pool."

"Ah, yes." Zeruhn's face relaxed as he calmly put away the camping stove. "That was my prize."

"Your *prize*?" I balked.

"I was hunting you," he said, like it was the most rational explanation ever. "And then I caught you. That kiss was what I earned for capturing you, doe eyes." That wicked smile returned. "Along with your name, of course."

My head shook in utter disbelief. He had the skills to convert a propane stove into a solar-powered one, but then he said bizarre caveman shit like that.

"But...then you let me go."

"I did," he said with a nod. "It will be a while before I can hunt you again, but next time," his tongue darted out to wet his lips, "perhaps you will reward me with more."

11

ZERUHN

I awoke early when it was still dark. Ariadne's silhouette was the first thing I saw, the shape of her hidden by the blankets she'd pulled over herself. But that didn't dampen the desire to pull her flush to me until her body molded to mine. I would honor my promise to not touch her, but that didn't mean I didn't want to.

Using the wall for support, I pushed myself up to standing and hopped to my crutches on my good leg. My injuries still ached with a persistent soreness, and I bit my tongue to not groan or make any noise. There it was again, that confusing, instinctual need to keep Ariadne comfortable and looked after.

Or just to keep her in general. These infernal instincts spoke to me like guiding voices, like humans with their gods or their mental illnesses. I wished they'd shut up.

Even so, the idea of keeping Ariadne around was a pleasing one. I liked having her in my cave, sharing a meal, and even sleeping near each other, despite not touching. She seemed just as confused as I felt, and there was some comfort in knowing I wasn't the only one thrown by all this.

I had taken lives during a hunt before, but never a kiss. I'd never allowed anyone to live in the labyrinth as long as she has. For as long as I've dealt with the humans and shifters thrown in here, this was completely new territory.

Lago had curled up to sleep near Ariadne, allowing just enough distance that his antlers wouldn't poke her. He stirred and turned in a small circle as I secured my crutches under my arms, then promptly fell back asleep.

I huffed a soft laugh as I made my way out of the cave. The little creature was already smitten with her, and I saw her pet him a few times before she drifted off last night. I'd never be able to keep her, but I wanted to savor her presence in the labyrinth for as long as possible.

Several yards away from the cave seemed far enough to take a piss. I leaned my crutches against another boulder and carefully put some weight on my bad leg. Already the pain and swelling had gone down. When it came to healing from injuries, being lab-created certainly had its perks.

I tried not to think of Ariadne as I handled my cock. Tried to not stroke myself at the thought of her wide, stormy eyes and her hands on me as she stitched me up. I wanted her to trust me, wanted my promises to line up with my actions when it came to her. For some reason, being honest with her mattered when it never had before.

Maybe because she was the first person to have ever been honest with me.

Everyone played a game in the labyrinth. People did what they thought would help them survive the longest, whether that was pretending not to fear me, trying to befriend, or fuck me.

Ariadne was confused, scared, brave, compassionate, and refreshingly genuine. She didn't pretend to be anything else. Maybe that was why she tickled my instincts in a different way.

I finished pissing and turned toward the wall with my crutches, hopelessly lost in thoughts of my pretty prey. So much so that I didn't notice the robotic arm emerge from the wall. The next thing I felt was a metal collar snapping around my neck, holding me in place with an unyielding grip.

My mind instantly returned to the lab with its blindingly bright lights, stainless surfaces, and the smell of toxic cleaning products. I struggled with the collar like I did back then, pulling at the metal clamp that pinned me like an animal next in line for slaughter. Humans never saw shifters as anything else, really.

Next to where the arm emerged, a slab of rock slid aside to reveal a doorway. Another fucking hidden door. I thought I'd found them all but apparently not. I snarled as a human man stepped out, regarding me like a cockroach he'd just found in his bathroom. He was dressed in a tailored suit with an ornate MT logo pinned to his lapel. A high-ranking MinoTek official. That was surprising. These types usually didn't bother with me face-to-face.

"Take it easy, Zero-Nine," the man told me in a placating tone. "I'm Simon Gibbs, Prime Minister Minos' Chief of Staff. You'll want to calm down and listen."

"You'll want to secure more than just my neck if you really want me to listen." I gripped the collar, trying to put as much space between my neck and the metal as I could.

"Now, they told me you were the most rational of the proto-types." Gibbs cocked his head. "The one with the most human-like brain. I'd hate to be disappointed."

"*They* gave me an IQ of 162, but sure." I allowed a small shift, letting my horns grow longer. "Believe what they tell you."

His already-thin mouth pressed into a frown. "You still have a live prisoner in here. Ariadne Saavas. She's been in the labyrinth for over a week."

That made me pause. I'd always figured the labyrinth was monitored, but I didn't know to what extent. It also didn't make sense to me that this man would care about the petty criminals that ended up with me. People were thrown in here because men like him didn't want to bother with an actual criminal system.

"And? What do you care how long I toy with my prey?"

"The labyrinth is meant to be a death sentence to all who enter. She must be put to death."

"She will be," I said. "When I'm done with her. This is my domain. Can't I have a little fun?"

Gibbs clasped his hands behind his back, puffing his chest out slightly. "The Prime Minister has a vested interest in seeing that she dies. Soon."

If he thought I gave a fuck about what the prime minster of MinoTek wanted, he was sorely mistaken. "Tell him to come kill her himself then."

Such a thing would never happen, and we both knew it. I wasn't entirely convinced that the Prime Minister was a real person. His lackey only rolled his eyes at me. "What if we arranged for an incentive if you killed her as soon as possible?"

"Depends on the incentive." I only ever killed on my own terms, but now I was curious.

"Freedom," he answered. "Well, freedom within reason."

I snorted. "I think you and I have very different ideas of what *within reason* means."

"You will be granted conditional citizenship with the ability to become a full citizen if you meet all the conditions," he said. "And free modifications."

"Modifications?"

"You could lose those horns. And the, uh, extra appendage."

He nodded at my tail, which was flicking curiously. "They might even be able to do an iris implant to give you a normal eye color. You could live as a human man, doing whatever you please, going anywhere you'd like."

A long pause hung between us. "Within MinoTek," I clarified.

"Yes, of course."

"And all I have to do is kill the woman?"

"That's correct." His Adam's apple bobbed as he swallowed. "Shouldn't be too difficult for you, considering you do it regularly."

My curiosity got the better of me. "Why is the prime minister interested in this girl? She's nothing special."

"I'm not at liberty to say." Gibbs' posture stiffened, clearly at his limit of dealing with a lowlife like me. "So, will you do it?"

"Sure, whatever." I tugged at the collar once more. "Just don't use this fucking thing on me again."

"Do this task, and you'll have nothing to worry about." He smiled, pleased. "Remember, do it *soon*. And there should be no doubt of her death. Leave a body behind, if possible."

"Oh, I'll leave her corpse nice and pretty for the prime minister. Are we done here?"

He swallowed nervously again, then turned toward the doorway. The robotic arm finally released me as the slab of rock slid closed after him. I spent a few moments just rubbing my throat and thinking back over that bizarre conversation.

So the most powerful man in the entire city-state wanted my stormy-eyed prey dead. Interesting. Luckily for me, I was good at lying and didn't give an iota of a shit what government officials wanted. But it was still interesting. If they wanted her dead so badly, there had to be a reason.

I returned to the cave just as dawn began to illuminate the labyrinth, so I set up the stove, grabbed a carton of eggs, and started to cook breakfast. Ariadne and Lago roused just as the food started to sizzle.

"Smells good, Zeruhn," she said through a yawn, rubbing her eyes.

The compliment shouldn't have affected me, but my chest sparked with pleasure. It seemed to be doing that more often lately.

"What happened to your neck?"

"Ah." I brought a hand to my throat, still lingering with soreness from that fucking collar. "Got hit by some tree branches when I walked out to take a piss. I forget how tall I am sometimes."

"You been up a while?" Ariadne sat upright, her expression becoming more alert, if even suspicious.

"Not too long." I flipped an egg over. "Did you sleep well?"

"Yes, actually." She stretched and raked fingers through her mane of thick, dark hair. "Best night of sleep since I ended up in here." Her hands flopped down to her sides with a sheepish smile. "I'd kill for a hairbrush, though."

"Oh, here." I leaned over to the nearest set of drawers and rummaged around until I found my prize—a rectangular brush with most of the bristles still intact. "Will this work?"

Ariadne stared at me for a few moments before taking the brush from my outstretched hand. "It'll do. Thank you."

I returned my gaze to the stove, unsure how to respond. Watching her brush her hair seemed almost perverse. Not as bad as stroking my cock, but it felt like too intimate a thing for what we were.

"How are you feeling?" she asked softly.

That question made me deeply uncomfortable. I'd never

been asked that in my life. "I'm recovering," I muttered in response.

"That's good."

Is it really? I wondered.

"I'm still thinking about that price," Ariadne mused after a few moments of silence.

"Price?" I was distracted, not as vigilant as I should have been. Probably due to the fact that I could still feel the metal collar around my neck, on top of finding her brushing her hair arousing.

"The price you wanted for spilling your secrets." Ariadne used the brush in her hand to gesture around my cave. "For how you got all this stuff, how you know so much."

I straightened, turning off the stove. "I know I left it up to you, but I have an idea."

"Oh yeah?" She sounded truly curious, without an ounce of fear in her voice.

"Tell me about you." I slid some cooked eggs onto one of my plates with the fewest chips and handed it to her. "And I'll tell you about me."

It seemed like an even exchange. I wanted to know more about this doe-eyed beauty. And maybe I'd find out why some scumbag politician wanted her dead so badly.

"Oh, that's all?" She seemed surprised. "I mean, there's not much to tell," she added with a sheepish laugh. "Thank you for breakfast."

"Thank me by telling me your life story." I sat back with my own plate while Lago hopped out of the cave to graze.

Ariadne used one of my many mismatched forks to cut delicately into her egg. "Well, um, I was born and raised in Mino-Tek, but my mom came from outside the city-state."

"Where?" Places outside of MinoTek fascinated me. All my

life, I'd been dying to know what existed outside of this infernal city.

"A place called New York City." Ariadne looked to the ceiling as she chewed on that thought and her egg. "She said it's not there anymore, but it was a big city. Not a city-state, but it was also in a state called New York."

"What brought her here?"

"The city was falling to ruin, and everyone was displaced. She said she hopped a high-speed rail as a young woman and just rode as far as she could, all alone." Ariadne smiled to herself. "Kind of wish I'd have been able to do that."

"Don't we all," I mumbled around a mouthful of runny yolk. "And she met your father here?"

Ariadne shrugged. "I guess. He was never around, and she never talked about him. I don't even know his name or what he looked like."

That surprised me. It went against everything I'd read about human family dynamics. "Aren't two parents supposed to raise children together?"

"It doesn't always work out that way." Ariadne set her plate down in her lap. "Sometimes a child is unexpected, even unwanted. Raising children can also be stressful, especially if you grew up poor, like us. You need more money and things to provide for them. For some parents, walking away is the easier choice."

It disturbed me how casually she said all this. Like all shifters, I was made sterile so my fucked-up genetics wouldn't poison natural gene pools. But if I *could* make a child, abandoning it along with its mother seemed unfathomable to me. Shifters were made with specific purposes in mind. We didn't have the freedom to find partners and make families. It was something completely out of my reach, and I hated that humans, who could breed so easily, seemed to take it for granted.

"I kept asking her about my father one time," Ariadne continued, her voice wavering slightly. "I don't know why I had such a bug up my ass back then. I was just being a teenager, I think. But I kept pushing and pushing her until she snapped. She yelled at me to stop and then just started crying. I'd never seen her so upset before." Ariadne set her plate aside and placed her hands in her lap. "I never asked her about him again after that."

"Do you know why she was so upset?" I asked. Human behavior confused me during the best of times, but such a reaction about a man who created a child with her was baffling to me.

Ariadne's eyes flicked up to mine, a steely hardness in them that heated my blood. "I've never told anyone this before, but if I had to guess," she released a deep breath, "when she got pregnant with me...I don't think it was a consensual act." Her gaze lowered again. "That was why he was never around, why she never mentioned him. It was just... a traumatic experience for her." Ariadne shook her head, her eyes blinking rapidly as she sniffed. "It didn't occur to me until years later, and I never even apologized for upsetting her."

"You didn't know." A heavy ache settled in my chest, an uncomfortable, near painful sensation simply because of seeing Ariadne's pain. "You couldn't have known. I'm sure she is not angry at you for that."

"Yeah, well. She still deserves an apology." Ariadne sniffed and quickly wiped her eyes.

Silence passed between us as I tried to think of what to say next. I liked Ariadne's sharp tongue and smiles. Her sadness was something I wanted to banish forever.

Something else gnawed at me that I was desperate to know. "What you believed happened to your mother." I tried to say it as delicately as possible. "Do human men do that...often?" It reminded me of the one who'd tried to touch Ariadne in her sleep, and the thought brought my rage to simmering again. If there was one kill I would never regret, it would be that one.

Ariadne huffed out a mirthless laugh in response. "They do it enough that we treat all men as dangerous until they prove that they aren't."

"I've proven myself to be extremely dangerous," I pointed out. "But you don't seem to treat me as if I am."

She picked up her plate of food again, smiling down at the cooked egg. "For some reason, I'm not afraid of you doing *that* to me." She took a bite and chewed thoughtfully. "You haven't hurt me yet. Which is crazy to think about, because you're probably the most dangerous person in the whole city."

"I definitely am," I assured her.

"Are you *going* to hurt me?"

"No."

"But you've *hunted* me," she pointed out. "You said you'll do so again once your leg is better."

"I did not hurt you the first time, and I don't intend to hurt you any other time." I let my fork clatter loudly against my plate. I was supposed to kill her, but that was the last thing I wanted to do. I had no doubt that the human, Gibbs, would come back if I didn't carry out that task. I wasn't worried about him, though. I'd deal with him whenever he decided to come back. The more I talked to Ariadne, the stronger the need to protect her became.

"And in case I haven't made it clear," I added, "I will never force myself upon you."

"No, you'll just steal kisses instead," Ariadne shot back. Oh, there it was, that beautiful storm in her eyes.

"You are welcome to give them to me whenever you'd like," I replied.

She huffed again and stabbed violently at her egg, her cheeks reddening.

12

ARIADNE

top flirting. Stop flirting.
Stop. Flirting.
Stop getting distracted, for fuck's sake.

It was almost...pleasant having breakfast with Zeruhn. He seemed to be in a good mood, despite his injuries. He teased me, smiled, and asked me questions about myself, on top of cooking meals. It almost felt like I was on a date with a guy.

A really good date.

Maybe it was because I knew he never really talked to anyone else, but I felt okay with opening up to him about my mom. I still didn't entirely trust him, but that came more from a place of not knowing him yet, not because of what I did know.

He killed people. I still needed to escape the labyrinth. Both of those facts were important. But the longer I sat eating and talking with him, the less urgent those things felt. Guilt washed over me at the thought. I was sitting and eating breakfast, flirting with an attractive man, while my mom was probably worried sick and suffering from her arthritis.

"Where does the water from the stream come from?" I tried to sound casual as I stacked our empty plates.

"A waterfall at the far edge of the cavern." Zeruhn answered me easily, taking the plates and putting them to the side. "I'll take you there when my leg is healed. It's actually quite beautiful." His eyes lingered on me as he said that last word, and my face heated up again.

"You'll take me there before or after you hunt me down again?" *God damn it, what did I say about no more flirting?*

Hearing that was promising, though. If he took me directly to an escape route, that would be all the easier.

The minotaur grinned, and I resented the resulting flutter in my stomach. "The hunt is no fun if you know when it's coming, doe eyes."

He'd used that pet name several times too, and I was trying not to let on how much I liked it. Everyone always shortened my name to Ari as a nickname, so it was nice to hear something different.

"Alright, so?" I held my hand out, palm up, expectantly.

Zeruhn stared at my palm, then flicked his gaze back up to mine. "Yes?"

"I paid up and told you about me. Now it's your turn."

He chuckled and reclined on his elbows, gingerly stretching his legs out in front of him. "What would you like to know?" Lago hopped up to his side then, and Zeruhn scratched the base of one antler.

"How did you two become friends?" I decided to start with the easiest topic.

Zeruhn's expression softened as Lago stretched out and flipped to his back. "He's like me. A lab-created prototype."

"I figured as much."

"The scientists who oversaw my development created him

during their downtime. He was the laboratory pet. Apparently lots of labs made their own creations to just keep around for entertainment."

His voice took on a sad note, and I started to regret choosing this as a first topic.

"He had lots of health issues, as these genetic experiments often do. His antlers grew faster than the rest of his body, and he wasn't strong enough to lift his head most days."

"The scientists didn't do anything to help him?"

Zeruhn shook his head with a scoff and a roll of his eyes. "Experiments were scrapped and started anew all the time. They didn't care."

"Poor little guy."

"Both of us were left alone for hours when they weren't running tests on us." Zeruhn stroked down one of Lago's long ears while the jackalope's eyes began to fall shut. "So we bonded over that, because neither of us had anyone else."

My gaze drifted to the photo of the pregnant woman next to his bed. If it was just him and Lago, what was her significance? When I looked at Zeruhn again, his gaze was intensely focused on me. Shit, he'd caught me.

"What happened to the lab?" I asked in a rush of breath. I couldn't ask him about her, not yet. He might tell me but asking felt too invasive.

"It was shut down." His focus returned to petting the jacka-lope at his side. "All the funding went to more profitable labs, the ones that successfully created the shifters you see now." His head tipped back, a huff of laughter escaping his mouth. "So many of the scientists were crying. *'My life is ruined!'* he mocked.

"Because...they had lost their jobs?" I guessed.

"Yes." Zeruhn continued to chuckle. "Seven-figure salaries reduced to nothing overnight."

"And you find that funny?"

"When they casually tortured and then slaughtered every genetically imperfect creature that they created?" His golden eyes brightened, lips pulling back into an even wider grin. "I couldn't stop laughing that day, doe eyes."

That's cruel, I wanted to say, but I stopped myself. Zeruhn, Lago, and probably countless others encountered cruelty I could never fathom. Could I really blame him for seeing the scientists' misfortune as poetic justice?

Poverty was the cruelty I knew. The constant struggle and unfairness I could relate to, but I'd never really been mistreated by the people in my life. In that sense, I was extremely lucky. There was never a doubt in my mind that my mom loved me. My neighbors had also been my friends and babysitters. I couldn't imagine the loneliness of growing up without my community.

"Were they really so horrible to you?" I asked.

Zeruhn shrugged, but I saw the tension coiling in his wide shoulders. "Sometimes they talked to me and treated me like another human. But that was primarily to test the parameters of my intelligence and learning abilities."

"They made you really smart, didn't they?" I asked.

He looked uncomfortable with that question. "Yes," he bit out. "I was designed with a genius-level IQ. Mainly just to see if a highly intelligent shifter was possible." He scratched absently at the base of his horns. "It's possible that my brain matter is what stunted my shifting ability, but they never found out for sure. What they did find out," his hand dropped to his lap, "is that the government preferred shifters with much lower intellect."

"Makes sense," I said. "Makes them moldable and obedient."

"Keeps them from laughing their asses off when your entire future goes up in flames." He smirked.

This time a laugh escaped me too. "You're awful," I said with a shake of my head.

"The absolute worst," he agreed, grinning wider.

Shit. This *no-flirting* mantra really wasn't doing anything.

"So, you learned how to read and write in the lab?" I asked next. "How to, I dunno, make things solar-powered?"

"Converting to solar power is easy, given that you have the materials." Zeruhn bent the knee of his good leg and propped his arm on it. "But yes, I did graduate university-level physics and engineering courses. I completed at least four PhD programs by the time I was thirteen."

"*Thirteen*?!" I squawked.

"For some reason, I was slow to figure out that the lab interns were having me do their schoolwork for them." Zeruhn looked away, a sheepish expression crossing his face. "No one taught me how manipulative and self-serving humans would be. I found that out on my own."

"You're not the only one," I said. "It's a difficult lesson for many people, no matter what stage they are in life."

Zeruhn nodded sagely before pinning me with another bright, golden stare. "The more I talk to you, the more I realize you're a rare kind of human."

Now *that* was funny. "Me, rare?" I snorted. "Definitely not."

"But you are," he insisted. "Do you think I've had conversations like this with everyone who enters the labyrinth?" His head tilted, his gaze curious and heated. "I've seen all kinds come through here and...you're the first person I've truly spoken to. Or had a meal with."

I swallowed, unable to hold back the statement in my throat. "Because you killed them all."

"Yes." The answer was calm, almost whispered. I expected a

more heated response, some amount of aggression. But the minotaur almost seemed tired.

"Why?" I asked against my better judgment. "I was sentenced here for reading pamphlets. I'm completely innocent of any actual crimes. Surely I wasn't the first one."

"Probably not."

I shook my head as I stared at him, trying to reconcile the man I was just flirting with with the monster who left skeletons at the entrance.

"So why kill them?" I repeated.

"What people do outside of this cavern is of no concern to me." There it was, the undercurrent of aggression. A growl rippled from Zeruhn's throat. "In here, a person's true nature is always revealed. And do you know what I see, Ariadne? Every single time, no matter if it's a man or woman, whether they're innocent or a true criminal?"

"...What?"

"Someone who wouldn't hesitate to kill *me* if given the chance."

"That can't be—"

"It's true, Ariadne," he said. "Sometimes they try to befriend me, manipulate me, fuck me, or just beg and cry, but the end result is always the same." Zeruhn's voice softened again. "I kill them before they kill me. That's all it is." He shook his head, staring off into the distance. "It used to bother me, but so many years have passed. There have been so many people through here, all the same."

I could only stare at him in shock, wondering how many people he had killed. My gut feeling told me he was being honest, that it truly was about survival. He didn't look remorseful, exactly, but it was clear how heavily this all weighed on him.

Zeruhn's gaze returned to me. "When you stitched my

wounds instead of finishing me off, that was when you broke the pattern. You showed me you were different." He angled his head, his horns catching a beam of sunlight. "*That's* why I'm curious about you, doe eyes."

That probably should have terrified me, and it did, a little.

But what I didn't want to admit was how much it warmed me from the inside.

13

———

ARIADNE

I stayed with Zeruhn another full day because, well, it wasn't like I had anywhere else to be. And weirdly enough, I was finding that I really enjoyed his company.

Zeruhn's ankle felt much better by the next day, and he quickly became restless. "Let's go to the stream and rinse off," he suggested after our breakfast of eggs and some potato-like root vegetable. "Then we'll see how my ankle feels about going to the waterfall."

"After two days?" I asked, shaking out my blanket before folding it up. "You can't possibly be ready to walk on it so soon."

Zeruhn huffed as he secured his crutches under his arms. "When you're a lab-created freak, anything is possible."

Don't call yourself that, I wanted to say. I bit my tongue before it came out, my brain catching up to the fact that I wanted to *reassure* this man, to say something that would encourage him to not be so self-deprecating.

It seemed ridiculous if I looked at it objectively. Why should I care what a self-admitted murderer thought of himself?

But I did care.

So help me, it seemed like I was starting to care about *him*.

We spent all of yesterday just lounging in the cave and talking. I told him about my childhood, which he could not seem to get enough of. Zeruhn seemed fascinated by the idea of a community, of my neighbors who helped each other in times of need. The occasional celebrations and block parties we had that almost always got shut down by the shifter police. When me and the other neighborhood kids would run around and play pranks on the adults. Those wide, golden eyes never strayed from my face as he asked for every last detail.

And I was happy to tell him about it, to have someone truly listen. His wide-eyed fascination was adorable, in a way.

He did not supply as much about himself, however, and I still couldn't bring myself to ask about the photo of the woman.

Today, though, Zeruhn and Lago buzzed with a similar amount of energy. The jackalope ran in zigzags, jumped, and twisted in the air. He reminded me of the stray puppies from my neighborhood, and I couldn't stop laughing at his antics. Zeruhn was definitely faster on his crutches, putting more of his weight on his bad leg than I expected.

The sun was at its peak when we reached the stream, and the air was pleasantly warm. Everything felt...okay. For a moment, I could pretend that I wasn't in a prison, out on a stroll with a killer.

A killer that I couldn't stop staring at, especially when he knelt at the edge of the stream, cupped water into his hands, and splashed his face. The water dripped down his neck and bare chest—I still hadn't seen him put on a shirt at any point.

When Zeruhn looked at me and smirked, I had to make sure that no saliva was falling out of my mouth.

"The water's cold. It feels good," he said, carefully swinging his legs around in front of him.

While he gingerly unwrapped the compression bandage around his ankle, I splashed my face as well, gasping at the brisk temperature on my skin. Fuck, it felt *great*. My last bath was days ago in the stone pool, and I quickly became aware of how grimy I was.

Zeruhn had rolled his pants up to his knees, and when he finished unwrapping his ankle, miraculously, it was only slightly more swollen than the other one.

"Wow," I said, openly staring again. "You're almost as good as new."

"Told you," he answered before dipping both feet in the stream. "Ahhh," he sighed, his head dipping back while his eyes fell shut.

Okay, the freezing cold water must have felt amazing on his ankle, but did he *have* to look so hot doing that?

"I'm going to get in, I'm filthy." Zeruhn leveled a gaze at me. True, he still had dried blood on him from the fight, but that final word sounded sexually charged too.

"Me too," I blurted out. Yep, a dip in a freezing stream was exactly what I needed.

His eyebrows went up as if in surprise, but he didn't comment. "I'll be taking my pants off, just so you're aware."

Oh, right. Shit. Obviously I had lost some brain cells in my blatant ogling.

"I...I won't look." I averted my gaze to his amused laughter.

"Suit yourself," he said before adding, "I won't look at you either."

Well, that was chivalrous of him. Although he'd been pretty chivalrous with me the entire time I'd been here. Except for the whole hunting and stealing a kiss thing.

My face heated at the sound of rustling clothes, and while I wasn't trying to look, I caught a glance of Zeruhn's wide, muscular back as he entered the stream.

And his ass.

Oh, fuck, I just saw his ass!

I looked away, but it was too late. I'd seen enough to know that it was perky and oddly cute on such a big, scarred body. The stream only came up to his knees, so I also saw his thick, muscular thighs. And his tail, which was an oddly curious thing.

The base of it sat just above his ass, between the dimples at the base of his spine. It was covered in short, dense fur, tufted with some longer hair at the end. The appendage swished over the stream's surface like it had a mind of its own. I dared another glance back, watching it splash water over Zeruhn's legs like an extra hand. With its help, his backside was thoroughly rinsed in minutes.

And damn my stupid brain, but I couldn't help but wonder what the front side looked like.

"You alright?"

Zeruhn's face tilted to the side, though he still didn't look behind him. I noticed the profile of his lips and the straight length of his nose and realized I must have been staring too obviously.

"Um, yeah! Yeah, of course. Why?"

"You're just quiet back there. We can go to the bathing pool if you'd rather not get in the stream." He then bent over—why was I still looking?—and splashed handfuls of water on his torso.

"Oh, I'm okay. We can go to the bathing pool later. It is kind of cold, but I would like to see the waterfall, if you're still up for it." I reached into the rushing water and then brought my hands to my forehead and neck, trying to cool myself down.

"It's a climb, but I'm feeling up to it." Zeruhn poured more handfuls of water over his hair. So much for my resolve. I guess I was just going to keep on staring.

"Why is that area different?" I asked, mainly to distract myself. "Where the pool is, I mean. Like it was an actual building with hallways and rooms, while the rest of the labyrinth is…more wild, I guess."

"The labyrinth is a chasm created by a massive earthquake," Zeruhn said matter of factly as he splashed water over his arms. "Centuries ago, the earth ripped apart and created this place below the surface. Unfortunately for the humans at the time, whatever was on top of the fault line fell inside the chasm."

"Oh, that must have been devastating."

"Yes. People died. Cars, buildings, and all kinds of infrastructure were destroyed." Zeruhn looked to the side again, in the direction of the bathing pool. "Except the church. There was some damage, of course, but it was still largely intact."

"A church?" I cocked my head, unfamiliar with the word.

"Yes." I saw the edge of his smile as he returned to rinsing off. "A place where people gather to worship a god."

"God?" I repeated. "That doesn't sound like something MinoTek would approve of."

"You're right. The state has morphed into its own religion of sorts." Zeruhn shook his head with a huff. "Controlling every aspect of daily life and being an ever-present force."

"How do you know so much about this? How life used to be?" I asked. "My mom said there were no shifters when she was a girl. And before she came here, she and her family could just leave the city whenever they wanted to."

"History books," he answered succinctly. "And she's right. Shifters are a fairly new invention."

"And where do you get history books in a deep chasm in the

earth?" I kicked my feet in the stream. "Or solar panels? Or crutches, for that matter? Do the guards give them to you?"

"Nothing is given to me." Zeruhn turned around slowly, and I hid my eyes at the last minute. The cold water on my neck and face was all for naught as my skin heated again, burning hotter to the sound of his throaty laughter. "I'm decent now, doe eyes. You can look."

I peeked through my fingers, unsure of whether to be relieved or disappointed at the sight of his brown, canvas pants sitting low on his hips again.

"Shall we hike to the waterfall?" Zeruhn's tail swished playfully behind him as he placed his hands on his hips. "I'll show you where all my goods come from."

✳ ✳ ✳

WHEN HE SAID HIKE, HE WASN'T KIDDING AROUND. IF IT WERE UP to me, I'd say rock climbing was a more accurate term.

What started as a brisk, uphill walk turned into getting my hands, knees, and feet abused by boulders, shallow cliffs, and rocky outcroppings. Zeruhn, of course, didn't break a sweat. Neither did Lago, for that matter, who took his own route jumping from rock to rock. But me? I was out of breath, and my hands were raw and bloody within an hour.

"I didn't realize this would be so difficult for humans," Zeruhn said, examining my palms with a frown.

"Not all humans, I'm sure. I'm just out of shape," I panted.

"Here." Zeruhn turned around and sank down into a crouch. "Climb onto my back."

"What? No!" My heartbeat spiked with panic, and maybe something else, at the thought of touching so much of his bare skin.

"I'll carry you, it's no trouble," he insisted.

"No, your...your ankle," I sputtered. "You should still take it easy. Adding weight to your back could injure it again."

Zeruhn tilted his head back to look at me. "I'll be fine, doe eyes. But we're still a mile out from the waterfall, and you won't make it much longer like this. Just let me carry you."

Damn, I really did want to see it. And I wasn't exactly repulsed by the thought of taking a piggyback ride on him. Actually, I was uncomfortable with how much I liked the idea.

"Okay," I relented. "But set me down whenever I get too heavy."

"Certainly."

With that, I leaned over his back and wrapped my arms loosely around his neck. I planted my feet wide and allowed him to scoop under the backs of my thighs, lifting me up.

"Comfortable?" He brought my legs forward so I could wrap them around his waist. "I'll need my hands to climb, so hold on tightly with your arms and legs."

"Mm-hm, got it. Wait. Hang on, what's that?"

Something was touching my butt and my back. I looked behind me to see that Zeruhn's tail was gently pressed along my spine, as if to offer extra support while I held onto him. The furry end flicked back and forth near my shoulder blade.

"Sorry about that. It's got a mind of its own." He started hiking again, taking long, great strides.

"It's okay." He walked across a relatively flat area, so I released one hand around his neck to pet the furry tuft tipping his tail.

Zeruhn stopped dead in his tracks, and his whole body shuddered. "Warn me before you do that," he groaned.

"Oh, sorry!" I returned my hands to loop around his neck.

"It's fine, really. It's just...a sensitive area."

"The end of your tail or the whole thing?" I didn't know why I asked, why I wanted to know about *any* sensitive parts of his body.

"The whole thing, but the tip especially." He continued walking and added quietly, "The base of it too."

Again, I didn't need to know that. So why did it feel like I was mentally filing away that information for later?

He started climbing again, scaling short cliff sides by simply jumping, grabbing the edge, and pulling us up. Even with me, a human-sized backpack, he didn't slow down or tire. Lago zigzagged his own way up but kept pace with us easily.

The sunlight was brighter up here, and there were more plants, trees, and bird nests in these cliffs. I even saw a couple of stray cats jumping from rock to rock, heading nimbly for the nests. That brightened my hope of getting out even more. We had to be close to an escape route now.

"Oh my God, are those nectarines?" I pointed at a tree on its own little cliff ledge with tons of reddish-pink fruit.

"I don't know what they're called," Zeruhn admitted. "But I've eaten from that tree. The fruit is delicious."

"It has a pit in the middle?" I said. "The skin is smooth and kind of pops like a membrane when you bite into it? It's really sweet and juicy on the inside?"

"Yes to all of the above," he chuckled.

"Ugh, it's my favorite," I groaned. "Our next door neighbor had a nectarine tree, and she would always give us huge bags of fruit. We'd make jam, bake it into pies, or just eat it raw. I never got tired of it."

Zeruhn immediately turned toward the tree and started climbing the short ledges up to where it grew.

"Oh, no, Zeruhn," I protested. "You don't have to just for me."

I had barely finished talking when he pulled us up to the

cliff and stood before the tree. The air smelled so sweet here, and a hard pang of homesickness hit me right in the chest. Zeruhn plucked a couple of ripe fruits from the tree and handed one to me.

"They're my favorite too," he said so quietly that I almost didn't hear him.

We set off again, and I tried my best not to choke him with a one-armed grip while I ate my nectarine with the other hand. He carried his fruit in his teeth while he climbed, and I did my best to look at the scenery, not the muscles in his jaw as he chewed.

It was truly beautiful up here, and I ate my nectarine happily. But the higher we trekked, the more sadness and despair clouded over me. Zeruhn had superhuman strength and agility. He scaled ledges and cliffs that were ten, maybe twelve feet tall, over and over again. Maybe a world-class athlete could do that, but an average labyrinth prisoner? There was no way in hell.

"Here we are," he said, barely even panting as we stood before our final destination.

I slid down from his back and looked up, my neck craning back further and further. The opening in the cavern was closer than it had ever been and yet still so far away, maybe a hundred feet up. There was nowhere left to climb here, the rock wall leading up was smooth, likely shaped over centuries by the cascade of water tumbling over the edge.

"Up there is a restricted area just outside of Upper Mino-Tek," Zeruhn explained. "People use it as a dumping ground, and sometimes the water carries things into here. That's how I've gotten my books and all of my supplies. The products for the bathing pool too. Pretty much everything, except for food."

I heard him, but everything he said was noise. I couldn't stop staring at the water coming down over the ledge. Here it was, my last chance of escape.

And it was fucking impossible.

"Ariadne?" Zeruhn touched my shoulder. "Are you alright?"

"Fine," I said flatly. "It's really pretty up here. Thank you for showing me."

He said nothing, and I knew the poor guy had to be confused. I'd been chatty and excited all morning, and now my attitude had done a complete one-eighty. I never told him I was hoping to escape, so I couldn't explain now why I was so disappointed.

"Is something wrong?" Zeruhn moved in front of me, blocking my view of the cresting water, of the only way out.

"No." I couldn't even look at him now, couldn't drink in the details of his attractive face, horns and all. All I could think about was how I was well and truly trapped here.

I would never see my mom again.

"No, I'm fine. I'm just...worn out, I guess." I turned away, not wanting to let him see me wipe tears away.

"Do you want to rest? I'll leave you be while I look for supplies."

"Can we just go back?" I squeaked out, trying to hide my sniffle.

"Go back to the cave? When we just got here?"

"Yes, sorry. I'm just...I can't..." I was full-on crying now and couldn't bring myself to look at Zeruhn. If I saw his face, I might be tempted to explain everything and couldn't risk it.

He was warm and kind to me now, but would he stay that way if he knew I planned to leave? He was also flirtatious and oddly possessive of me. *You don't touch what's mine,* he'd said to Rich after goring the man with his horns. What would the minotaur do to his prey if he found out I'd try to escape him once and for all?

"Yes, we can go," Zeruhn said, to my relief.

He crouched before me, and I climbed onto his back without another word. Our descent into the main valley of the labyrinth was equally wordless. I half expected him to lash out at me, to prod me and demand that I explain myself. He had admitted that human emotions were something he didn't grasp as well as facts and figures. But he never said a word.

We returned to his cave, which, in a sense, had become my cave as well. Since there would be no leaving this place for me. Would he even want me to stay in his space for the foreseeable future?

I'd cross that bridge when I came to it. Right then, I wanted to wallow in my newly found grief. Never again would I walk my familiar streets, talk to my neighbors, or laugh at the children running with the stray dogs.

I would never hug my mother again, cook a meal for us, or hear her voice again.

The weight of it all settled over me like a concrete block, to the point where I could barely breathe. Even when things were bleak and scary before, at least I had something to hold onto. I at least had a goal to get me through this.

Now I had nothing.

I laid down on my blankets on the floor of Zeruhn's cave and just...wished I could blink myself out of existence. My heart pumped blood. My lungs contracted and expanded. But I didn't feel alive anymore.

At some point, I must have fallen asleep. What a shame that I had to wake up.

I was stiff and aching from lack of movement and turned

over to get more comfortable. I couldn't wallow in misery forever with a sore ass now, could I?

Next to my bed, there was something that hadn't been there before. Something that poked a little bit of feeling back into the cold, numb shell I'd become.

A wooden crate overflowing with nectarines.

14

ZERUHN

I couldn't begin to understand it. One minute, Ariadne seemed excited and happy. She'd been looking forward to seeing the waterfall since the day before. The next minute, she became sullen and withdrawn, her lips turned down in a constant frown.

The worst part of it was that she stopped talking to me.

Her barrage of questions stopped, and for the next three days, she barely responded when I asked her anything. She barely ate and completely ignored the crate of fruit I brought to her.

Ariadne's doe eyes had lost their shine. Instead of stormy and bright, they were dull and lifeless. Her gaze focused on nothing, even when Lago and I were right in front of her. Her mind was off somewhere else, and I was desperate to bring her back.

I didn't realize before how much I enjoyed having her here. Not just as my prey to hunt, but as a companion, someone to talk to and pass the time with. Every minute that stretched on without her voice or her presence was torturously long.

I didn't even care about my strange instincts, my unusual urges, when it came to her anymore. I just wanted this fixed. I wanted to erase this dark cloud that had settled over her and wished she would tell me how to do that.

Lago stayed glued to her side, nuzzling her as gently as he could with the edges of his antlers. I found myself wanting to touch her in similar ways, to hold her against my chest and wrap around her as if I could protect her from whatever was going on.

When she rode on my back to the waterfall, the way her body wrapped around me was my new favorite physical sensation. No one else had touched so much of me before. She covered my back like a blanket, arms and thighs gripping me with a tightness that I never wanted to be released from.

But I knew she did not enjoy being touched by strange men, so I kept my distance. When she sat by the stream as night fell, I placed a blanket over her shoulders and let her be. I tried to ask her what was wrong, and she only answered, "There's nothing you can do."

I tried asking different questions and told her more about the labyrinth in an attempt to distract her, but I never got a response.

By the end of the third day, I was at the end of my rope. Ariadne seemed to be in pain in some way, and I had tried to coax her out of it gently. She wasn't responding no matter what I did, and I was desperate to get any kind of reaction out of her. Anything to tell me she was still here, even if that reaction was extreme.

Like anger. Or fear.

She sat at the stream again the next morning, watching the water rush by. I stared at her unmoving figure for a few moments before beginning my shift.

My feet stamped the ground as massive hooves. Muscles

exploded in size and density all over my body while my horns grew long and sharp enough to tear through a human easily—as I had done many times before. My face transformed last as I gave in to the odd sensation of my skull growing and rearranging to that of a bull.

I stamped a hoof once more and tossed my head with a great huff of breath. It was the only warning Ariadne would get. Her shoulders tensed, lifting slightly toward her ears, but she otherwise didn't move at the sound.

Fine. You could've had more of a head start, prey.

I started toward her and saw her body tense up with every step I made. But she still did not move. She was off in her own mind and pretending I wasn't there. Well, she wouldn't be able to pretend for much longer.

I came up to stand directly behind her. Sitting on the ground, she barely reached my knees in this form. I leaned down and gripped her nape in one hand, eliciting a gasp of shock—and maybe even a little fear.

Ariadne struggled, but I held fast. Not enough to hurt her, but just enough to pin her in place. She was forcing my hand, she had to understand that. I had tried to draw her back to me as a man with no result. Now, she would succumb to me as a beast.

"Zeruhn!" she cried out, small fingers scrambling to pull and pry my hand from her neck. "What are you doing? Let me go!"

I did the opposite and squeezed just a fraction harder. Then I leaned closer until my mouth touched her ear. She flinched at the contact from my bull's head, and that stirred the first rush of excitement through me. *Finally, a reaction.*

"Run for your life, prey," I said, the words slurred and heavily accented through my inhuman mouth, but she got the meaning.

I released Ariadne's neck, and just as I had hoped, she scrambled to her feet and took off running like a shot.

The scent trail she left behind was tinged with fear, but not as much as the first time I hunted her. Good. I wanted her shaken up but not too afraid to speak with me after this.

I bellowed a roar at her shrinking form, following her at a leisurely pace. Even if I lost sight of her, that tantalizing scent would lead me to my doe-eyed prey. She would have to look at me then and really *see* me. Whatever pulled her mind away had nothing on being in the clutches of the minotaur.

Her panting breaths got my cock hard, and I wrapped my hand around it, trying to choke the thing into submission. I wanted her, but that wasn't the point of this chase. If she would let me conquer her in that way, then I would. But right then, I wanted *my* Ariadne back. The one that blushed when I teased her, who asked questions, and cared for my wounds when no one else did.

My cock wasn't listening, however, so I released it to re-focus on my pursuit. She was out of sight at the moment, but her scent zigzagged through the grassy field next to the stream. As if that would stop me.

She had headed in the direction of the church, which was surprising. After the last hunt, I figured she'd try somewhere new. Besides, I could navigate these tunnels with my eyes closed while she would become hopelessly lost.

I told you not to make it too easy for me, I thought with a click of my tongue. I just might have to spank her for that when I caught her.

Ariadne's scent was stronger in these stone walls, the air more stagnant than outside. There was a sweetness to her, almost like those nectarines she loved so much. Her scent clung to my skin, almost like she herself was draped over me, pliant and welcoming of my touch.

I turned down a corridor, following the smell of her like a

dog after a bone. My cock was rigid and straining now, dying to sink into our warm, soft prey. The organ would absolutely destroy her in this form, but fuck, it was fun to imagine her taking it.

My hooves echoed on the stone floor, no doubt alerting Ariadne to my pursuit. Good, I wanted her to know I was right behind her. That I would never stop until she was mine.

I sensed movement down another corridor, then felt the vibrations of small, hurrying feet. I roared until a series of echoes were created. She would get completely turned around that way, thinking I was right behind her when I was right here, lying in wait.

Just as I predicted, Ariadne rushed out of a side doorway looking frantically behind her. She bumped into my chest, the force making her teeter backwards. I grinned at the sight of her —flushed face, panting breaths, and wide, alert eyes. Such perfect, beautiful prey.

With a small shriek, she took off running again. I went after her, keeping my strides short to allow a bit of distance between us. She looked over her shoulder and picked up the pace, pumping her arms with the effort. I kept pace with her, knowing she would fatigue soon. My human was fragile. She *needed* me to catch her.

My animal instincts did most of the talking while I hunted, while the human side of me took a backseat. I couldn't rationalize *why* I needed to hunt, why this pursuit thrilled and excited me so much. Ariadne took it to a whole new level for me. She brought a thrill to the hunt I'd never experienced before. And she was prey I wanted to capture and keep.

Forever.

I didn't care about the why anymore. I only knew that I had

to keep her, that I needed her voice and her curiosity like I needed air to breathe.

Ariadne was slowing, holding her side with one hand while the other pressed to the wall for support. She kept moving, although her run had slowed to a brisk walk. Her breaths came in wheezes, almost like she was pained. Time to end the hunt soon then. I wanted her exhausted but not dead.

I caught up to her quickly and scooped her off the ground with an arm around her waist. She kicked and thrashed, but her struggling was weak, and she did not tell me to let her go. I wondered if this was progress. Was she truly less afraid than before?

In a few long strides, I hauled her to the flat surface in what was once the chapel. I had read in history books that this was an altar, a place to put offerings to the gods and saints of the old religions. My doe-eyed prey would make a fine offering, but she was mine to keep.

I laid her back flat on the altar, wedged myself between her thighs, and pinned her hands down just as I returned to my human form. She was less afraid of me like this and seemed to enjoy looking at me in this form.

"I've caught you, Ariadne." I hovered low over her, savoring her ragged breaths, dilated eyes, and flushed, parted lips. "Will you give me my prize now, or do I have to take it from you?"

I would never take more than a kiss from her. I would hunt her but never violate her. I wondered if she knew that or if she saw me as exactly the same as Rich, the human whose blood had coated my horns because he dared to touch *my* prey. And like a coward, trying to touch her while she slept.

Thinking of him aroused my bloodlust, made me want to gore some other pathetic human waste. But he was gone and no longer a problem. It was just me and her now, exactly how I wanted it.

Drinking in the sight of my sweet conquest laid out before me, I waited for Ariadne's response. And what she did shocked me.

She lifted her head from the altar, wrapped an arm around my neck, and crashed her mouth to mine.

15

ARIADNE

y heart had already been racing. My lungs were already constricted from the exertion of running away from him. Now my heart and breaths slammed into overdrive while I kissed that very same man.

It wasn't just a kiss, though. I couldn't begin to describe it or explain what drove me to do it. It was a battle for control, a scraping of lips and teeth and a wild press of tongues. And it wasn't just Zeruhn doing it to me. I gave as good as I got. Fuck, I *started* it.

The minotaur's mouth molded to mine, and he matched me for every beat. He moaned when I bit his lip, surged his tongue into my mouth when I gasped for breath, and dug his fingers into my hips with a possessive hold. His own hips rocked forward, and I gasped at the heavy press of the erection in his pants. My core pulsed greedily, the ache for him to fill me up already bringing whimpers to my throat. It had been so long since I'd been touched or kissed, and it had never been so all-consuming like this.

I wanted to give in, to keep floating on the high of Zeruhn's deliciously soft mouth, to hold him in place with my thighs until he gave me what I was craving. After feeling numb for days, I finally felt *good.* Even better than good—exhilarated. In hindsight, that chase felt like foreplay. It shook me out of my rut and got my blood pumping. Best of all, it distracted me from the misery of the past few days.

But I couldn't be doing this, shouldn't be aroused by a man who was also a beast. Someone who killed so many people and did so easily.

"Zeruhn, wait," I said when our lips parted for a breath, pressing a hand on his chest. "Stop for a minute. I just...just need a moment."

I braced myself for what would come next. Anger, certainly. Maybe some of that violence I knew all too well burned inside him. Men didn't like it when their fun was stopped. Many of them were pushy and forceful, especially with us girls from the slums.

But the minotaur only eased back with a lopsided grin, looking thoroughly pleased with relaxed, hooded eyes. "I didn't expect such a prize from this hunt. You taste divine, Ariadne." He tilted his head and edged his nose along the length of my neck. "And your scent. Just mouthwatering."

The slight contact from the tip of his nose was enough to make me shiver, and I pressed a hand to his shoulder. "Please, can I just get some space for a minute?"

Zeruhn pulled back farther, his brows pinching together, but not in anger. He seemed to be concerned. For me. Those golden eyes burned into me, silently demanding to know what was going on. It was too intense, too much. I hopped off the flat table he'd placed me on and walked a few steps away.

"Don't leave again," Zeruhn growled out. "Not when I just got you back."

I turned to look at him, confused. "Leave? I haven't gone anywhere."

"You haven't been *here,* with me, for the last few days." He approached me warily, his tail flicking behind him. "You've been off somewhere else, somewhere I can't reach. You're not eating. I've barely heard your voice. Your eyes, they don't *see* me. Not like they used to, before the waterfall." His tail hugged close to his body then, nearly tucked between his legs, and only the tip flicked hesitantly.

"Oh, Zeruhn..."

An ache filled my chest with the realization of what he was saying. He *missed* me. Missed...whatever this was between us. He'd been trying to get my attention, because of course, he had no idea why I had completely retreated into myself. And he'd been concerned, trying to keep me fed, warm with blankets, and cheering me up with a crate of nectarines. He was worried about me and didn't know how to shake me out of my funk besides hunt me.

This bestial man, who'd killed dozens, if not hundreds of people, cared about me. And damn everything, I'd started to care about him too.

"I'm sorry," I said. "I should've told you why I acted like that, but I didn't know how you'd react."

"React to what?" He moved closer, though still giving me the space I asked for.

"I wanted to see where the water came from to see if it would allow me to escape."

"Ariadne." Zeruhn reached out and stroked tentatively along the side of my face. "You could have just asked me, and I would have saved you the trouble."

I met his gaze, seeing warmth, affection, and even sympathy in his stare. "So, is there?"

"A way to escape the labyrinth?" At my nod, he said, "Not while your heart is still beating." I closed my eyes in defeat, and he gently stroked a thumb under my eye. "I'm sorry. If there was a way out, I wouldn't be here either." His thumb then traced my jaw with a featherlight touch. "And I never would have met you." His tone lifted at that last sentence, like my being here made it better for him somehow.

"I have...someone who needs me outside," I admitted. "Someone vulnerable who depends on me. And if I can't get out, they have no one."

"A child?" Zeruhn asked, almost sounding hopeful.

"No. My mother, actually. She has arthritis. Her joints get really painful, and it's difficult for her to move around."

"I see." Zeruhn's fingers moved on to stroking my neck, the touch warm and relaxing. He was still a full arm's length away, and my need for space was quickly diminishing. I wanted to feel the press of his chest and hands on me again. "If I could get you out so that you could go back to her, I would."

"You would release your prey?" I asked with a mirthless laugh. "For good?"

"I never met my mother," he answered, his face still dead serious. "You are lucky to have been raised by yours. And she is surely more deserving than me to have you tend to her."

I peered up at him. "Wait, I thought you were made in a lab."

"All shifters are born from human surrogates. I am not genetically related to her in any way, but she carried me." Zeruhn's throat bobbed with a swallow. "I was told that she wanted to adopt me once it was discovered that I was a failed prototype. But it's against the law, an executive order from the prime minister himself."

"What? That's terrible. Why would it be illegal to adopt prototypes?"

"Some bullshit liability reasons. They said it was because they didn't know what would happen once I reached puberty or adolescence. The rush of hormones could make me violent or reveal more issues with my genetics."

"Is she the woman next to your bed? The photo."

"Yes, I stole it from a file."

"And you never got to meet her?"

He shook his head. "It was to keep the lab creations from forming familial attachments. Couldn't have emotional responses interfering with test results."

"I'm sorry, Zeruhn."

He shrugged one shoulder, the corner of his mouth ticking up. "I didn't bring her up to compare my story to yours. Just wanted to explain why I absolutely would return you to your mother if I had that ability." He sucked in a breath. "As much as it would pain me to lose your company."

"I...like your company too," I admitted. "I'll always worry about my mom, of course. But I suppose it could be worse."

"True. You could be stuck in a labyrinth with Rich."

"Okay, now I dislike your company immensely."

A dry chuckle left his throat, and his fingers drifted from my neck to the edge of my hand. "Do you want to eat something? And maybe wash up in the bathing pool?"

I snorted. "You telling me I stink?" I already knew I did. I wasn't exactly focused on self-care in the last few days.

"I suppose you could smell worse," he cracked back at me with a teasing smile. "Wait for me in the bathing pool. Can you find your way?"

"I'll manage."

He swayed toward me like he was going to kiss me before he left, then seemed to change his mind. Instead, he abruptly turned around, tail sweeping behind him as he jogged out of the ruin.

I found my way to the bathing pool after only a few wrong turns through the maze of hallways. The stone fish was still pouring water from its mouth, and the baskets of soaps, toothbrushes, and towels were neatly arranged along the walls.

I grabbed a few handfuls of the small soap bottles and started dumping them in the water. For one reason, I really wanted to get squeaky clean and erase this layer of sweat and grime from my skin. The second reason was to create enough bubbles so that Zeruhn wouldn't get a free look at the goods once I undressed.

Once a thick layer of bubbles floated on the surface, I stripped down and climbed in, letting out a sigh as I let the water rise to my shoulders.

Mom, I'm so so sorry. I wish there was a way to tell you that I'm okay. You don't have to worry. I'm alive, unhurt, and...

"...Safe." I breathed that final word out loud, though it was barely audible over the trickle of water. I had to say it because it seemed impossible to be true, and yet it was true.

I was in the most dangerous place in the city, the prison where death was imminent. And yet I felt *safe* with the person who had caused so much death.

"What have you done?" Zeruhn's voice was light and amused as he stepped into the room, carrying a small bag of nectarines in one hand and a large bowl in the other.

"I...wanted to get really clean." Shyness over my nudity overtook me, and I sank to my chin in the water. I realized I hadn't been fully naked in front of him before now, because I'd been too chickenshit to undress in the stream.

"You certainly will be." He came to the edge of the pool and held out a nectarine to me. When I went to take it with my hand, he pulled it back with a shake of his head. "Open your mouth."

I did as he said, our eyes locked together as he held the fruit out again. Our gazes held as I took a bite, my teeth gently scraping the pit in the center. I had to make an obscene sucking sound to keep the juice from running down my chin, and I swear Zeruhn's eyes dilated at the sound.

When I pulled away to chew, Zeruhn brought the small fruit to his mouth and took a large, sucking bite out of the other side. Most of the nectarine flesh was gone just from that, the pit bared in his hand.

I swallowed, and the soft fruit seemed to leave a lump in my throat. "Are you going to get in?"

Wordlessly, Zeruhn set the food aside and stood, reaching for the clasp on his pants. "Are you going to pretend to look away again?" he asked, a note of teasing in his voice.

"I—no. I wasn't pretending!" I stammered. "I was trying to give you privacy last time."

"Mm-hm," he said skeptically. "I don't understand privacy, to be honest." With that, he stripped off his pants in one quick shove down his legs and then was wading into the pool.

"Uh—what! I mean, what don't you understand about it?" I tried to look away at first, but once he was underwater from the waist up, I could almost pretend we weren't both naked. Together.

He shrugged as he grabbed another nectarine and handed it to me. "I've either had people constantly in my face, or I've been completely alone. Never in-between, and never of my choosing."

"So you've never had the chance to keep something for yourself," I said.

"No. The idea of it is just very strange to me. I've read about it, but I don't understand it."

I chewed on that while also chewing on my nectarine. "Privacy can also be between multiple people. Something between you and another person that no one else gets to experience."

"Like what you and I have."

I paused on my bite, my teeth clenched together. He'd said aloud exactly what I'd been thinking. "What do we have, Zeruhn?"

"I don't know." His eyes flicked away, and I could see clearly how feelings were strange, uncomfortable territory for him. "I just know that I've never done this with another person before."

"What do you mean by this?" I pressed. "Can you describe it?"

"I..." He rubbed a hand over his face, and right then, the fearsome minotaur looked flustered and adorable. "My mind is always focused on you."

I tried not to choke on my nectarine as I forced another swallow while my heart jumped into my throat.

"At first, I was annoyed by it," he said. "That you occupied so many of my thoughts since the beginning. I didn't understand it. When I first hunted you, I was...dissatisfied. Not by you, but myself. You were afraid of me, and it bothered me that I made you feel that way. I wanted more of your sharp tongue and the storm in your eyes." He braved a shy glance up at me. "When you tended to my injuries and we started spending time together, it started to make sense."

"What did?" I whispered.

"That I was not meant to kill you, but...to keep you." Zeruhn rubbed his forehead, then his gaze became more determined. "I want to hunt you only if it chases away your sadness and ends in pleasure for both of us. I haven't laughed like I have with you in years, only when Lago does something stupid."

That got a chuckle out of me, and I felt his hand caress my arm under the water's surface.

"I want to protect you from anything that would harm you." A growl tinged his voice as he spoke and his fingers wrapped around my upper arm. "And I would kill anyone that tries."

"Please don't talk about killing." I lifted a hand out of the water to touch his soft, bearded jaw. In doing so, I also got a little bit of suds on his face, and we both laughed as I tried to smooth it away.

"What should I talk about instead?" Zeruhn lowered his forehead to mine, and I took the opportunity to run my hand up to the base of one horn.

"You spoke of pleasure," I said, my skin breaking out in goosebumps from the tension and the all-consuming effect this man had on me. "How about more of that?"

"Only speaking?" he groaned, leaning his head into my hand that massaged where his horn jutted out. "Or doing?"

I hesitated only a moment, realizing I had him literally in my hands. The massive minotaur smiled as he allowed me to pull him down by the horns for a scorching kiss.

16

ARIADNE

His hands went around my ribs as we kissed, skimming the edges of my breasts. I sucked in a harsh breath at the touch, not realizing how sensitive they were.

Zeruhn broke the kiss but kept his mouth hovering over mine. "If kissing is the only pleasure you want, please tell me now." He was growling again, but this time with a sexy undercurrent of desire rather than aggression.

"No. No, that's not all I want."

Part of me still felt oddly disassociated from all this. The fact that we were naked and making out and that he'd confessed his incredibly sweet feelings for me, which I didn't know how to respond to. And that I quite possibly returned those feelings.

Was this right? Was this okay? Could this ever work between us? How was this supposed to end? He was still property of MinoTek, wasn't he? The state's personal execution machine?

All of that thinking threatened to pull me from the moment, which was the last thing I wanted. He made me feel better, made me feel *good*. I was sick of feeling terrified, scared, sad, depressed.

For the time being, he was all I had.

And fuck, I could sure do worse than a muscle-bound, golden-eyed man with horns and a tail who had a crush on me.

"What do you want, doe eyes?" Zeruhn nipped at my lips, forearms molding to my back as he drew me forward into his chest. "Tell me before I lose control and devour you like a nectarine."

His chest muffled my peal of laughter, so I kissed him there, letting my arms wind around his waist to explore him. I found a scar on his chest and kissed him there too, and then another.

"You've really...been attacked so much." More scars came into my view, ones I hadn't noticed before.

"Those are from the lab," he said. "See how clean they are? Scalpels." He directed my hand to a long, jagged scar near his collarbone. "That was an attack. A human with a sharp rock."

"You let him get this close to you?" I traced the scar with my fingertip, watching the muscles in his neck feather under my touch.

"It was a group of them," he answered. "Maybe ten or so. I... handled them all, but they drew a few scratches."

It was more than a scratch. The scar tissue was thick and created a pale stripe across his collarbone.

I wound both arms around his shoulders, no longer caring that my breasts pressed to his chest and that we were flush together without a lick of clothing between us. Just skin sliding on skin.

"I want *you*, Zeruhn," I confessed in a whisper against his neck. "All of you, everything."

The next thing I felt was him lifting me out of the pool with ease. Water and bubbles sluiced down my body as he perched me on the edge, my feet still dangling into the pool. He was so tall that he still had to lean down to kiss me, forcing my thighs open as he wedged himself between them.

"Sweet, pretty prey," he murmured between rough kisses. "I've dreamed of the day you would completely submit to me. I'll leave you wrung out and hoarse." A promise and a warning, all in one.

Zeruhn's mouth fell to my neck while his hips canted forward. Sharp teeth and plush lips teased and nipped at my pulse as the hard length of him left a trail of heat on my inner thigh. I clutched at his arms, holding on for dear life at the sensations he wrought through me. My legs squeezed around his waist, my toes in the water brushing along the length of his tail, which made him shudder and groan against my neck.

"Oh, I want to mount you like a beast," Zeruhn growled.

That pulled a gasp from me, both of shock and at the bolt of pleasure that struck my clit. What a depraved thing to say, and yet, why did it excite me so much?

"But I won't, at least not yet," he went on. "I'll take my time with you. And I only want to destroy you if it's pleasurable for you too." His hands slid up my ribs to cup and knead my breasts. I wasn't especially small-chested, but those palms completely covered my girls up. And when his thumbs rolled over my nipples, they pulled even more sensitivity and *need* from my body.

"You like this, doe eyes?" he asked at my resulting whimper, gaze rapt on me.

"Yes," I sighed. "You can—yes, that!"

He'd already begun skimming that mouth down my chest and paused to kiss the swells of my breasts. "You're so soft," he groaned into my cleavage. "Your skin, your scent...I can't get enough."

He continued on, pulling the dark tip of my breast between his lips. I whimpered again at the scraping of teeth against the sensitive bud. My hands slapped to the floor at my sides and I arched, pushing my chest into his face for more of that wicked mouth.

Zeruhn released my nipple with a long, pulling suck to give the same treatment to the other one. While he lavished attention on me, I stared at his cock.

It rested on top of my thigh—hot, pulsing, and the biggest one I'd ever seen, not that I had a large sample size to compare to. I wanted to touch it, though. To feel that heat against my palm and see what kind of bestial sounds it would pull from my minotaur. He was already pleasing me so thoroughly, and I wanted to make him feel good in return. But shyness or something, maybe my last shred of common sense, was holding me back. I knew his tail was sensitive too, and for some reason, that felt a lot less intimidating than touching his cock.

I ran a hand down his muscular back until I found the base of his tail. When I wrapped my fingers around it and gave it a stroke, his hips drove forward with a loud bellow.

"Fuck, Ariadne," he grunted into my chest. "Are you trying to make me come all over your gorgeous skin? Because I will if you keep touching my tail like that."

"The thought is tempting," I admitted. It would be hot to see the sole survivor of the labyrinth lose control because of some tail petting, all because of me.

"Hm," Zeruhn grunted with a bright gleam in his eye, his hands moving to rest on my hips. "Seems I have to take matters into my own hands."

He lifted me again and set me back down gently, now with my pelvis perched at the very edge of the pool, almost hanging over. I placed my hands behind me to retain my balance. "What are you doing?"

He answered by lowering to chest-height in the water, and transferring my legs from around his waist, to over his shoulders. *Oh shit,* I thought, panic and arousal surging through me in equal measure. *He's eye-level with my pussy. He's going to—*

A shiver ran over me as he placed a scorching kiss inside my knee. His lips trailed higher before turning his head to kiss my other thigh.

"You don't have to do this." A tremor filled my voice. I was both eager and fearful of what was to come. The first guy I messed around with had made a comment about girls tasting or smelling weird down there. Since then, I always redirected when guys started heading that way, which wasn't too often. Most men seemed happy to skip it.

But Zeruhn pinned me with a burning stare that said skipping this was absolutely *not* an option.

"You don't understand, doe eyes." He turned his head to suck another wet kiss halfway up my inner thigh. "I *need* to do this. Or I'll go feral with the need to have your taste coating my tongue."

Holy shit, he wasn't kidding. This wasn't even dirty talk, just him being brutally honest. His kisses grew more ravenous as he approached my center, his beard scraping my sensitive skin, heightening every sensation until he reached his destination.

His whole mouth covered my cunt like he was sucking a bite out of that nectarine, but there were no teeth here. Just the most sensational pressure of his lips and tongue taking a long, decadent lick.

"Oh, fuck!" My hand flew to his head and grasped a horn. He gave an encouraging moan and leaned into my grip.

I directed him toward my clit, and he made a delicious humming sound against the small bundle of nerves. The infuriating minotaur licked all around it, avoiding direct pressure until I bucked against his face, on the verge of begging and whining. Then I almost cried out with frustration when he moved away, lowering to tease his tongue against my entrance and suck on my lips.

"Zeruhn, please," I finally said. "Higher, my clit. I'm so close."

"Oh, my sweet prey." His voice vibrated against my skin, tickling my nerves so much that I might just get there if he kept talking. "What if I like you squirming and begging? You're at my mercy. Exactly where I want you."

"But I...I don't like this! It doesn't feel good."

He paused then, raising up to watch my expression. I was biting my cheek so hard, I thought I might draw blood. I willed my expression not to crack, but he saw right through me.

"You're not a very good liar, prey."

I gasped at the thick, blunt finger pressing through me, stroking through my slick heat.

"I'll give you credit for cleverness, though," he added. "But now I'll keep you at my mercy even longer."

And damn him to all the gods that were once worshiped in this place, he did just that. Toying with me was his favorite thing, and not just during a hunt. He pumped his fingers hard through me, curling and spreading the thick digits to find the spots that made me scream and beg the loudest. He teased my clit, alternating hard and gentle licks to keep me teetering on the edge of release. Every time I thought he would finally be merciful and let me come, he pulled back or switched things up.

I was one huge bundle of frayed nerves by the time he was finally ready to put me out of my misery.

"Sweet, beautiful, prey," Zeruhn murmured with a kiss to my clit. "You've begged so beautifully for me. Now take your release."

I could have sobbed with relief. His fingers stroked me expertly while his tongue flattened over my clit hood. It was mere seconds before I was gone, hurtling into the most explosive orgasm I'd ever had. Every strike of his tongue and fingers seemed to draw it out for longer, my whole body contracting and releasing as if I was a heart pumping blood.

My mind felt blissfully soft. All the worry, stress, and fear felt far away, across a foggy landscape.

No one had ever teased me that much. So few had tried to get me off at all. But Zeruhn treated it like the most important mission in his life.

"Come back to me, doe eyes." Even though he was no longer attached to my cunt, I felt the vibration of his voice on my skin, though softened due to the fog in my head. "I'm not done with you yet."

"Mm, not going anywhere." I felt drunk, that kind of loose, uninhibited giddiness like when a group of neighbors passed a bottle around. I returned my arms to around Zeruhn's neck and pulled him in close. How could such a hard-bodied man have such soft lips? I wondered this while another very hard part of his body notched where I was still pulsing and sensitive.

"Last chance to stop me," he whispered in a harsh breath against my mouth. "I needed your cunt wrapped around my cock days ago, but if you don't—"

"Don't stop," I begged, finding the base of his tail again. "Don't you dare stop now."

He groaned through a kiss and thrust forward without any preamble. The intrusion made me flinch and tense up. It didn't hurt but, oh fuck, was that intense. He stretched me more than I thought he would.

Zeruhn's hand immediately went to my clit, massaging it while he made small thrusts to acclimate me to his size. "You're already taking me so well," he purred. "And you feel fucking incredible."

It wasn't long before I was craving more, and like he read my mind, he started fucking me deeper, taking long strokes in and out of me. I watched his length disappear inside me, then marveled at the massive cock that pulled nearly all the way out. It almost seemed absurd that he would fit, but *oh* he did.

Not only did he fit, he seemed to press against every single nerve ending that signaled pleasure to my brain. I felt him in my nipples and not just because they scraped his chest each time he pressed all the way inside. I felt him inside my thighs and not just because my legs clamped to his waist in a death grip. With every kiss, I felt the same pulse in my lips that was in my cunt. His teeth as they scraped my shoulder, the desperate, possessive grip of his hands on my waist. I felt him everywhere in an unforgettable way, like he was leaving a permanent mark on me.

"You'll come for me again, Ariadne," Zeruhn snarled, his voice rough and feral. "And because I'm such a merciful predator, I won't torture you so badly this time."

"Oh yeah?" Contrary to him, my voice went high and breathy. "Or is it because you're close to coming too, you filthy beast?"

I paused, wondering if that last bit had gone too far. But Zeruhn only let out a sound somewhere between a moan and a growl while his hips rutted faster into me. "You'll be my undoing."

"Who's the prey now?"

The words tumbled out before I could think, but their truth struck me with the same bright clarity as my minotaur's eyes. For this moment at least, he was in *my* control. He would do anything I wanted—wring another orgasm out of me or stop entirely if I wanted him to. He'd struggle, but he would do it.

Because this man didn't want to just fuck and conquer me. I was a prize, and he wanted to *win* me.

"Make me come already, minotaur," I goaded him, high on my freshly-realized power over him.

Zeruhn pulled out of me with a snarl, picked me up, flipped me over, then drove inside of me again, accompanied by an echoing *smack* of his palm against my ass. It all happened so fast, I was still processing the stinging pain on my cheek as he stuck new, deeper, *better* places inside me.

"I'm yours, Ariadne," he grunted against my ear. "But make no mistake. I am no one's prey."

Water splashed over the edge of the pool with each one of his punishing, delicious thrusts. His hips smacked against my ass with obscenely wet sounds that echoed off the stone walls. Every stroke of him inside me was *almost* too much, on the border of pain and intense pleasure.

And when his fingers circled my clit again, I knew I was right. He was rough, bestial. Domineering and a complete predator. A killer. But the chink in his armor was me. He didn't want me frightened, hurt, or even mentally distant. His greatest desire was having me consumed by pleasure.

"Tell me what you are to me." The harsh command contrasted with his light touch on my clit, too light to get me there.

"Yours," I panted, wriggling for more friction.

He gave a small slap to my clit. "My what?"

"Your prey!" I all but screamed.

He hummed approvingly, returning to a light, stroking touch. "And what do predators do with prey?"

"Mm! Uh, they hunt."

"Very good." He pressed harder, circling his fingers only

slightly faster but still not enough. "Tell me again, and I'll let you come."

My whole body buzzed with pent-up energy, the need for release coiling up like a spring. All the while, he fucked me at a steady, brutal pace. I was so, so close, dangling over the edge by a thread.

"I'm your prey," I moaned deliriously. "I'm yours to hunt, yours to fuck. Whatever you need, I'm fucking yours and no one else's."

"Mine," Zeruhn agreed with his last grip of control. "Mine to please, mine to protect. Ariadne, you're mine to kill for."

My orgasm erupted and his followed right after. Heat spilled and pulsed inside me. My body gripped and squeezed his length like it never wanted to let go. Zeruhn's hands slapped to the ground on either side of us, like he would fall into the water if he didn't keep his balance.

And I couldn't fight the smug thought, nor resist saying it out loud while I rubbed the base of his horns. "Guess I'm not the only one wrung out and hoarse."

17

ZERUHN

Ariadne and I walked back to the cave—our cave—with our hands joined, interlaced at the fingers. Such a small, innocuous touch, but it sent pleasure surging through my chest. She grabbed my hand after we finished washing up in the pool, and we remained joined like that until we reached home.

Lago sunbathed on a patch of grass just outside, and Ariadne released me to pet his belly. There was something just... satisfying about this. And not just in the way a fuck provided. I liked that we were returning home together, that we would eat an evening meal and talk some more before we slept.

When she finished petting the jackalope, I picked her up and hoisted her over my shoulder just to hear her shriek of laughter and feel her small palms on my back.

"Is this what I have to deal with now?" she asked when I laid her down in my bed—our bed—and proceeded to kiss her, because a twenty-minute walk was too long without. "Being picked up and carried away to be ravaged?"

"Yes," I grunted, nudging my way to the soft skin of her neck. "You are prey. You don't get to choose."

She snorted at that, and it pleased me even more. She knew it was a fib and trusted me that it was. She knew I would carve a tunnel out of the labyrinth with my bare hands if she asked me to.

"Zeruhn?"

"Mm." I was on my way to her breasts again. Fuck, they were so lovely and soft. How they swayed when I fucked her was mesmerizing.

"That wasn't your first time, was it?"

"Hm?" Her voice had become serious. It was an important question, so I lifted my head. "What wasn't?"

"What...just happened. At the pool."

"Oh. No, it wasn't." I lifted up to kiss her, reassure her. Perhaps it was her first time, and she was feeling self-conscious. "But that doesn't make you any less mine, doe eyes."

Ariadne's lips were stiff against mine. "So, you've slept with others? Here, in the labyrinth?"

I watched her expression, searching for clues to gauge her mood. She felt something was wrong, and I needed to understand it. "Yes, before I knew you existed. Is that a problem?"

Her mouth fell open as she sat up, scooting away from me. "You're telling me you've fucked people and then *killed* them?"

I cocked my head. It sounded bad when she said it like that, but it was more or less what had happened. "Well, yes."

"Oh fuck. Oh my..." She turned pale and scooted even further from me, out of my reach. I'd had a countless amount of injuries in my lifetime, but nothing hurt quite like that.

"Ariadne, I would never harm you." My chest tightened with panic. I didn't understand, except that I was losing her. Right after she declared herself mine and had been thoroughly pleased just moments ago. "I would never—I don't understand where this is coming from. I thought you were...happy."

"It's been running through my head ever since we did that." Her hands shook as they raked through her hair. I yearned to pull her into my chest but knew she would not allow it. "You're *really* good at sex, even though you've spent most of your time alone. It seemed weirder the more I thought about it. How could you know how to please me so well without a decent amount of experience?"

"Again, I don't understand the problem." My frustration rose like the swell of angry waves, but for her, I tried to keep it at bay.

"How could you sleep with someone and then kill them?" she demanded. "You said you killed for survival. It was either you or them, but how—"

"It *was* for survival," I barked. "You think they fucked me because they actually wanted me?" I let out a bitter laugh. "Oh, doe eyes, you have no idea what people will do in their darkest, most desperate moments."

Ariadne went quiet for a moment. "What do you mean?"

"The women in the labyrinth knew they couldn't overpower me with brute force. So they usually tried a different tactic— seduce the monster, no matter how much he disgusts them, until a human man gets thrown in so that she can run to him for help. Then the two of them tried to kill me together. So that," I sat back against the wall, holding Ariadne's gaze the whole time, "is how I end up fucking people and then killing them."

Ariadne slumped, her gaze in her lap. "I'm...sorry, Zeruhn. I didn't realize."

"Well, thank you for the unwavering faith in me," I bit out.

She flinched like I'd struck her. "I'm just not used to anyone being so...casual about death and killing. It's a big deal where I'm from, to have a life taken away. My community was so tight that whenever someone died or disappeared, *everyone* mourned for them."

"How nice for you," I scoffed. "I don't have the luxury of considering how the deaths I cause will affect the people in their lives."

"It's not a luxury, it's just decency!" she argued. "Even those who have nothing can take a moment to show respect for the dead."

"Why should I respect anyone who tried to take *my* life?" I rose to my feet, the cave suddenly too cramped for me and my burning temper. "I don't know how to make you understand it from my perspective, Ariadne. It's either them or me, every single time. That's it, that's all it is!"

"Life isn't that simple, Zeruhn. I mean, what if you had gotten someone pregnant?"

"Impossible. All shifters are sterile. So, nothing for you to worry about," I added with a sneer. I didn't want to speak to her cruelly, but I was feeling defensive, like a cornered animal. "I've memorized hundreds of complex processes, but when it comes to my survival, it *is* that simple. It's been proven, over and over again."

"What about me?"

I sighed tiredly. "You're different. I've told you this. You're the one exception."

"But I'm not different!" Ariadne brought a hand to her chest. "Who do you think raised me? My mother, my neighbors. I've known dozens of people who've been picked up by the MSP over the years, never to be seen again. They probably ended up here." Her face took on a pained grimace. "Some of them are probably those skeletons you leave by the door."

A tense silence brewed between us, and I could feel her mentally pulling away from me again, retreating to that fearful creature I first met.

"I don't know what to tell you, doe eyes. Some were probably innocent like you. Others were like Rich, or worse. But in the end?" I shrugged. "People will do what they must to survive, like try to eliminate a threat. So far, you're the one person who's proved me wrong."

And in a cruel stroke of irony, an electrical humming sound gently vibrated through the labyrinth.

"What's that?" Ariadne stiffened.

"The doors," I said. "Another prisoner is about to get thrown in."

Ariadne's wide eyes locked onto me. "What'll you do?"

"What I always do," I answered bitterly, turning to leave the cave. "Live another fucking day."

"Zeruhn, wait!" I heard Ariadne scramble after me but didn't look back, not until she grabbed my arm and pulled. "Please, just—"

"Just what?" I growled, shaking out of her grip. "Wait for them to hunt Lago and cook him over a fire? To bring a rock down on my head while I sleep? Just *what*, Ariadne?"

She stood firm despite my outburst, the storm in her eyes brewing. "Just give them a chance. Like you did with me, alright?" Her hand slid into my palm, fingers lacing with mine in that way that made my chest spark with light. "I promise you, I'm not all that exceptional. Just allow them to show that before you..."

"Kill them." I couldn't understand why saying the word, or even the idea of it, was so difficult for her. It was my everyday life.

"Yes, that," she said with another flinch.

I untangled my fingers from hers. "If I do as you ask, I hope you're prepared for the chance that I won't return."

With that, I turned and headed for the doors.

154

18

ARIADNE

I hope you're prepared for the chance that I won't return.

Zeruhn's parting words rolled around in my head while I paced the small cave. In truth, I wasn't prepared for that at all. What did I know about hunting small birds for food? What if the solar panels on the cooler busted? What if I ran out of water purification tablets? I couldn't go to the waterfall to collect supplies for myself. I didn't know how to defend myself, let alone fight shifters to the death.

And all that was just in terms of strict survival. In the few days I'd really gotten to know Zeruhn, I didn't want to think of going on without him.

He was kind and caring towards me despite his callousness about killing others. But not just me, Lago too.

I paused in my pacing to pet the jackalope, who was munching on a leafy plant growing just outside of the cave entrance. "He's good to you too," I mused, running my fingers through the impossibly soft fur. "He'll protect you, no matter what."

Lago stretched under my petting and then promptly flopped

155

over, encouraging me to continue my ministrations on his belly. I did so with a smile, knowing full well that Zeruhn would do the same. He'd never harm this little guy. That made sense to me, so why was it so hard for me to reconcile that he killed humans and shifters out of necessity?

It's murder was the simplest answer. But from Zeruhn's point of view, it was self-defense. Survival. And how could I fault him for that?

I brought my head to my hands with a groan and, for the hundredth time, stared in the direction in which he went. He'd been gone a while, and it was getting dark. More time passed and night fell. Crickets sang and other insects hovered around the solar-powered lamp I set by the cave entrance. And there was still no sign of him.

"Lago, what should I do?" I scratched the base of his ears. "Should we go after him?"

The jackalope shook his head before nuzzling an antler against my thigh. He'd hardly left my side since Zeruhn left. He was sweet and clearly could understand my distress to some extent. But nothing would ease my worries until that tall, horned man came back to me.

"What if it was another bull-shifter?" I wondered aloud. "Someone who is *actually* an equal match for him? He wouldn't be stupid, though. He wouldn't try to appease me that badly. Not if he went up against someone really dangerous."

Lago rubbed his antler against my leg in a nodding motion as if he agreed with me.

Then I heard something over the crickets and trickling stream, like a heavy footstep. "Zeruhn?" I shot up from my seat, stepping a few feet outside the cave. It took a few moments for my eyes to adjust, but the heavy steps continued. Slowly. Someone was definitely approaching.

I could have collapsed with relief when I saw those long, golden horns like two torches in the darkness. Zeruhn was in his bull form, his heavy snorting breaths growing louder as he approached. But why was he moving so slowly?

"Zeruhn." I started out of the cave toward him. "Are you okay?" His form staggered, and I started running. "Zeruhn!"

He'd fallen to one knee and was starting to tip forward. I reached him, and he nearly fell backward with the force of me throwing my weight against him. Something was definitely wrong if someone like me could topple the minotaur.

"What happened? What's wrong?" I cradled his massive bull's head between my hands. Even on his knees, he was eye level with me.

Right away, my palms felt sticky. The light from the cave barely reached this far, but I knew the dark substance coating his face and horns was blood. Whether or not he murdered another person was the furthest thing from my mind right then. All I cared about was this person right here.

"Where are you hurt?" I demanded, my hands dwarfed by the sheer size of his skull as they felt around his head.

Zeruhn shifted back, his face pale and teeth gritted against the pain. "Head's fine," he bit out. "It's...down here. And my thigh."

His hand was pressed to his stomach, blood seeping out against the edges of his fingers. And on his leg was a series of small open wounds, five clustered together in inch-long slits. All of them bleeding a steady trail down his leg.

"He smuggled in a knife," Zeruhn hissed. "They're not deep, but I think the blade was coated in some kind of blood thinner. I've already lost a lot."

"Shit. Keep your hand there." I whipped off my shirt and ripped it down the middle to make a long bandage. I successfully tied it around his leg, but his thigh was so thick that I couldn't wrap it more than once. And he *needed* more pressure on those wounds, fucking fast.

"Don't move, I'll be right back. Keep your other hand over your thigh." I ran back to the cave without another word, grabbed the first aid kit, then ran back to him.

"Nothing in there will work." Zeruhn sounded tired, his eyelids blinking heavily. "I'm bleeding too fast."

"*Something* has to work!" I frantically dug through the kit, pulling out all the gauze pads inside. "Here."

But he was right. His blood soaked the gauze like it was tissue paper under a faucet.

"Ariadne." Zeruhn touched my cheek with one blood-soaked hand. "So beautiful. My doe-eyed woman."

"Stop." My hand shook as I pressed his palm back over his thigh. "We are not done. Keep putting pressure on there. We're going to stop the bleeding, Zeruhn."

"I never thought...I would have with anyone...what I have with you..." His forehead leaned heavily against mine as his consciousness faded.

"Zeruhn, you need to stay with me." I smacked a quick kiss to his lips, the metallic tang of blood coating my mouth. "I need to kiss you some more. I need to be hunted by you. I need you to capture me and fuck me like crazy again. Don't you want to do that?"

"Mmm..." A small smile pulled at his lips but he was otherwise unresponsive.

"Zeruhn!" I screamed, inches away from his face. "Don't leave me!"

"Ari...adne..."

He slumped forward, his weight too much for me to hold. I was pinned under his bulk but kept my hands pressed to his stomach and thigh, fighting the current of blood leaving his body.

"I'm sorry," I sobbed against his ear. "I shouldn't have told you to hesitate. It's my fault."

Something twitched near my finger, and I thought it was just the reflexes of his hand. He'd seemed fascinated by the small intimacy of holding hands, and I yearned to curl my fingers around his, to hold him in that way for his final moments. But more than anything, I wanted to keep him alive as long as possible. So I kept my palms sealed against his wounds and placed kisses on his neck and shoulder, hoping he could still feel that I was here.

This time, something *bit* my finger, and I figured out we weren't alone.

"Lago?" I craned my neck and could just see the tip of his antlers on the other side of Zeruhn. The jackalope raced around to my side, dropped something, and promptly bit my finger again, thumping his rear feet impatiently. "What's that?" I squinted in the darkness, not wanting to pull my hands away from my dying minotaur.

The jackalope responded by lowering his head and stabbing me in the arm with his antlers.

"Ow! Okay!" I removed my hand from Zeruhn's thigh to feel around in the dirt. A sharp blade nearly sliced my finger, and there was something small, made of some hard plastic. My thumb rubbed over a small wheel with grooves in it—a lighter.

It hit me then, a bright spark of hope. But I had to act fast.

"Stay with me, Zeruhn." I shoved at his shoulders, pressing with all my might to get him on his back. "I'm not done with you yet."

It felt like moving a three-hundred pound, unwieldy boulder, but I finally rolled him faceup in the grass. His heartbeat was weak, his breathing shallow as I flicked the lighter in a panic. A tall flame jumped from the top, more than what a lighter this size would normally put out. Zeruhn must have modified this thing too, thank fuck.

I held the knife blade in the center of the flame and waited, unsure of how long it needed to heat to cauterize a wound. When it started to glow red, I figured that was enough. Time was not on my side.

"I'm so sorry if this hurts," I muttered before pressing the side of the blade to the largest of Zeruhn's stomach wounds. There was sizzling, smoke, and a foul burning smell, but he didn't react. I only hoped that didn't mean I was too late.

Over and over, I heated the knife blade and sealed off every one of Zeruhn's stab wounds. My hands were burned and painful by the time I was done, but that was the least of my worries. I applied burn cream from the first aid kit only after I saw that he was no longer bleeding and had sprayed his wounds thoroughly with the anti-infection solution.

Everything ached, and I wanted to collapse from exhaustion, but now my biggest fear was waking up and finding out that I'd acted too late.

I hovered my ear over Zeruhn's mouth, my hand light on his chest. His pulse and breaths were consistent but weak. I couldn't stop listening. I had to make sure the next breath came and the one after that. And the one after that.

I listened until I could no longer hold myself up. So I laid next to him, my hand still on his chest. That soft, steady heartbeat was the only anchor I had left.

19

ARIADNE

I awoke with a start just as dawn approached. Zeruhn was still motionless next to me, a gray blanket covering us both. I sat up and pulled it back in a panic, bringing a hand to his chest.

Thump-thump. Thump-thump. His heart was still beating, the sound stronger and clearer than last night. I slumped back to the ground in relief, rubbing my face in exhaustion.

"Lago?" I croaked, peering down at the jackalope at my side. "Did you drag a blanket all the way out here for us?"

His nose twitched and his moth wings fluttered.

"You're the sweetest," I said, scratching between his ears. "We're so lucky to have you."

He nuzzled closer to me, and I allowed myself a few moments of petting him before sitting up to check on Zeruhn more thoroughly. The cauterization seemed to work, and he hadn't bled any more since last night. I had been clumsy with that damn knife, though, and burned some of his healthy skin too.

"I'm so sorry," I whispered, twining my fingers through his.

The touch seemed to stir him, and he let out a pained groan.

"Don't move." I pressed on his shoulder as he started to roll up. "You lost a lot of blood."

"Ariadne?" He blinked, those golden eyes shining like suns. "How...how am I still alive?"

"Because of Lago." I petted the jackalope's soft fur again. "He gave me tools to cauterize your wounds and stop the bleeding."

Zeruhn let out a soft huff of breath, looking down at his stomach and leg before resting his head back on the ground. "I thought that was it. A human with a stupid little knife."

Guilt speared through me, and I fiddled with the blanket, looking away as I pulled it over his waist again. "You need to rest. I'll get you food and water. When you're ready to walk, we can go back to the cave."

"Ariadne, come here." He started to roll up again.

"No, don't move! You need to rest while your body replenishes blood."

"Come *here*, doe eyes." Zeruhn sat up and batted away my attempts to push him back down. He all but wrestled me into his arms, cradling me against his chest.

"It seems you've saved my life again," he whispered against my forehead.

"I almost killed you!" I choked out with a sob. "I told you to give them a chance, and look what happened."

He scoffed, holding me tighter as I tried to pull away. "It wasn't your fault, Ariadne."

"Yes, it was!"

"He looked unarmed, but the knife was hidden. I let my guard down, plus he was fast. It was my own mistake, not anything you said." Zeruhn's beard nuzzled my cheek. "I heard your concern, but I'll admit I did not listen. While your intentions are good, I know how the labyrinth works, Ariadne. I know why I'm still here." Rough fingers stroked down the length of my arm. "I'm sorry that violence upsets you, but he did not get a chance to hurt you or Lago. And I'll never be sorry for that."

"I...I'm starting to understand that it's necessary," I admitted. "The labyrinth. It brings out the worst in people. It drives them to do terrible things."

"Hm." Zeruhn made a noise like he disagreed. "I think it reveals people's true nature."

We were silent for a few moments until I leaned my palm on his chest. "Alright. Now lay back down. You need to rest."

"What I need is the woman who saved my life." He groaned into my neck, tongue sliding out along my pulse.

"Zeruhn!" Why was I already panting? "You're still covered in dried blood."

"Then strip me down and wash me, doe eyes."

"I will if you let go of me."

"Never." Still, he loosened his hold with a crooked smile. "You've made me insatiable for you."

"Do you *ever* fucking rest?" I laughed in spite of the harrowing last few hours. If he was flirting, it meant he had to be feeling better.

"Not when it comes to pleasing and protecting you." He pulled me forward, sucking a kiss along the length of my shoulder. "I mean it, doe eyes. I've mostly recovered. My genetics allow me to heal quickly. Let me celebrate being alive by feasting on your cunt."

"As wonderful as that sounds, I would feel a lot better if you took it easy." I pulled back, already itching to erase all traces of the last few hours. "Let me wash you, like you suggested."

He flashed me a toothy grin. "And then?"

"And then you can do whatever you'd like with me."

"Hm." Zeruhn finally released me fully, planting his hands

on the ground behind him. "I can't decide if I want to hunt you or just perch you straight on my face."

"Somehow I doubt your leg is up for a full-fledged hunt, even if you are feeling better."

He frowned, rubbing just below the series of stab wounds on his thigh. "You may be right. My muscles are locked up and cramped here."

"All the more reason for you to rest." I stood, stretching out my own stiff muscles. "Can you make it to the water?"

"I'll manage." The stream was only a few yards away, but I still hovered around Zeruhn as he gingerly got to his feet. He was definitely limping, and I saw the tightness in his jaw despite his effort not to show pain. The poor guy couldn't catch a break.

"Take your pants off, and sit on the edge," I said, a plan already forming in my mind.

Zeruhn obliged, watching me with a heated gaze while he left his pants on a grassy bank and lowered his feet into the chilly water. "And where will you be, doe eyes?"

Now that my shirt was gone, I removed my camisole first—the bloodstained, threadbare garment was not sexy at all at this point, but I felt the weight of his stare as tangible as a touch. Doing my best to pretend I was alone and ignore the heated flush covering my skin, I turned away to unfasten my pants. Zeruhn inhaled sharply as I slid them over my hips, slowly uncovering my ass. I delighted in hearing his, "Fuck," as I bent over to peel them off my legs.

I'd never felt inclined to do a striptease in my life, and I wasn't sure why the urge to do it came over me right then. Maybe it was like he said—a celebration of being alive.

Completely naked, I slid into the water and hissed at the frigid temperature coming up to my waist. But I didn't look at him until I found my way between his thighs. Zeruhn's cock was already thickening on his leg, his hands in a death grip on the bank.

"What's wrong?" I teased him, lifting a hand to drip cold water onto his leg. "You seem tense."

A frustrated groan worked up from his throat. "So many have tried and failed to kill me, but it is you, sweet Ariadne, who will be the death of me."

"The cold water should help with that." I rubbed my wet hands over the dried blood on his legs, being careful around his wounds, and knowing full well that the cold water was *not* helping.

"You can't just touch me and expect me to not...be aroused. And you're cold, doe eyes. Your skin is covered in bumps. Come here and let me warm you, my love."

My heart skipped a beat with that last word, but I quickly brushed it off. He was trying to seduce me, and I couldn't let it work *that* quickly.

"I'll let you warm me when all this blood is washed off." My hands went higher, dripping water over his hips and waist while I ignored his cock.

To Zeruhn's credit, he didn't attempt to touch me. But when romance didn't work, he switched his tactics to dirty talk. "Your nipples are so tight," he rasped. "I want to suck them and feel how hard they are, see if they'll soften from the heat of my tongue. I bet your cunt is scorching hot in that cold water too."

"It's not," I tried to insist with a straight face.

"Let me taste it and see," he pressed.

"Your face is filthy." I wet my hands again and scrubbed the dried blood from his beard, cheeks, and forehead.

"Yours is beautiful," he answered, his gaze like liquid fire. "You're truly the most beautiful woman I've ever seen."

"Stop talking, and let me concentrate!" I laughed with a small swat to his chest.

"If you want me to stop talking, you'll have to kiss me."

"You're impossible." Clapping my palms to his cheeks, I placed a chaste kiss on his now-clean mouth. "Stubborn as a bull."

He grinned against my mouth. "That's why you're drawn to me, my sweet, pretty prey."

"Hm, I can think of a few other reasons." My touch skimmed higher, tracing the base of his horns while I scratched his scalp.

Zeruhn angled his head. "It really doesn't bother you that I'm a lab-created failed prototype?" An abrupt question, one I had no problem answering.

"Not at all," I said. "The only thing that bothers me is that you never got the chance to make your own choices. Be your own person. You never asked to be experimented on, to be thrown in here to fight for your life. I wish you could've had a family. A community to support you."

Zeruhn was silent for a while, his intense gaze studying my face. "I have you," he said simply.

"You do," I agreed. "And I...have you."

"Always, Ariadne."

It felt like we were making some kind of vows to each other. Not exactly marriage but we were promising mutual solidarity and understanding. He probably didn't know what he was missing, couldn't relate to being ripped away from loved ones. But he understood losing that had hurt *me,* and that empathy from a horned, feral man floored me.

Zeruhn angled my chin in his hand and kissed me with sweetness that had me melting. But I also noticed that he was shifting his legs, trying to pull me into his lap.

"No sex," I insisted, breaking away from the kiss. "I'm telling you, you need to rest."

"I can rest if you ride me," he suggested with a teasing laugh.

"Something tells me you're not a 'sit back and let the girl do all the work' kind of guy."

"Hm, what gave it away?" he mused. "The fact that I can't keep my hands off you? That I'm addicted to your taste and how you squeeze around me when you come?"

"Zeruhn." I slapped a hand to my burning face. "Stop. Talking. Like that."

"Kiss me." He traced the edge of my jaw. "And make me."

Emboldened, I wrapped a hand around the base of his of cock. "I've got a better idea."

20

ZERUHN

My breath felt stuck in my chest when she gripped my cock and gave it a tentative stroke from base to head. I didn't expect it from my shy, doe-eyed human, but she had surprised me with boldness before.

"You have the wrong idea if you think that'll shut me up." I wrapped a hand around hers to tighten her grip, guiding her along my length. "I'll just start singing the praises of your hands, on top of everything else about you that drives me wild."

Then she did the absolute last thing I expected. She leaned down and *licked* me.

My hips jerked at the sensation, and I was, for once, truly speechless. My thoughts spun for something to say, to convey how that little swipe of her tongue made me solid as iron and sent waves of pleasure through me like never before.

Ariadne seemed to enjoy my lack of speech. She wore a tiny, smug smile as her tongue circled around my blunt head. The wet softness of it was *so good*. I needed more. I needed the heat of her mouth and her lips running over me.

But she was set on torturing me in the best way, running her tongue up and down the shaft, circling the head and flicking the underside in a way that made me gasp for air. Her hands stroked me leisurely, spreading the wetness from her mouth with light, almost tickling pressure.

"Ariadne..." Her name was the only plea I could utter, the only word to express all the rush of sensations she was making me feel.

"Zeruhn," she answered back, a lilt of teasing in her voice. Oh, her *voice*. She said my name with her lips resting on my cock, and the movement of her mouth was just *everything*. I was the most feared monster in the city-state, and this human woman could do absolutely anything she wanted to me.

When she finally slid her mouth over me, I could barely breathe. That sweet tongue pressed to the underside of my cock while her lips sucked around me with the sweetest pressure. I didn't dare move, and with all her insistence that I should rest, she must have known that would happen.

"What...are you doing to me?" It took all of my mental fortitude just to string a sentence together. If an enemy came up behind me right then, I would be done for.

And I'd die happily, with my woman's mouth wrapped around my cock.

Ariadne answered my question with a hum that vibrated down my length to my fingers and toes. She knew what she was doing, knew the power she had over me like this. Her hands and mouth worked in tandem, gliding over my full length from root to tip in practiced, coordinated motion.

I didn't know if I wanted to kill or thank every other man she'd done this to. On one hand, I saw red at the thought of anyone else touching her. On the other, she likely wouldn't have been rendering me stupid like this without practice. She covered her teeth with her lips, sucked and stroked me with constant, steady movements. My doe-eyed woman handled a cock with confidence once she got over being shy.

"Ariadne..." I repeated her name like a chanting prayer, my fingers finding their way into her wild mane of dark hair.

She continued on steadily with a soft hum while I slowly fell apart. Every stroke and lick marched me closer to release and unraveled every thread of control. The pleasure was almost unbearably good, but I wanted more. More of *her*. I wanted her skin sliding against mine. Her tongue, her cunt, or her nipples filling my mouth. My hands clenched at my sides, aching to hold on to her ass or waist while she wrung pleasure from my cock.

I wanted to beg her to ride me so I could touch and taste her in all the ways I wanted to, but the only sounds I could make were her name and the groans she wrought from me.

My chest tightened with desperate breaths, and every muscle in my body seemed to lock up. Pleasure coiled inside me like a spring, threatening to snap under the building pressure.

"Ariadne." Her name dragged from my tight throat. "I'm going to come soon."

"Mm-hm," was all she said, working me with those hands and mouth at that constant, steady pace.

It was that—her calm control seeing me through to the end —that set me off.

"Fuckkk," I hissed through my teeth as the release of pleasure hit me with the force of a tidal wave. All my strength left. All the feeling in my body concentrated right where Ariadne had her hands and mouth wrapped around me. I felt faint after that first wave of pleasure hit, my vision darkening. Maybe she was right that I didn't have enough blood in my body yet.

It took minutes to catch my breath, long after Ariadne had released me, and the intense pulsing throughout my body eased to a tolerable level.

"What...was that?" I panted.

She smiled up at me, forearms resting on my thighs. "Well, we call it a blowjob where I'm from."

It took a few more breaths before I could formulate a response. My mind was pleasantly blank, even more so than usual after a good fuck.

"That's a terrible name," I grunted out. "You did the exact opposite of blow."

Ariadne dropped her arms from my legs, a crease forming in the center of her brow. "I put in all that work and that's all you have to say, huh?"

"No." I reached for her shoulder, drawing her back toward me. "I mean, you wanted me to stop talking and I just..." I shook my head. "I have an extensive vocabulary and...there are no words for how you just made me feel."

The storm in her eyes brewed, scheming and cunning. "You've never had that done to you before?"

"Never." She was standing between my legs again in the perfect place. I brought my hands to her waist. "Now it's my turn."

"Zeruhn—what?!" she shrieked as I lifted her straight up from the water, higher and higher as I tilted my head back, until her cunt perched directly on my waiting mouth. Oh, she was scorching hot alright, not to mention fragrant and slick, and not just from the water. Did my sweet woman get aroused from sucking me off? What a delectable thought.

"Oh shit, I'm gonna fall!"

I directed Ariadne's hands to my horns while I licked the cold water from her skin. My tongue would warm her, please her as she pleased me. I didn't know if her feet could touch the ground like this and, frankly, I didn't care. She was exactly where I wanted her.

It didn't take long for her to stop flailing and use my horns as leverage. She rested her body weight against my mouth, giving me plenty to lick and suck. I didn't pay attention to her clit yet. I wanted to remove the taste of the stream until the only wetness filling my mouth was hers.

The squeeze of her palms around my horns sent a pulse straight to my cock. I'd be ready to fuck in moments if she would let me, even though it'd be a long shot.

"You're supposed to be resting," Ariadne moaned, all the while grinding and rolling her pussy over my face.

The only place I'm supposed to be is inside of you, I thought with a chuckle to let her know I'd heard her.

I thrust my tongue inside her to illustrate this, squeezing both sides of her ass in a rough grip. This was what I needed—to have her in my hands, her taste coating my tongue and filling *all* of my senses.

"Zeruhn..." Now she chanted my name as I had hers, her body spread open and at the mercy of my pleasure.

Unlike me, who had been still while her sweet mouth worked me, she tried her best to wiggle and squirm, to control where my attention would go. I growled against her cunt and reached up to grab a breast, plucking the nipple until she whimpered and stilled.

"You're cruel," she whined from above me. I could picture the little pout on her face and laughed. She had seen my cruelty, and it wasn't even in the same world as this. She would never experience cruelty again, I decided. Not as long as I was around for her to sit on my face like this. If she wanted to be queen of the labyrinth, I would be her throne.

Just to show her how benevolent I was, I licked a stripe up to her clit, that pleasure center she was dying to have touched.

Ariadne cried out and held on to my horns like her life depended on them. "Yes, Zeruhn! Please, please…"

I would have called her greedy if she hadn't pleased me so selflessly moments before. And the truth was, I didn't have the patience to draw her pleasure out. I wanted her release filling my mouth and dripping drown my chin like the juice of a nectarine.

So I let her grind and rub against my mouth all she wanted, keeping my tongue and lips pressed to that hard bud that sent her into a frenzy, because I wanted her release just as much as she did.

And when Ariadne finally came, her head thrown back with a cry and her legs trembling with convulsions, I sucked and drank from her, knowing full well I was the greedy one.

I wanted to be the only reason for every moment of her pleasure.

21

———

ARIADNE

"I need to go back to the waterfall today." Zeruhn brushed the words in a kiss over my brow, his arm tightening around me as he said them.

"Why?" I traced a scar on his chest, far too comfortable to move, especially with his body under me as a pillow.

"Because we need supplies."

I lifted my head, propping my chin on his sternum to look at him. "Are you sure you're up for all that hiking and climbing?"

"It's been three days, doe eyes." He tugged at a lock of my hair with a teasing grin. "I think all of my blood has been replenished by now, don't you?"

It was true. He seemed perfectly healthy and probably had been since at least yesterday. His cauterized wounds were already scarring over, adding to his extensive collection. I figured out quickly that my minotaur did not like to rest. The sleeping cave, which had become a cozy little home, seemed well stocked. So I wondered if it was truly a matter of supplies or that he just needed to move around.

"I won't be long," Zeruhn assured me, running an affectionate touch up my arms. "You should stay here with Lago. Stay even if you hear the doors open, and tell me when you get back."

"Why do you want me to stay?" I asked with a frown.

"Because the waterfall makes you unhappy." Heavy, calloused fingers rubbed into the nape of my neck. "I don't want to see that storm in your eyes fade away ever again."

I never exactly knew what he meant by the storm in my eyes, but I understood the sentiment, and it was sweet. He didn't want me to become upset like last time.

"I'll bring you more nectarines," he promised with a kiss to my neck. "And anything else useful I might find. It really depends on what the outsiders decide to throw away."

"You know." I turned my head, catching his next kiss on the mouth. "I think I would like to come with you."

Golden eyes widened in surprise. "You would? Why?"

"For a fresh start, I guess. A do-over." When the confusion didn't leave his face, I added, "Last time, I was only focused on escaping. That was what upset me, when I realized it would be impossible. Now?" I took his hand and linked our fingers together. "I'd like to go just to see it and to be with you."

Zeruhn's hand tightened around mine. "And if it saddens you again?"

"Then I'll tell you," I answered. "I won't fall into a depressive dark hole again. At least, I'll try not to. But whatever happens, I won't shut you out this time."

"Good." Zeruhn's other hand slapped down on my ass and groped me there. "Otherwise I'll have to hunt it out of you."

"Yeah, yeah, caveman." I leaned down to kiss him, letting myself go pliant on top of his hard body.

"I mean it, Ariadne," he said solemnly after a few kisses. "I'll chase away your sadness however I can. When you withdrew like that, it was...so distressing. I felt...helpless, unable to force the outcome I wanted. It pained *me* to see you like that. I couldn't stand it, I didn't know how to turn it off. How to make you happy again."

"That's sweet of you, big lug." I planted another kiss on him. "But you need to understand something."

He frowned. "Yes?"

"I'm not always going to be happy. Sometimes I'll be sad and just need to process things, to grieve what I lost out there."

"Out of the question." Zeruhn shook his head defiantly, horns cutting through the air. "If that happens, I will stop at nothing until your spirits are lifted again. Whether that's by bringing you the last nectarine on earth or tonguing your cunt until—"

"Neither of those things will reunite me with my mom," I said. "I love that you want to make me happy, Zeruhn, but sometimes the things that will cure my sadness will be out of your control. And while I'm..." I blew out a long breath, "...learning to accept that I'll never see my mom again, I'll still miss her. There will be times where I'll just wish I could hug her again, even though I know it's not possible. Sometimes I'll just need to let myself miss her and be sad over it, until it passes. Does that make sense?"

He was silent, pondering for a minute. "I understand that you will need this, and it's important to you. But I still don't like it." He rolled us up to sitting, arms and legs wrapped protectively around me like shields. "What should I do when you have these moments? If I can't fix them for you."

"Just be here." I leaned my head against his shoulder, curling my legs up and melting into the solidness of him. "Give me some space to deal with my shit, but be here when I'm ready to come out of it."

"It doesn't feel like enough," he grumbled. "You've saved my life twice and ask so little of me in return."

"I dunno, killing anyone who poses a threat to me is a pretty big deal."

"But you don't like it when I kill people." He let out a dry chuckle, swatting my hip. "Fickle woman."

"Really, Zeruhn." I nudged my forehead into his neck. "Being patient with me, being *here* for me is huge." A smile pulled at my lips. "And I supposed being hunted would get my mind off of things and provide some much-needed endorphins."

"Now that is something I can do." He kissed the bridge of my nose, then quickly pulled away to look at me solemnly. "But only when you're done being sad."

I beamed back at him, running my fingers over his bearded cheek. "Yes, exactly."

How could he be so...perfect? Ruggedly hot, intelligent, adaptive to the worst of circumstances. Protective, if brutally so, but also stunningly kind. He may not have fully understood that he couldn't always cure my sadness, but he respected me enough to listen. And not to mention the sex with him was on another level. The thought of being 'hunted' by him now sent a shivering thrill through me, and I was already craving that exhilarating type of foreplay again.

Holy shit.

Was I falling in love with the minotaur?

"Ariadne." He said my name in that low, sexy growl with a nip to my earlobe.

"Mm-hm?" I squirmed under his affection, the friction of his beard on my skin sending tingles through me.

"I said, do you still want to go to the waterfall?" Zeruhn kissed my shoulder, making sure to rub his beard on me there too. "I don't like the thought of you unprotected, so I would actually prefer it if you did. But if you'd rather not, Lago will let you know if anyone approaches."

"No, I'm good, really! I'll go." I smiled at him. "I think if I go with a different mindset, then it'll be okay."

"Okay then." He stood, pulling me up with him. "And if you stroke me while riding on my back, I won't complain."

"Oh, for fuck's sake." I rubbed my forehead with a groan. "You're the horniest man on earth, I swear."

He started to point toward his head. "I mean..."

"I know, I know. Walked right into that one." I swatted his ass on my way toward the stream. "Let's see some romantic water-falls, caveman."

* * *

THE SECOND TIME AROUND WAS A LOT MORE ENJOYABLE AND LESS anxiety-inducing. I was able to actually enjoy the scenery, from the trees somehow growing in the tiny crevices of the rock walls to the rock formations themselves.

Zeruhn carried a large backpack, wearing it on his chest so that I could ride on his back. He only let me fill two side compartments with nectarines since we needed to fill the pack with supplies we actually needed. He was hoping for some new solar panels to replace the ones going out. I had my heart set on a new change of clothes or a few. They wouldn't even have to fit —I had repaired enough of my own clothes over the years to alter anything. But I knew the people of Upper MinoTek could afford much sturdier, high-quality fabrics than what we got in the slums. If I could make a whole new outfit from some rich person's dumped goods it would make my day.

"How often is stuff ruined by the water?" I asked Zeruhn once I felt that cool mist on my face.

"With electronics, almost all the time," he said. "Sometimes I get lucky if I set things out in the sun to dry, but anything with working electrical components is rare. I usually find books, clothes, home decor, random kitchen accessories, things like that. And that's if they're not broken by the fall. It's a fifty-foot drop from the ceiling to the next flat surface down here."

"So many people from my end of the city could use stuff like that," I muttered. "I wonder why there isn't any kind of donation thing set up."

I took it back the moment I said it because I already knew. No one cared about the people from my side of the city.

"Most of what's dumped down here, I don't use," Zeruhn admitted. "It is a waste if there are others who could use these things."

He straightened as we reached the final cliffside next to the waterfall, and I slid from his back to peer up at the cascade of water.

"Do you ever see anyone up there?" I asked, shielding my eyes.

"I did once. A group of teenagers were doing drugs and sitting on the edge. I changed into my bull form and they scattered off, screaming."

"Mean," I laughed.

He smirked. "Would've been terrible if one of them had fallen in."

"*You're* terrible!"

His smile brightened as he turned to face me, that intense gaze searching again. "You're in good humor, doe eyes."

"Yeah, I feel alright." My chest fluttered, touched at his concern. "It's really pretty here actually."

"It is. I enjoy coming up here." He grabbed the nape of my

neck and placed a firm kiss on my lips that left me breathless. "Shall we see what we can find?"

Heat surged through me, and I would have preferred getting fucked under the spray of the waterfall right then. But we really did need supplies, and maybe we could still do that later.

"Yes," I breathed against his lips.

He kissed me once before releasing me and turning away, his tail swishing happily behind him, almost like a dog would wag its tail. I smiled as I went to check out some soggy books and papers near a cluster of rocks. It was cute that he had some animal qualities to express his mood.

"I'm going to see what's down there." Zeruhn pointed to a small series of ledges near the base of the waterfall. "I see something reflecting light. Might be panels."

"Okay. Just be careful." The rocks down there were the slipperiest.

"I will, my love."

There was that word again. It jump-started my heart like an electric shock. He said it so casually as he climbed down our ledge to his target below. Did he even realize the weight of that word, how saying it would affect me? Or did he read the definition in a book and just figured it applied to our situation?

No, Zeruhn wasn't stupid or emotionless. He wouldn't say something without fully understanding its meaning, right?

I sat in a daze, his use of that word bouncing around in my head like an echo on a cave wall. I never wanted it to fade, wanted to keep hearing it in his rich, deep voice over and over.

"Guess that means I feel the same way," I admitted quietly to myself.

I basked in that giddy, warm feeling until I heard his voice again, yelling over the crashing water. "Not solar panels! Just a damn broken mirror."

"Oh! That's too bad," I yelled back.

"I'm going to keep looking. There's more stuff down here."

"Okay."

Firmly back in reality, I returned to the piles of paper materials situated inside a cluster of rocks like a nest. It looked like a plastic bag had burst open on impact, allowing the waterfall's spray to expand what was inside.

I dug through soggy, ruined paper, occasionally glancing at pages to see if I could read the running ink. Most of it looked like typical junk mail. Letters and notices, insurance and bank statements, boring stuff.

I was almost ready to move on when my fingers touched *dry* paper. It was in the center of the pile, near the bottom. The top layers had insulated these lower materials from getting wet. A small shriek of laughter escaped my chest when I saw several issues of *The Black Papers* in the bottom of the pile, mostly dry and undamaged.

I lifted them out and quickly flipped to the inside cover to see when the issues were dated. Most of them I'd read before, but two had been published more recently—*after* I had been sent to the labyrinth. Crossing my legs with the pamphlets in my lap, I opened the most recent one and scanned the list of articles in the table of contents.

Ooh. This issue had quite a few scandalous stories about the prime minister of MinoTek. That was bold of these journalists, firing straight at the top. They must have had pretty good dirt on him to publish. I flipped to the first article and started reading. *The Prime Minster of MinoTek is a Sexual Predator,* stated the headline. The anonymous author of this article had the code name Mercury.

My eyes couldn't read the words fast enough. It detailed multiple accounts of Prime Minister Minos discreetly visiting slum neighborhoods as recently as ten years ago. He and his inner circle would then sexually assault women, sometimes even teenage girls. If anyone tried to intervene, his bodyguards would draw weapons and threaten their lives. The journalist listed all of Minos' men by name.

He and his inner circle did this because these people had no power in the city. Even if the assaults were to be reported, they would be tossed out as quickly as they were filed. He terrorized people who were already struggling to survive, just because he could with no consequences.

There was no warning as to when the prime minister would arrive. It was simply at his whim. Sometimes he and his henchmen came in a beaten-down, unmarked car, dressed in street clothes that would help them blend in with us. Other times it was in a MSP squad car that drove around for a while like it was doing routine patrols. Even if people figured it out quickly enough to hide in their homes, he and his men would force their way in.

Because the homes had been granted to us by the MinoTek authorities, they technically belonged to him.

My jaw hung open the whole time as I read. This journalist, Mercury, was indeed thorough. They included multiple quotes from interviews with the victims, carefully concealing any identifying information, of course. But not only that. They claimed one of their informants was a scientist at a prestigious university in Upper MinoTek, and this scientist was acquainted with the prime minister.

The scientist had successfully taken a DNA sample from the prime minister and tested it against multiple samples taken by Mercury from the victims' children. Over forty percent of them were an exact match.

The prime minister of MinoTek had sired over a dozen

confirmed children in the poorest neighborhoods of the city as a result of his sexual assaults. And those were only the ones whose mothers had agreed to speak to the journalist and consented to DNA swabs.

This irrefutable evidence is being kept in a safe location within our anonymous network, Mercury wrote. The identities of the children and victims will also remain unpublished, in order to protect them from the State who will surely seek to keep them silenced. MinoTek authorities were already becoming aware of my investigation before the publication of this story. If they uncover my identity, this may be my last article for The Black Papers, *but do not fear, readers.*

They want to silence us because they're scared. They are few, and we are many. The power they hold over us is little more than brainwashing. They've been grinding us down so long, we've never tasted anything but dirt. But there is plenty of sky and clean water for us too. We don't have to stand by and watch them assault our loved ones and treat us as sub-human. We only need to come together and take back the rights we've been denied.

"What are you reading?"

Zeruhn brushed a kiss against my cheek, the contact and warm rumble of his voice startling me.

"Oh, hi!"

He gave me that sexy, lopsided grin, easing down next to me to read over my shoulder. "I watched your eyes move back and forth for a whole minute. Must be entrancing, whatever it is. Erotica?"

"No!" I laughed, slapping his bicep. "This little publication," I closed the booklet to show him the front cover, "is what got me arrested and thrown in here with you."

"Oh?" His eyebrows lifted, intrigued.

"It's like a gossip column but better," I explained. "Because it's all about criticizing the State. The journalists are completely anonymous, and these are just left out in public places. Everyone reads them."

Zeruhn frowned. "So why were you singled out?"

"Beats me." I shrugged, then flipped to the story I was reading. "This one's crazy. It says Prime Minister Minos went around to slum neighbors and assaulted dozens of women and ended up fathering a bunch of kids."

My minotaur's brows knitted even tighter together. "Is it true?"

"No one really knows," I admitted. "They say they have DNA evidence, but of course, they can't publish it without risking the privacy of those involved. A lot of their stories are like that. They say they have proof, but we have to take them at their word." I thumbed through the pages. "I'm sure there's some truth to it, which is terrible."

"Did you ever see him?" Zeruhn fired the question at me with surprising intensity. "Come to your neighborhood and assault women?"

"The Prime Minister? Uh, no. Not that I remember. I've heard rumors about it in other communities, though." I cocked my head at him. "Why? You look really hard-pressed about this."

Zeruhn sighed and smoothed out his features, but the tightness in his jaw remained. "It just sounds unbelievably cruel to me, abusing power in such a way. Women, especially living in those conditions, are no threat to him. And to abandon children he created too?" He swallowed and looked at me. "And you seem rather nonchalant about it, if I may say."

"It's not that. I'm just...numb to it, I guess," I admitted. "Men abusing power and taking advantage of vulnerable people is just another day in my world."

He shook his head with disgust. "How did human men become so terrible?"

"They are the worst," I agreed, then turned to stretch my legs into his lap. "But you, my minotaur, are better than all of them combined."

"Aren't you lucky that I'm only part human," he growled softly, skimming his mouth over mine.

"The luckiest," I agreed, leaning into his kiss.

22

———————

ARIADNE

"I didn't find the type of panels I needed," Zeruhn grunted out in frustration. "None that were salvageable anyway."

I rubbed a hand over his chest. He was carrying me on his back again as we returned to our cave from the waterfall.

"How bad is that for us?" I asked.

"In another week, we might not be able to cook using the camper stove. The ones I have now are so corroded, they're barely generating any power."

"Well, we have your lighter, right? Can we make a fire and cook food the old-fashioned way?"

Zeruhn squeezed my thigh as he leapt from a boulder to the grassy bank of the stream. "You used almost all of the fuel in that to cauterize my wounds. And I don't have any left."

"Oh. Shit."

"It's alright, doe eyes." He chuckled, crouching so I could slide from his back. "More than anything, I'm glad to be alive."

"I'm glad you are too." My worry only grew as I stood and turned to face him. "But what's going to happen if we can't cook food? Is there anything else we can do?"

"Worst case, we'll live on raw eggs from the cliff nests for a little while." Zeruhn laughed at the face I made. "It's not so bad. I've done it a few times. But don't worry." He swung his backpack from his front to his back and picked me up again, wrapping his arms around my thighs and lifting until I straddled his waist. Then he settled his palms on my ass and kept walking. "I'll keep checking back at the waterfall. People dump random things every day, so some panels are bound to turn up."

I wrapped my arms around his neck and rested my head on his shoulder. "And if they don't?"

"They will." He pressed a reassuring kiss to my brow. "I've been here for twenty years and have gone through dozens of panels in that time. They always turn up."

The weight of those numbers took a moment to sink in. "Twenty years is a long time. You've been in here since you were...what, fourteen?"

"Yes, but I didn't look like a human fourteen-year-old. I wasn't much smaller back then than I am now."

"It's still crazy to me. You were a child, all alone. A child they created and were trying to kill!"

"It's okay, doe eyes." His hands laced together under my ass, hugging my sides with his massive arms. "I'm not alone anymore."

"No, you're not. But you don't have to carry me everywhere, you know." Despite what I said, I leaned my chest against his, enjoying the support of broad muscle underneath me.

"I like to carry you," he said. "You are small and fragile, like a doe."

"Excuse me?" I demanded in mock outrage. "Fragile? Who saved whose life again?"

Zeruhn chuckled, bouncing me in a way that deliberately rubbed against his thickening erection. "I don't mean fragile to say that you're weak. But you fall apart so beautifully when you're filled with cock." His grip on my ass tightened, almost punishingly. "And you will only ever fall apart for me. Do you understand?"

"Yes," I groaned, already breathy and fluttering for him. Only him.

"Good girl," he praised with a rough pat to my ass.

"Sounds like you want to go hunting," I mused, my heart already speeding up with the anticipation of running from my sexy, horned monster.

"Mm, tomorrow." His hands went to my waist and set me on the ground. "It's been a long day. You should be at full energy when I hunt you."

One glance around told me we were already back to his cave. *Our* cave. His long strides had gotten us there in record time. And at the first sight of our blankets on the floor, all I wanted to do was curl into them and sleep.

"Tomorrow then," I said, suppressing a yawn. "I'll make sure to stretch before running around the labyrinth."

"Oh, I will stretch you just fine, doe eyes."

"Hey, if you're gonna have a smart mouth," I tapped my lips with a finger, "put it to good use."

My minotaur approached me like the predator he was—golden eyes blazing, hand outstretched to caress my cheek as he kissed me. The moment our lips made contact, the caress became a possessive grab, a fist closed around the hair at the nape of my neck while his tongue plunged into my mouth.

Just as quickly as he started that fiery kiss, he ended it. "Lie down and let me hold you, doe eyes."

"Ugh, you are infuriating sometimes."

"Save your strength for tomorrow." The edge of his smile touched my lips. "You'll need it."

"Well, I'm definitely not going to be able to sleep with that kind of promise hanging over my head."

"It'll be worth the wait," he murmured, hands falling to wrap around mine. "Now lie with me."

Even when he was unbearably sweet, his voice carried a command that made me limp and unable to resist. We lowered to the bed together, snuggling into each other and sharing small kisses as we pulled the blankets over us.

"I'll be returning to the waterfall early in the morning," Zeruhn said into my hair, his massive body curled around mine like a shield, one thick arm draped over my waist. "A lot of the dumps happen before dawn. If I can be there early enough, I might be able to salvage some panels before they get too damaged."

"Okay. Want me to come?" I was already fighting to stay awake, too warm and comfortable in his embrace.

"No, my love. You rest." A warm kiss fell to the crook of my neck. "I'll be back before you even wake up or just shortly after."

"Okay, be careful."

"You too. Remember, don't leave the cave until I return."

"I won't."

* * *

ZERUHN WAS STILL GONE WHEN I AWOKE, WHICH I TRIED NOT TO BE alarmed by. Sunlight bathed the open valley in bright light, which meant it was already midmorning at the earliest, and I'd slept in late.

At the cave entrance, Lago sat alert like my little fluffy, horned bodyguard. Occasionally he flicked an ear or his nose twitched, but he otherwise seemed calm.

"You'd know if something happened to him, right?" I asked the jackalope. "You seem to know things."

He looked at me and thumped a rear foot on the ground.

I smiled back. "You understand me, yes?"

Another foot thumb.

"Does one thump mean yes and two mean no?"

One thump again.

"Is Zeruhn only four feet tall?"

Two thumps.

I went to sit next to him with a laugh, reaching to scratch the base of his antlers. "Zeruhn is lucky to have you. I know it's because of you that he hasn't felt totally alone here."

Lago thumped one foot.

I laughed again. "Modest little guy, aren't you?"

Another thump.

We sat together for a while, just waiting for our favorite minotaur to come back. Lago stretched out next to me and thumped yes when I asked to pet his belly. His eyes fell closed after a minute, paws hovering in midair, when something startled him. The jackalope's eyes snapped open, and he scrambled upright, ears stiff and alert.

"What is it?" I asked. "Is Zeruhn coming back?"

Lago thumped twice on the ground.

I froze, barely breathing while my heart made a racket in my chest. Then I heard it, the barely discernible, distant hum of machinery.

"Someone's coming?" I whispered. "Another labyrinth prisoner?"

The jackalope softly thumped once.

Shit. I didn't know what to do. I thought the part of me that hoped for human company was dead and withered. After Rich, the shifters, and the one who stabbed Zeruhn, the last thing I should have expected was a friendly human face.

And yet, some small part of me thought maybe this time was different. Maybe, just maybe, this person was innocent, like me. And wished no harm on others.

Zeruhn would never believe it. He'd immediately go on the offensive to protect me and Lago. But he didn't know humans like I did.

Did *I* really know them though?

Maybe it was just a primitive part of my brain that was eager for someone else of my species to connect to. Whatever the reason, a mixture of hope and anxiety roiled in my gut like a stormy sea.

Without warning, Lago took off like a shot out of the cave.

"Hey! Where are you going? Lago!" I started going after him but was no match for his long, jackrabbit legs. He headed upstream toward the waterfall, so I could only imagine he was running to get Zeruhn.

Fuck. The thought of Zeruhn dealing with another human amped my anxiety up to another level. Over the last few days, I'd almost forgotten about how many people he'd killed. He was just my smart, sexy, horned...boyfriend? Lover?

I had a better understanding of *why* he killed now, but that didn't mean I was more comfortable with the idea.

"Hello? Is someone there?" a voice called. A *male* voice.

Oh no.

I turned around slowly, now painfully aware that I was in plain sight and out of the protection of the cave. A man in the distance walked toward me, his arm raised in a wave. I gave an awkward wave back.

As he got closer, I could tell that he was nicely dressed in a blue polo shirt and khaki pants. Not someone from the slums, but he didn't look like Upper MinoTek stock either. He was also young, maybe my age, with blonde hair and a healthy tan.

Damn it. He's kind of cute too. Zeruhn was going to lose his shit when he saw him.

"Hey!" He waved again, showing a white-toothed smile as he jogged closer to me. "Are you..." He slowed to a walk, then stopped altogether with his jaw hanging open. "Holy shit, it *is* you! Ariadne, right? You're still alive in here?"

"Sorry, do I know you?" I crossed my arms, planting myself between him and my cave.

The man raised his hands, not moving from his spot. That was comforting, at least. "No, sorry. My name's Aaron, but I usually go by my last name, Theseus. I, um." He chewed the inside of his cheek. "Have you heard of *The Black Papers?*" It must have been obvious from my expression because he went on. "I work with them as one of their sources. I'm a—well I *was* —a lab tech for MinoTek Pharmaceuticals."

Now it was my turn to be shocked. "Like the DNA tests?" I sputtered out. "Of the prime minister's children?"

"Yeah, I ran a few of those." Aaron nodded. His eyes flicked around nervously before landing on me again. "Including yours."

"Mine?" My heart dropped into my stomach. "What do you mean? That's not—I never gave a DNA sample!"

"Your mother did," he said softly. "She told us you were at work. But she gave us a couple strands of your hair from a brush."

"No, when...*why* would she do that?" I felt dizzy. The ground threatened to tilt out from under me.

"A few months ago," he continued in a gentle tone. "And it seemed like she already knew. But she wanted to help build a case against the PM, and we promised anonymity for her and you."

The pieces of information started to snap together in my mind, and the world righted itself under my feet. I was in control once again. "Well, that didn't work out so well, did it?"

Aaron's jaw tightened, and I knew I was right. "You *couldn't* promise anonymity," I went on. "The authorities found your list of Minos' illegitimate children, didn't they? At least, they found my name. *That* was why I was thrown in here on bullshit charges."

"Ariadne." Aaron raised his hands placatingly. "I am *so* sorry. I guess your mother never told you."

"Don't try to blame this on her! She trusted you, and you failed her too."

"I'm really, really sorry. Truly! We only wanted to help people, and we still are. We're trying to build a case with actual evidence and take it to a court outside of MinoTek. The whole system needs to be rooted out, and the people at the top need to be charged with crimes against humanity." He lowered his hands slowly. "And it's still possible. There are people working within the system to dismantle it." He brought a hand to his chest with a sheepish smile. "I was one of them until, you know, very recently. And anyway, holy shit!" His hands thrust out toward me. "You're still alive! That's incredible."

"So what got you tossed in here then? And don't lie." Zeruhn might not have cared what crimes were committed to get thrown in the labyrinth, but it still mattered to me. And my alarm bells were ringing because Aaron Theseus seemed too damn cheerful for a man that had just been sentenced to death.

His cheerful attitude faded at the question, but not by much. "Okay, so...you're right. More of my test results for *The Black*

Papers were found by my boss. I encrypted everything, but he's a savvy son of a bitch and loyal to the State, of course."

"Great." I crossed my arms. "So more victims are going to be identified and hunted down. Fantastic."

"Look, it's not all bad." Aaron looked around and edged closer to me, and I promptly took a step back. He may have been fighting the powers that put me in here, the same ones that allowed Zeruhn and so many others to have been experimented on, but I still didn't trust him.

Aaron at least recognized that I didn't want him any closer and stopped where he was. "There are more of us in the system," he whispered. "We have help outside of here, and they're going to get us out."

"They're...what?" I heard the words, but my brain couldn't seem to process what he said.

"I have a buddy who's a shifter cop. He's gonna help me, well... us, get the fuck out of here." Aaron leaned to the side, patting down his pant leg. "But we've got to make sure the minotaur doesn't get us first, right?"

"...What?"

I could only blink, watching dumbfounded as he reached under his pant leg and produced a syringe with a dark, viscous liquid inside.

23

ZERUHN

I'd never had so much difficulty leaving my bed to scavenge before. Ariadne's body was warm and soft, curled into a shape that fit perfectly against me. She breathed deeply in her sleep, lashes sweeping over her cheekbones, lips slightly pursed. I never wanted to let go of her or to stop watching her.

But if I didn't find some intact solar panels soon, we would struggle to eat. Providing for her was what mattered most. That sole purpose was what my instincts focused on, and I was done fighting them. Her happiness, comfort, and safety were now all that I wanted.

And once I returned, I would hunt my sweet little prey and claim her body, her cries of pleasure, as my victory.

It was a fight to lift away from her and face the chilly, gray dawn. Before I left, I draped a heavier blanket over her, making sure to cover her from feet to shoulders. My body temperature was a good four degrees higher than a human's. So if I felt the chill, she would surely be freezing.

"Stay with her," I instructed Lago at the cave entrance. "If anyone enters, come find me immediately."

The jackalope's nose twitched, and he thumped one foot on the ground.

Despite every instinct telling me to stay at Ariadne's side, I turned my back to the cave and headed upstream toward the waterfall. I moved quickly, breaking into a run and scaling the rock walls and cliffs at a pace that had me sweating within minutes. The faster I got there and collected my spoils, the sooner I could get back to her.

I reached the waterfall in record time and took a moment just to stand in the spray of cold water. It cooled my heated blood and washed away the sweat on my skin. *Hm, I should fuck Ariadne under the waterfall.*

I remembered how her skin pebbled in the stream, how tight her nipples were when they rubbed against my thighs when she'd sucked me.

Ugh, I needed to focus. Needed to do what I came here to do, *then* sink into that cunt I would kill for.

She didn't like it, but I couldn't change these instincts that ruled me. My human side could only wield so much control, and there was no holding back this need to protect what was mine.

I forced my thoughts away from her to look at my surroundings. Everything seemed the same as yesterday. Nothing new had been thrown over the cliff yet.

My tail swished with aggravation behind me. I walked directly to the smooth, rock wall that the water cascaded over and looked up. The wall ended where the sky began, and at that junction was the strange world of humans. A world I'd never been part of and would never belong to.

And yet Ariadne, who was so perfect for me, came from that world. She even missed it, at least parts of it.

How different were we from each other, really? At the molecular level, we were completely different species. I had originated from humans, was even carried and nourished by a human mother, but my DNA, what structured my cells and my consciousness, was anything but.

And somehow, in a stormy-eyed human woman, I found everything I didn't know had been missing.

I brought my palm to the rock wall, letting the stone cool my heated flesh. "All I need are some fucking solar panels," I said to the wall. "Why hasn't anything been dumped this morning?"

No answer, unsurprisingly. I crossed my arms, looking skyward as I thought. I might just have to come back tomorrow, keep coming back until something turns up. If I was on my own, it would be no issue. I would ration my food portions and conserve my energy until I eventually got what I needed.

But now I was taking care of another person and burning faster through my food stores as a result. That changed everything. My own survival became less important, but hers was everything. I needed to make sure she had enough to eat and enough purification tablets so she could have clean water to drink.

A soft series of clicks broke through my thought process. I jerked away from the wall but still wasn't fast enough. A panel of rock slid aside, and the robotic arm lunged for my throat.

"Argh, fucking another one!" I roared, clawing at the metal hand now latched around my throat.

A door slid open next to the arm and a suited man walked out. This fucker promptly opened an umbrella to shield against the waterfall's spray.

"Do you like it?" Simon Gibbs nodded at the robotic arm

holding me in its grasp. "It's an upgraded model from the last one. Every part is coated with a waterproof solution so that it doesn't rust." He gave me a smug human look, the same one he gave me last time. "This one is also reinforced so that not even an animal like you can break it."

"An umbrella, really?" I rasped. "Will you melt if a little water touches you?"

His lips thinned. "I thought we came to an agreement, minotaur. The girl's life for your freedom. Why haven't you killed her yet?"

"Because I lied to you, that's why." Metallic fingers squeezed tighter around my throat, and I struggled to take in a breath. "I wondered why you wanted me to kill her so badly. And what do you know? Even a dumb animal like me figured it out."

"Your only purpose is to kill," he said. "That is why you're here, minotaur. You execute prisoners. That's the end of it."

"No." I shook my head what little I could. "The prime minister wants her dead because she's his daughter."

I knew it the moment Ariadne told me the story from the papers she'd found yesterday, but Gibbs' face sealed it for me.

"Yeah, you couldn't stop the story of him being a serial rapist from being published, so now you're looking to silence his victims." His name was on that list in the article Ariadne had been reading. How many people had he assaulted? He needed to die, but I couldn't move to get in his face. The best I could do was bare my teeth and snarl at the man.

"You falsely imprisoned a girl from the slums in the labyrinth, and you're *still* scared of her." I barked out a laugh. "You human men are pathetic. Never satisfied until everyone is crushed firmly under your boot. Women don't even want to fuck you, so you force it on them." I got enough of my fingers under the metal clamped on my throat to take a bigger breath. "I'm not the animal here. You are."

"If you won't do your duty for the State," Gibbs said stiffly, pointedly ignoring all my accusations. "Then we'll do it for you. And you, *minotaur*," he added with a sneer, "will be disposed of. Seeing as you are no longer useful."

"You can try," I growled back, my vision going red. "You might even succeed at killing me. But you will *never* touch her."

He scoffed and pulled a small black rectangle from his suit pocket. "Watch me, beast. I can track her ID chip with this." His thumb swiped over the screen a few times before showing it to me again. "Ah, look. She's only four miles from here. I can dispatch an officer and deal with her in minutes."

I didn't think, didn't feel. My body became overrun with the need to protect Ariadne, and I simply acted. My tail thrust out toward him. The sudden movement startled him, and he went stumbling. I couldn't grab his leg with my tail, but I could apply just enough pressure to his ankle to make him trip.

He went down with a heavy thud, and I had to make a decision quickly. This man needed to die by my hand. It was just a matter of whether or not I also died in the process. If I shifted, I would either break this robot arm holding me in place, or it would apply enough force to strangle me for good.

This is for you, Ariadne, I thought, and I let the change take over me.

My height shot up first, and I heard the creak and groans of protest where the arm attached to the wall. It remained clamped around my neck though, so I let the rest of the change happen and hoped I would still be breathing in a few seconds.

The metal collar held on even as my neck thickened, even while my musculature grew to three times the size of a human bodybuilder's. I stamped my hooves and grabbed for the metal arm, trying to get leverage so that I could tear from the wall.

My vision dotted with darkness. I felt an increasingly tight squeeze around my neck, and then I couldn't take breath. My head swung, trying to get free. But even my super-human strength was no match for this robotic arm.

"Stupid beast," Gibbs sputtered from the ground. "I told you you couldn't break it." He hadn't gotten up from where I laid him out. The soft old man probably broke a hip when he fell.

I was getting lightheaded now, my vision swimming in and out. My lungs were burning, and I wasn't getting any air. Well, I had already decided if I was going down, the least I could do was make sure this corrupt piece of shit wouldn't get near Ariadne.

He was reaching for something on the ground, stretching for something just out of his reach. My vision cooperated long enough for me to tell it was a small black rectangle—the remote!

I raised a hoof just as he grabbed it and brought my foot down as hard as I could through the top of his palm. His scream echoed off the many rocky walls, and a perfect C-shape indent now deformed the top of his hand, his broken skin filling in with blood.

I stomped down again and again to his ongoing screaming. My vision was all but gone, so I brought my hooves down wildly, blinding stomping down with what little remained of my strength. My body was so deprived of oxygen, I couldn't even tell if I was hitting a body or just the rocky ground.

All at once, the unbearable pressure on my neck released, and I pulled in the most beautiful, painful breath of air of my life.

I collapsed to the ground, gasping and coughing. Each deep lungful of air hurt a little less, and I was full of sheer relief that I came back from the brink of death.

When I had the strength to lift my head, the first thing I saw was the shattered handheld device he'd been reaching for. It was in pieces, both the outer casing and the small components inside. I glanced to the wall behind me and saw that the robot arm hung limp from where it had emerged.

I coughed out a laugh of disbelief. They reinforced the arm and controlled it from a handheld device, one that I'd been able to crush underneath my hoof. I thought I was done for but that blind stomping did the trick.

As for the man on the ground? He wasn't faring much better than his little device.

He cradled his bloody, mangled stump of a hand to his chest. His screams grew louder, and his legs flailed to get away once he realized that I was no longer collared. I approached him slowly, drawing out his fear. He couldn't stop staring at my horns, now longer than his arm span.

I let him scramble away until he teetered on the edge of the cliff. Falling to the rocks below probably would have been sweet relief for him, so I couldn't allow that. I grabbed him by the throat and lifted up, letting his fancy leather shoes dangle in midair.

His gaze met mine, his expression all twisted in pain and sobbing. The pathetic audacity only made me angrier. Did his victims cry and plead for him to stop as he was doing now?

The thought enraged me, and I squeezed harder around his neck, cutting off his air and ability to make sounds. The human side of my brain rang in warning, like an alarm bell. This man was an important figure to the State, and his death would have serious consequences. I would be arrested, and this time, they would likely stop at nothing to kill me.

But I couldn't bring myself to care. My animal instincts were in charge with only one goal in mind—protect Ariadne. Eliminate any threats to her safety.

And to do it painfully so that nothing would seek to harm her again.

I brought his face closer to mine until I saw my bull-headed reflection in his eyes.

"She is mine." My speech was distorted through my animal mouth, but he understood me.

"I won't...I'm sorr...no!" Gibbs could only mouth whispers until I released him, tossing him in the air like a ragdoll. When he came back down, I felt the weight of his body as my right horn impaled him, felt him tear open like tissue paper. And then the warmth of his blood trickling down over my head and face.

I shook him off with a roar, and he crumpled to the ground like the trash heap he was. He'd been impaled on the lower half of his torso and was still alive as he weakly tried to put hands over the gory wound. I snorted a heavy breath, my tail lashing behind me as I stood over him. I would watch him bleed out, let my face be the last one he ever saw. He was going to order *my* Ariadne's death, and I would see him suffer for it.

The breeze shifted as his blood pooled on the ground, and I lifted my head to take a deeper inhale. I swore my nose caught something strange...

A growl left my chest before I could control it. There *was* an unfamiliar scent, and it carried the markers of a human man.

Someone else was here with Ariadne and I.

I'd been so distracted by Gibbs that I hadn't noticed the humming of the doors opening. Sure enough, Lago came sprinting up the rocks moments later, his wings a bright green blur as they worked to get him more airborne. The jackalope was panting from exertion, and when he reached a flat rock within my sight, he thumped his foot in a rapid panicked beat.

Ariadne was in trouble.

I looked down at the dying man at my feet. He was fading quickly but still had the nerve to send up pained, pleading expressions at me.

"I'm going to give you a merciful death," I said. "But know this before you go—it's far more than what you deserve."

With that, I scraped a hoof along the ground. It was his only warning before my kick came crashing through his skull. I felt the bones shatter on impact but didn't stop to assess the damage. I'd killed rhinoceros shifters with similar blows. A human stood no chance.

My business with him was done. And then I sprinted down the series of cliffs to return to my woman.

24

ARIADNE

I stared at the syringe with the thick, sludgy liquid inside, unable to touch it. Unable to ignore the wave of danger signs and bad feelings that it brought to my body.

"What is that?" I finally asked, my throat dry.

"It's a powerful neurotoxin," Aaron said, almost proudly. "They use it to put down shifters that don't meet qualifications for the streets. A drop of this can make a human catatonic. A whole syringe can stop even the strongest shifter's heart in under a minute."

"And you want to use this on...?" I couldn't bring myself to say it, not even if I were to pretend to go along with his plan.

"The minotaur," he confirmed. "This was all top-secret, but the lab that created him was a sister lab to ours. When they closed down, we took in a lot of their old data and files. I'll tell you, I spent an afternoon reading about this thing, and *wow*."

"What did it say?"

"He was one of the earlier prototypes, before they put learning and mood inhibitors into their DNA and, holy shit, this guy was smart *and* violent. It was probably the deadliest combo, on top of being super strong and ruled by animal instincts. His whole genetic makeup is a recipe for disaster."

I was fuming inside, biting my cheek to hold back from blurting out any scathing retorts. Not that he was wrong, Zeruhn *was* smart and violent. But he was also generous and kind, warm, loving, and fiercely protective. He was a person, and so much more than a printout of data results from an experiment.

"He never cooperated with tests," Aaron went on. "Scientists reported injuries whenever they went to examine him, lots of black eyes and bruises. Just really fucking difficult."

"Isn't that what you are to the State?" I couldn't hold myself back any longer. "Difficult? A thorn in MinoTek's side, since you've been working with *The Black Papers* against them?"

Aaron seemed taken aback by my argument, his brows going up as he brought a hand to his chest. "*We* are human beings. We have rights that have been infringed upon. Shifters aren't people, they're lab-made to fill a specific role in society. They're mass-produced clones. They don't have, like, personalities or aspirations or anything."

"Does your shifter friend who's helping us escape know you feel that way?" I retorted.

"Look, I know how it sounds." Aaron waved a hand, shooting me a placating smile. "But he's agreed to help, and we've got to take care of ourselves, right? Once we're the hell outta Dodge, we can worry about the shifters."

I sighed and rubbed my forehead, knowing I wouldn't get anywhere with him. "So we...inject the minotaur with that, escape the labyrinth, and then what?"

"We head south as fast as we can." Aaron's face went serious again. "Steal a car, maybe shoot some people, do whatever we have to. It's gonna be risky as hell, and they're gonna be after us. But there's a port with boats that'll take us far away from here.

MinoTek won't have jurisdiction over us when we hit the water. And no matter where we end up, they can't extradite us back here."

He leaned in closer to whisper, "MinoTek is a big, black spot in the grand scheme of things. The outside world...it's not like this. This whole fucking city-state is a prison. Even the upper side is cut off from the rest of the world. They may be rich but they're not free. Out there?" He nodded to the crack in the ceiling. "It might not be as technologically advanced but people are taken care of. Everyone's basic needs are met, no police harassing you at every turn. You can live a life, a *real* life."

Aaron rubbed the back of his head sheepishly. "I was gonna enact this plan on my own, but since you're still here," he shrugged, "maybe us getting out together was meant to be." His gaze went over my shoulder to the cave behind me. "You've managed to escape the minotaur for how long, weeks? I mean, that's incredible. If we work together, Ariadne, I know we can do this."

My mind was screaming, *Zeruhn, where the fuck are you?* I didn't know what would happen when he showed up, probably nothing good for Aaron, but if what he was saying was true, that if we headed south and made it to the water, then we—Zeruhn and I—could be free. But if only...

"I have family in the city. If I do this with you," I said cautiously, "then we need to get my family member out as well."

Aaron pressed his lips together and gave a slow shake of his head. "If we take detours through the city, we'll lose valuable time and are guaranteed to get caught. And then they'll execute us on the spot, probably in public to set an example to everyone else. You know they did that before making the labyrinth a prison, right? I've seen old photographs, and they're not pretty."

"Either we get my mother or I'm not part of this," I said. "I wish you luck on your own."

"Ariadne." Aaron sighed like he was exasperated, and I was growing more annoyed every second. Least of all because he wanted to kill *my* minotaur. "I understand how important family is. Truly, I do." Something in his tone told me he didn't. "But we have to look ahead, to the future. We want the future generations to be free from an overbearing, tyrannical government, don't we? Sometimes we have to make sacrifices."

"I'm not *sacrificing* my mother." My voice rose, and I clenched my fists to hold back my anger. "And you don't even know me! Why the fuck are you talking to me about future generations like you plan to knock me up or something?"

"That's not—I'm not—" Aaron brought his fingers to his lips briefly. "I'm sorry. You're right. I'm just dying to get out of here before I get fucking skewered, you know?"

That did nothing to calm my mood. "Again, good luck with your plan, Aaron. I truly wish you the best."

"Ariadne, please think about this," he begged. "Look, once we escape, we can totally go our separate ways. We don't have to force anything that's, uh, obviously not here." He gestured to the two of us sheepishly.

Before I could answer, a bloodcurdling scream rang out and echoed through the labyrinth. I whipped around, facing the direction it came from—the waterfall. "Fuck, Zeruhn," I said under my breath.

"What the fuck was that?" Aaron demanded loudly. "Holy shit, are there more prisoners here? That sounded like torture if I ever heard it." He started vigorously shaking the syringe. "I'm not taking any fucking chances."

Fuck, I couldn't let him get near Zeruhn with that thing. I held my hand out. "Give it to me."

Aaron stared at me like I'd grown horns. "What?"

"I'll do it. I've..." I bit my lip, debating on how to spin this. "I've gotten close to the minotaur. He won't expect it coming from me because he trusts me."

Aaron's eyebrows shot up. "Whoa. Uh, okay. That...makes sense, I guess."

The judgment in his tone made me want to spit in his pretty human face, but I held back. "If you really want to escape, let me handle it. I won't go without my mom, but I can do this much for you."

Satisfied, he removed the plastic cover on the needle and placed the syringe in my palm. "Stick it anywhere you can, then press the plunger all the way down. He'll go down like a lightweight."

"Okay." The lie tasted bitter on my tongue, but I swallowed it down. "Stay here. I'll be back."

Out of nowhere, Aaron lunged forward and crushed me in a tight hug to his chest. A fake cologne smell filled my nostrils while my hands stuck out in midair awkwardly. What the fuck?

Just as quickly, he released me and stepped back. "Sorry, sorry. I just...thank you, Ariadne." He gave me an oddly heartfelt expression that, despite the fact that I did not like him, made me feel even worse about lying. "I can't imagine what you've been through down here. You're just brave, is all."

"Thanks," I said stiffly. "Well, I'm gonna..."

"You sure you don't want me to come with you? You know, as backup or something."

"No!" I held my empty hand up. "If he sees you, he could, uh, kill us both. He won't suspect a thing if it's just me. It'll work, trust me."

Those last two words made me wince, but Aaron didn't seem

to notice. He just nodded. "Right, makes sense. I'll just hang out then. Wait for you to get back."

"Okay."

With that, I turned and walked upstream with the deadly syringe in my hand. I wanted to throw it away the moment I was out of Aaron's sight, but I couldn't bring myself to.

"What the fuck is happening, Zeruhn?" I muttered to myself, picking up the pace. "What the fuck was that scream?"

I couldn't climb up the rocks very far, but it wasn't long before I saw a massive, horned monster rushing down toward me. He was lithe and agile for his size, almost mirroring the nimble jackalope following after him.

"Zeruhn!" I cried out in horror when he got closer. One of his horns was coated entirely in blood, and the red liquid dripped over his face and chest. He was in his bull form, and his face looked absolutely feral. His hooves crashed over the ground with each landing like a hammer striking steel.

His ears flicked forward, wild golden eyes taking me in when I said his name. "Ariadne!" My name sounded strange coming from an animal's head, but it was *him* saying it.

"Why are you covered in blood?" I demanded, taking him in as he stood in front of me. The blood looked fresh too, barely dried. "Are you hurt?"

Zeruhn's nostrils flared as he took a breath in, and he let out a frighteningly animal growl when he exhaled. "Why is there a human man's scent overlapping with your own?"

Oh, fuck. Aaron, you fucking idiot.

"A man...has touched you?" Zeruhn's ears flicked backwards, and I could hear the hurt in his voice. "Have you...doe eyes, *please* tell me why I smell a man on you."

"Listen, you big dummy." I climbed onto a nearby boulder and stood so that I was nearly eye level with him. I wrapped an arm around the back of his neck and pulled him down so that I could plant a kiss on that wide bull's nose. "I love you, okay? I'm yours, you're mine. There is no one for me but you." That might have been the first time I spoke those words aloud but the gravity of the situation didn't let me bask in those feelings for long.

"Then what is this scent?" Zeruhn growled. "Why is it all over you?"

"A man *is* here. He hugged me, that's all," I said quickly. "He told me about an escape plan. And I think...I think we could do it, Zeruhn. You and me."

"Escape?" he huffed. "With this unknown man who has touched you?"

My throat tightened as I showed him the syringe, but I choked the words out anyway. "No. He snuck this in to...to kill you."

Zeruhn stared at the needle across my palm, then picked it up and smelled it, instantly making a grotesque face. "He gave this to you? Why?"

"Because I...I told him that you trusted me. That I could get close to you and inject you with it without you suspecting anything."

My minotaur's head tilted, his eyes narrowing. "He believed you would manipulate me. Kill me to help him."

I nodded, swallowing despite the lack of moisture in my throat.

"But you didn't," Zeruhn went on. "You brought this to me and told me." He flicked his wrist, barely moving his arm at all, but the syringe shattered against a nearby rock. "Even though you know what I must do to him."

I nodded again, my heart punching a hard rhythm against my ribcage. "And I would do it again."

"Why?" The edge in his voice stung, but I knew it wasn't a slight against me. I knew he was coming from a place of being betrayed by everyone he ever knew.

"Because I'm loyal to *you*, Zeruhn," I said. "I'm on your side. I will fight for you. I will stand with you whether we're in the labyrinth or out there. You are *mine,* and no human man will take you away from me."

He was silent for several long moments before breathing my name, "Ariadne..."

"Wait." I pressed a hand to his chest. "I meant everything I said. I just have a question, and I need you to answer me honestly."

"Always, my sweet doe eyes." His arms falling around me covered my whole back. Even his tail thrust forward to wrap around my leg possessively.

"If we do try his escape plan and we make it out," I licked my lips nervously, "can we take my mother with us?"

"Yes, of course," he said without hesitation. "You said her joints pain her, so I will carry her myself."

It felt like I was falling, weightless with relief and such all-consuming love for this man. Not that there was any doubt before, but this was just another sign that I had made the right choice.

I chose the monster. Maybe that meant I was fucked up, but at least *he* had never seen me that way.

"I don't understand why you'd ask the question." Zeruhn's brow knitted, his bull face frowning. "She's important to you, so the answer is obvious."

"It's obvious to me too. I just...I love you so much, that's all." My arms barely went around his massive neck as I kissed him again. "Thank you."

"I love you too, my doe eyes." He held my chin, pulling back to stare intensely at me. "You *do* know what I have to do, yes? This man's scent is all over you. He sent you to kill me. I cannot hold back my instincts on this. He cannot get away with touching what is *mine.*"

"I know," I said with a nod. "I understand."

"Do you want to stay here?"

"No. I'll go with you."

Zeruhn sucked in a surprise breath. "You're sure?"

"Yes." I slid down from the boulder and took hold of his hand. "You'll stand with me through everything. So I'll do the same for you."

25

———

ZERUHN

"Will you tell me why you're all bloody?" Ariadne asked as we headed to the main valley. "It's clear you're not hurt. So who did you already kill today?"

I paused, at first hesitant about how much I should tell her. Death and killing was upsetting for her, but she asked the question calmly. And she seemed understanding of why I had to kill this next human, Aaron Theseus. Not just understanding but supportive. My doe-eyed human accepted me without trying to change me.

"He was a MinoTek official," I said, opting to hold nothing back. "Someone high up, the prime minister's chief of staff."

Ariadne's breath of surprise tickled my sensitive ears. "What did he want?"

"He wanted me to kill you. It was actually the second time he came through a hidden door to see me. When I didn't follow his order the first time, he came through to do it himself."

Ariande tossed her mane of black hair with a sigh. "Guess I'm popular around here."

"You're *mine*," I growled.

"I know that." She laughed humorlessly, then frowned. "So, he's dead?"

"Very much so."

"Zeruhn." Her grip on my hand tightened. "If he's a higher-up like you said, we're in big trouble."

"I know, I've been thinking about that." I squeezed her hand back, trying to reassure her.

"Like, they will probably send soldiers to swarm the labyrinth and corner us. There will be no hiding for us at that point."

"Yes, I think our time here is limited, doe eyes."

"So we *have* to escape."

"Yes, and we will. Us *and* your mother." I stopped and turned to face her. "But I have to do this first. I cannot let this human man go. Do you understand?"

"I do," she said with a solemn nod. "I won't get in your way."

"Good." My growl took on a purr at her decision to stand with me. I knew it couldn't be easy to support actions that went against her nature, no matter how intrinsic they were to mine. "After today, if we make it out safely, I won't ever kill again."

Ariadne's eyes widened. "Really?"

"Yes, I promise. I will protect you and your mother against any threat, but if we get out of the city," I placed a hand on her waist and brought her closer, "maybe the threat won't be so great anymore."

Ariadne leaned her head against my side. "Let's do what we have to, then." She pulled away from me, walking a few steps ahead. "I'll go a little bit ahead so that he doesn't run off at the first glimpse of you."

I huffed. "If he runs, I'll just hunt him down."

"That's the thing." Ariadne turned away, tossing a smile over her shoulder. "I don't want you hunting anyone but me."

It was hard to contain my groan, my aching desire for her and, well, contain how hard that made me. But I hung back, watching her long legs and perky ass crest the next small hill and go down the other side. I needed to sink into her one last time before we escaped, there was no questioning that.

I could not have asked for a better partner, nor more delicious prey to chase.

"Holy shit, you did it?" I heard a male's voice ask, and I pricked my ears forward to listen better. Just the sound of it made me see red.

"Well, there was a slight issue," Ariadne told him. I wanted to laugh. My doe-eyed human had hidden teeth and claws, better than any shifter. I was beyond proud that she was mine.

"What happened?" The male sounded dumbfounded. Every muscle in my body tensed, waiting for the right moment to show myself.

"You," Ariadne said, and I couldn't hold back my snort.

"Me? What are you talking about?"

"You came in here assuming you knew everything. Well, I'm sorry, Aaron. If you had just listened instead of talked, this might have ended differently."

"Ariadne, are you nuts? What the hell is going on—whoa!"

I stormed over the hill the moment he started talking, my rage too hot to hold back. The human male was puny, pathetic. His eyes and mouth hung open comically wide as he took in the sight of me, all hulking mass, horns, and covered in blood that hadn't fully dried from my last kill.

"You have no right to speak her name," I said, striding directly toward him. "You have no right to *touch* her!"

The human male started backing away but tripped over his

own feet and scooted pathetically on the ground while the stench of urine hit my nostrils.

"No...wait, wait!" He shot a panicked glance at Ariadne, and my rage hit a new high that he still had eyes to look at her. "But the syringe! Why?"

"Why did you believe I would be loyal to you instead of him?" she shot back. "I spoke to you for minutes, and all you showed me is that you don't care about anyone but yourself." She angled her head toward me. "I've known him for weeks. I've *seen* who he really is."

"Are you crazy, bitch? Look at that thing!" His panicked gaze swung back to me. "That is a lab experiment that's out of control. You can't possibly see him as a *person!*"

"I do," Ariadne said, her face softening into one of sympathy. Maybe even pity. "And it's really, really unfortunate for you that you don't."

"What is your escape plan?" I said. "Explain it before I lose patience."

"Fuck you, minotaur!" the human spat out.

I leaned down, picking him up by the front of the shirt. He changed his tune quickly once he was in clear sight of my horns. "Ah! Uh, my shifter friend! The cop. He's going to come to the main door at sundown. He'll knock twice. If you knock back four times, that means you're ready to go."

"Is that the truth?" Ariadne demanded. Her gaze was stormy, beautiful and furious.

"Yes! Yes, I swear! Please don't kill me. Please..."

I slid a glance to Ariadne. If she changed her mind, I was willing to put my rage aside, no matter how badly my instincts demanded vengeance. It was the last thing I wanted to do, but for her, I would.

She gave me the subtlest of nods in return, allowing me to

proceed. As if I could love her even more, my heart overflowed with appreciation for this woman. I would cherish her until the end of my days.

"I'll—I'll guide you both out," the human continued to babble. "It won't be easy, but, uh, extra muscle could be good, you know?"

"South, right?" Ariadne asked. "To the port?"

"Yeah, there will be a boat waiting. It's disguised as a party yacht."

"Good, thank you," Ariadne said respectfully before she turned away, walking in the opposite direction.

"Wha—where are you doing?"

"Do not speak to her," I snarled in his face. "She is finished with you."

"Oh fuck, what does that mean?" he whimpered.

"You touched what is mine. You sent her to kill me." I lifted him higher, angling him toward the sharp point of my horn. "Because your information will allow us to escape, I will not make you suffer much. But I cannot allow you to live."

"Oh fuck, please! I'm sorry! I—I didn't know!"

"You wanted her for yourself," I hissed. "You *touched* her!"

Something shifted in his demeanor then. Anger flashed through his eyes. "And you think she wants *you*?" he fired back. "You really think she'll fuck a monster-sized lab rat?"

I laughed. Just when I'd started to feel a modicum of sympathy for this human, he ruined it for himself.

"Oh, pathetic little man," I sighed. "Don't you know that she already has?"

His shocked face changed little when my horn went through him. There wasn't much blood as he was impaled, but it rushed out in a reddish-black stream as I lifted him off. I was a creature of my word and would minimize his suffering despite him being a prick to the very end.

He was staring in shock at the hole in his midsection and didn't notice my hands approaching the sides of his head. I snapped his neck quickly, like I would a bird. His body crumpled into a lifeless heap, and the surge of rage within me calmed, like the breaking apart of a storm.

It was replaced by something else, a rush of heat though my body. My cock ached to be squeezed in a slick, hot hold. Instead of bodies tearing on my horns, I wanted to feel hands grip them as I devoured a cunt.

I spun around, but Ariadne was nowhere to be seen. I could smell her, though, and the sweet nectar of her desire. A deep, yearning growl filled my chest as I followed her scent like it was a string guiding me to salvation. My sweet prey wanted to be hunted, and she was anticipating my capture.

And capture her I would.

You can run, but you can't hide, doe eyes.

26

ARIADNE

I knew a head start would only get me so far, so I ran while Zeruhn was preoccupied. He could settle his beef with Aaron, and I wouldn't have to stick around to witness it.

Maybe it was out of habit, or just nostalgia at this point, but I headed toward the ruins of the church. Besides the cave where we ate and slept, the church felt like "our" place in the labyrinth. It was where he first kissed me after that confusing-but-also-arousing first hunt. It was also where we first made love, where I first started to come to terms with my feelings for him.

It held a lot of memories for such a short time spent together. And soon, we'd have to leave and hopefully make new memories.

I slowed to a walk once I entered the maze of tunnels, letting my hand trail along the stone wall as I caught my breath. I could feel it again, that spark of hope that I thought had been crushed into dust. That dangerous little bit of optimism that sent me into a deep depression when I realized it couldn't be achieved.

But this time was different. Now I wasn't alone. If I spiraled again, I had someone to support me through it, to hold me above water when it felt like I was drowning. Or at the very least, chase me until I was too ragged to think about it.

I had only reached the end of the first tunnel when I heard the great crashing of hooves on stone. My pulse jumped as I sharply turned a corner just as Zeruhn called, "Where are you, doe eyes?"

Oh, the urge to answer back with some sass forced me to bite my cheek. I couldn't make it too easy for him to find me.

"I can smell your desire," he went on. "You *want* to submit to your monster. I can taste in the air how badly you want to writhe under your great, horned beast."

My thighs snapped shut but it only amplified the dull throb between my legs. My legs rubbed together as I slid along the wall, intensifying the need on my sensitive skin. When I saw Zeruhn's shadow looming in the entrance I'd just come through, I bolted.

The ground shook as he gave chase, and exhilaration pumped in my veins. After weeks in the labyrinth, my feet were tougher, my lungs stronger. He would always catch me, but at least I had better endurance to drag this foreplay out.

I also knew this maze of corridors better than before and zig-zagged in a formation that I knew would confuse Zeruhn's sense of smell. It was basically circling back to where I'd started, creating a single loop of my own scent.

After completing my loop, I flattened myself into a small alcove where two hallways connected. It would be easy to miss me if he didn't look closely enough. I breathed as quietly as I could, listening for my minotaur's approaching hoofbeats.

He was close, but I knew my trick had fooled him. I heard him circle in place, sniffing the air in confusion. "Clever little prey," he mused. "I see what you've done, but you can't be far. Where are you hiding?" I held my breath, trying to become even quieter. "I will give you twice the orgasms if you show yourself to me now," he teased.

I held back a snort. We both knew he liked a hunt to be challenging. The longer I stayed hidden, the more he would want to please me.

"You don't want to see a monster who is desperate for his prey," he warned. "I may not be able to control myself."

Oh, that was exactly what I wanted to see.

With a mocking huff of disappointment, he continued on following my scent in hopes of finding me in another shadowy corner. I jumped from my hiding place and went to tackle him from behind. Of course, because he was so tall, I just ended up hugging him around the waist.

"Caught you!" I laughed into his back. "I win."

He scoffed like a sore loser but smiled as he turned to face me, his form shifting so that I was staring into his human face again. "I knew you were there," he insisted.

"Then why didn't you drag me out?"

"Maybe I wanted to get caught for once."

"A likely story," I said skeptically. "The predator becoming the prey."

Zeruhn lowered until his arms wrapped them under my ass and he lifted up again, holding me in place for a rough, possessive kiss that we'd both been craving. "You may be my doe-eyed prey, but I'm the one who's been captured," he whispered before pulling away to stare at me intently. "Do you really want to escape with me, Ariadne? I've...I've never left here."

"Yes," I insisted. "We can go somewhere completely new, where we can just be ourselves, together. There's so much more outside of MinoTek." Truthfully, I was just parroting what Aaron had told me, but I clung to that story of an outside world like a life raft. It *had* to be real. There *had* to be a better place out there.

And if we died trying to find it? At least we had each other.

"I'll tell you as often as you need to hear it," I whispered. "I want *everything* with you."

"And your mother?" he asked. "How will she see me?"

I didn't know how to answer that. Mom was generally wary and distrustful of men, which made perfect sense now. But if I could see how amazing Zeruhn was, surely she would too?

"We'll cross that bridge when we come to it." I kissed him hard before he could respond, forcing my tongue between his lips to thrust against his. "Now, you have prey to devour, don't you?"

That was all it took. He kissed me deeply with a groan, hands groping my ass as he turned to press my back against the wall. "I'll pin you here while I devour you," he promised darkly. "I can't wait another moment to lie you down somewhere soft."

"Fuck me already," I begged. The weight of the day was catching up to me. Two deaths. The prime minister of MinoTek being my father and wanting me dead. The possibility of escape and seeing my mom again. It was all too much, and I needed to feel the thick press of him inside me to keep me sane.

But Zeruhn only chuckled as he gently brought my feet to the ground and then kneeled. He was just as tall as I was, horns included, while kneeling at my feet.

"I will fuck all of your worries away, doe eyes," he said while yanking my pants down to my ankles and helping me step out of them. "But first, I need your juices on my tongue."

"You're showing an awful lot of restraint." I held on to one of his horns for balance as I stepped out of my pants.

"Oh, trust me, I want nothing more than to rip these to shreds," he said while folding my pants into a neat pile. "But you will not be escaping bare-assed. I'll have to kill a lot more people who dare to look at what's mine. And I don't think you'll want that."

"You're such a brute." My laughter quickly morphed into a moan. "Ohh, Zeruhn..."

He wasted no time, his head diving between my legs to lick a long stripe along my pussy. His moan was a rough vibration on my skin. "Delicious."

I brought both hands to his horns while his tongue made me see stars. Dried blood flaked off where I touched him, reminding me of the brutal acts he'd done just moments before. Was it fucked up that I didn't care right then? All I cared about was that this killing machine, this monster, kept licking me again and again, in *that* spot, right there...

My first orgasm shuddered through me, the convulsions making me grind on Zeruhn's wicked tongue to wring even more pleasure out. He hummed delightedly, like he was enjoying his favorite meal. Large hands gripped my hips and steadied me, holding me above his face so that his tongue could thrust inside at *just* the right angle.

I scrambled for purchase, yanking on his horns and scratching over his head while he continued to devour me. More dried blood flaked off, and I couldn't bring myself to care.

"I like your little claws, prey," he groaned before returning attention to my clit, sucking a wet kiss over the hood. "They make me even harder for you."

He propped one of my legs over his shoulder so he could tongue me deeper, and I expanded my scratching down his neck and over his shoulders.

"Yes, dig those little claws into me," he growled, rubbing two fingers over my wet lips before stroking them inside me. "Show me how badly you want me."

His lips sealed over my clit as his fingers curled against my slick walls, and I would have drawn blood if I scratched him any harder. My minotaur drove me to another orgasm, twice as explosive as the first, with his well-coordinated fingers, tongue, and that deep growl that kept vibrating along my skin.

If it weren't for him holding me pinned to the wall, my jelly legs would have collapsed beneath me. Zeruhn then stood to full height, taking me with him. He held me with one arm slung under my ass and undid his pants with the other.

"'Kay, now you're just showing off," I muttered, my brain still fuzzy from the orgasms.

"This is nothing," he chuckled. "You are so light."

"Whatever, just fuck me already."

He clicked his tongue, then delivered a light swat to my ass. "So demanding."

I felt the blunt tip of him notch at my entrance before I could say anything smart back. He was holding me, standing up, so I didn't have the leverage of a wall or the ground to sink down onto him. My monster, my predator, was in complete control of me.

"Please," I begged, rolling my hips and wriggling over him as much as I could.

He smirked. "Oh, *now* she asks nicely."

"Please, Zeruhn..."

"You want my cock filling you up?" He thrust his hips just slightly, making him slide through my wet, sensitive folds. It felt *so* good, but it wasn't nearly enough.

"Yes!" I cried, surprising myself at how much I needed him right then. We were about to be running for our lives. Who knew when we would connect like this again?

He gave me a kiss, one filled with passion and pent-up need. "I can never refuse you, my doe eyes." Then he impaled me on his thick length.

My scream echoed down the stone corridors, as did the slaps of his hips against my spread-open thighs with each brutal thrust. He controlled everything—the pace, the depth, the speed. My minotaur was feral, eyes like tarnished gold in the sunlight as he fucked me with abandon.

Zeruhn had such a firm grip on me that I didn't even *need* to hold onto him, but I did anyway. I wrapped my arms around his shoulders, digging my nails into his upper back while I whimpered and moaned into his ear about how good he felt. He dragged his teeth along my shoulder in return, whispering back that my cunt gripped him so well and I made him lose control.

We were both covered in flecks of dried blood now, fucking in the middle of a hallway in a prison where we'd both been condemned. And yet, the labyrinth was where we had found each other. Who knew how far we'd make it outside these stone walls, if we made it at all. But this place proved that each other was all we needed. Where so many had died, *we* had survived. And that meant something.

Zeruhn caught my mouth in a sharp, biting kiss, shifting the angle of his thrusts so that he struck my clit with each drive of his hips.

"Oh fuck, I'm not gonna last," I gasped against his lips.

"Took the words right out of my mouth," he groaned.

Less than a minute later, convulsions rocked me to the tips of my toes. He swelled inside me, which just extended my pleasure as my body squeezed around him. His own release spilled, and he slapped a hand to the wall in order to keep standing. His arm actually trembled as he continued holding me tucked against his body, his cock still pulsing inside me.

"Want to put me down?" I asked, smiling lazily with my cheek on his shoulder.

He snorted in reply, tightening his hold on me. "Never."

I kissed his neck, hugging around his wide shoulders. "I'll never let go of you either."

Zeruhn straightened again, already catching his breath as he secured both arms around me. "Promise?"

That single word held so much gravity in that moment.

"I promise."

27

ARIADNE

"He tracked my ID chip with a handheld device?"

"Yes." Zeruhn held Lago in his lap, gently stroking the jackalope's long ears. "I believe there is some kind of network with the ID chips. He would have been able to send your location to an officer with the push of a button."

We had just cleaned each other off in the bathing pool and were hashing out an escape plan before waiting for the signal from the shifter officer. Not that we had much to go on since we didn't have a map of the city, or anything really.

There was also the possibility that the shifter wouldn't help us at all since Aaron was no longer with us. So many variables were against us, and so few were in our favor. But we had each other, which didn't seem like much, but we had better advantages than anyone else attempting escape.

Zeruhn was highly intelligent on top of having his brute strength. I knew my way around the slums pretty well, which were south of the upper side, on the way to the port. Assuming my mom was still okay and at home, we could pick her up on the way.

"You know what we have to do before we leave here," I said, a warning in my tone. At Zeruhn's confused stare, I held out my wrist and rubbed the small, hard spot where my ID chip had been implanted at birth. "We have to cut out my chip and destroy it so they can't track us."

"I was afraid you'd say that," he sighed, gently stroking the inside of my arm.

"It shouldn't be too difficult," I said. "But I'll need your help."

Zeruhn frowned in obvious distress. "I never want to do anything that hurts you."

"It'll be a minor cut," I promised him. "We'll just pop it out, destroy it, and I'll be fine with the stuff in the first aid kit." I leaned forward and kissed his forehead, touched and a little amused by his concern. He gored people to death with those horns but didn't want to give me the equivalent of a paper cut. "It's sweet of you to worry, but we have to for our best chances of escape."

"I know," he sighed, his thumb rubbing the patch of skin just above where the chip was embedded. "I just don't want to see you in pain."

"The sooner we do this, the sooner I won't be in pain." I shifted in my seat, scooting closer to him. "I'm just not sure I can do it myself," I admitted.

"And you think *I* can?" he scoffed, but pulled out his knife and gently ran his thumb against the blade to test its sharpness. "Let's get this over with then."

He took my wrist in his lap and I looked away, not trusting myself to not flinch when he cut me. As he did, Lago hopped away from him and around to me, rubbing his antlers against my knee.

"Thank you, little buddy." I scratched the fur at the back of his head. "You're a good distraction—ah!"

I felt the pain of the first cut, then the warmth of blood dripping down my wrist as Zeruhn gently prodded with his fingers.

"I can see it," he told me. "Just trying to push it out through the incision. Fuck, my fingers are too big."

"Here, let me." I took a deep breath before I looked. My wrist was a bloody mess, and so were Zeruhn's fingers from trying to remove the chip as gently as he could. I pressed down with my thumb, gritting my teeth against the aching pain as I tried to slide the tiny device out from under my skin.

"Shit, it's really not going," I hissed.

"I don't want to cut you any more," Zeruhn said. "I don't want to hit one of your arteries."

"Give me the knife." I held my other hand out, noticing how much it shook.

"Ariadne..."

"Just give it to me. We're running out of time."

Zeruhn relented, passing the handle to me. I took several intentional breaths to gather my courage and find clarity through the pain throbbing up to my shoulder. Then I made another small incision directly over the chip, which was no bigger than my pinkie nail. I cut another line across that one, making an X that quickly welled over with blood. I pinched the sides of the cut I'd just made, scooping up with my fingers as I sucked in a hiss of pain.

"Ariadne." Zeruhn breathed my name in awe. "You did it."

Pinched between my thumb and forefinger was a small computer chip. I could hardly believe it myself, and a laugh escaped me. "I fucking did it."

Zeruhn took my arm and quickly pressed gauze from his first

aid kit to my bleeding wounds. "You're brave, doe eyes," he murmured with a kiss on my shoulder. "I'm proud of you."

I let him tend to my arm while I examined the chip in my opposite hand. This tiny little thing, which MinoTek touted as such an incredible invention, was the source of so much discord in my community. Removing it was a crime, but we never had the option to *not* get it implanted. The State claimed ID chips were for safety and keeping accurate population data, but we all knew it was just to keep tabs on us. To be constantly present in our everyday lives, watching our every move for the smallest infraction against our overlords.

No one deserved that.

A realization hit me as Zeruhn finished tying off the gauze on my arm. "I'm gonna have to remove my mom's chip too."

He gave me a curious look. "Will she let you?"

"I don't know," I admitted. "Honestly, I'm not even sure she'll want to go with us. But I can't imagine escaping the city without her."

"Just give me the word and I'll fling her over my shoulder." Zeruhn gave that wicked, crooked smile. "Or if you want to leave the choice with her, I will support you in that as well."

"I do want to give her the choice," I said. "I really hope she comes with us. With the prime minister's people hunting his victims down, she could still be in danger if we leave."

"I'm confident she will come." Zeruhn brushed his knuckles against my cheek. "After not knowing what happened to you, she won't want you to leave her sight." He cocked his head frowning. "I hope she allows us privacy to fuck, because that would be strange if—"

"You animal!" I cackled and slapped his chest, which immediately sent pain shooting up my arm because it had been my bandaged one.

My minotaur then chastised me for hurting myself before he wrapped me up in a hug and smothered me in kisses. After our laughter died down, we kissed quietly, wrapped up in each other as light began to fade in the labyrinth.

Our last day here.

"You want to hear something crazy?" I said, my head resting on Zeruhn's chest.

"From you, always." His chin rested on top of my head while his hand ran in light passes up and down my back.

"I'm going to miss this place."

He chuckled lightly, placing a kiss on top of my head. "So am I, strangely enough."

We were sitting near the door, the one where I and dozens of other prisoners had come through, so that we'd be ready for the signal from the shifter on the other side. Sundown was still an hour or two away, and Zeruhn stiffened out of nowhere.

"What's—"

"Shh!"

I hardly breathed while he cocked his head, appearing to listen intently. Lago had also stilled, long ears straight in the air like radio antennas.

"They're quiet, but I hear them," Zeruhn whispered, patting me so I would get up from his lap. "They're coming from the far side, trying to ambush us."

"Who?" I demanded.

"Cops, soldiers, does it matter?" He got to his feet, heading straight for the door. "Whoever they've sent to kill us."

"Shit." Not that I blamed him for killing a corrupt, likely evil, MinoTek official, but it really threw a wrench in this escape plan.

Zeruhn banged his fist on the door four times. Barely five seconds passed before he knocked four times again.

"The shifter isn't supposed to get here until sundown!" I whisper-yelled at him. "What if he's not even on duty yet?"

"Then they'll ignore it." He knocked again. "I've thrown rocks and all kinds of shit at this door. It's indestructible, so they don't care what kind of noises come from the other side."

"Zeruhn!" I squeaked, catching sight of a long line of shifters in matching dark uniforms by the cliffs near our cave. They would definitely find our belongings there and then us soon after.

"I know, doe eyes." He banged his fist four times against the door again. "Come on, fucking shifter. We need you now."

One of the shifters already in the labyrinth was looking out over the main valley. I couldn't tear my eyes from him, hoping he wouldn't see us. But just as I feared, he turned in our direction and froze. Pointing directly at us, he motioned to the others with his other hand.

"Zeruhn, they see us!"

My minotaur pounded at the door four more times before glancing over his shoulder. "Ariadne, I want you to hide."

"What? No, I'm not leaving you!"

The shifters had taken on their animal forms. Wolves, big cats, bears, gorillas, and even two rhinoceroses were stampeding towards us. The ground shook, and terrifying growls and roars filled the once-quiet labyrinth. I had no question that their orders had been to slaughter us on sight. Against that many, not even Zeruhn would stand a chance.

"My love, you need to run." He pounded on the door again before turning away from it, his own shift beginning as he faced the stampede.

"No, they'll kill you!" I screamed.

"You can still get out," he told me, his face now that of a

bull's. "Take Lago with you. He deserves a life outside of here too. Get your mother and escape together."

"I said I would never let you go!" I cried, clutching onto his arm. "And I fucking meant it!"

The shifters would be on us within a minute. They kicked up a cloud of dust, and I could make out individual facial expressions now. I steeled myself, wrapping all of my limbs around my minotaur. I wouldn't leave him alone, not for anything.

"Ariadne," Zeruhn growled, human pain and desperation twisting his animal features. "I am not worth your sacrifice. Go *now!*"

"Yes, you are!" I screamed back. "You are worth it, you are the only thing that's worth it!"

With a curse, Zeruhn shoved me behind him, squaring up to face the stampede. Even until the end, he would protect me. I pressed my arms and face to his back, trying to focus on the warmth of his skin and the strength coiling in his muscles.

"I love you," I whispered against his spine. "I mean it."

He kept facing forward but reached back with one of his hands to grab mine. I held on tightly and braced myself for the painful impact. The roars of animal sounds hurt my ears now, drowning out our racing heartbeats and everything else. Dust clouded the air and got in my lungs. They were so close. Any moment now.

Thump-thump-thump-thump.

I looked down for the source of the noise to see that Lago had hit the door with his foot. A green light pulled my gaze up, and I couldn't believe my eyes when I saw that the panel had changed colors.

"Zeruhn," I whispered in disbelief.

Then the door the slid open.

28

ZERUHN

I couldn't take my eyes off the stampede in front of me, couldn't let my guard down even as I heard Ariadne whisper my name. I loved her, but she was damn foolish to not run and hide. Even if the horde of shifters tore me to pieces, at least she could still have a chance.

She and her mother could still find freedom. She could meet a human man who hopefully wasn't a complete piece of shit and have a future with him.

The mere thought, even as a last resort, sent my temper boiling. *Ariadne is mine.*

"Zeruhn!" she yelled louder, and I felt her tug on my waist like she was trying to pull me back.

I dared a glance over my shoulder and, to my complete shock, saw that the door was open. A uniformed shifter stood over the threshold, gesturing wildly at us to come through. Ariadne scooped up Lago, and I shoved them both through before running in myself.

The shifter hit a panel and the door slid closed. Moments later, the entire tunnel shook with the force of a dozen massive animals crashing into it. Claws scratched and predators roared in fury on the other side. They would have been tearing into *us* if that door hadn't opened.

"Thank you." Ariadne spoke to the shifter first, her hand on her chest as she panted for breath.

The shifter ignored her, staring at me. In human form, he looked like a boy, no older than eighteen, but on a too-big frame with too many muscles.

"You're the fucking minotaur," he declared, his voice a mixture of fear and awe.

Congratulations, you can see. I bristled, but he did save our lives, so I paused before speaking. Being with Ariadne had taught me that I sometimes had to choose words carefully when speaking to others.

"Yes, my name is Zeruhn," I said. "Thank you."

"Where's Theseus?" the shifter demanded, looking between the two of us. "Why was a whole squadron after you? Those are my coworkers, they've seen my face now!"

"Your human friend is dead." I chose not to think of kind words this time, preferring to get straight to the point. "It tends to happen when people attempt to kill me."

I thought Ariadne might chastise me, but she didn't. She only stood supportively by my side, still cradling Lago in her arms.

"So you'll help us escape," she said, not as a question.

"Do I have a choice?" the shifter grumbled. "I'm dead either way."

"We're leaving the city with or without your help," I informed him.

"Well, you'll be a lot more successful with me." He shrugged, eying my horns, which scratched the tunnel ceiling if I wasn't careful. "Can you shift or are you," he gestured at me, "stuck like that?"

I shifted to human, decreasing my height and horn length. The shifter continued to gesture at me. "Keep going. We're gonna need you to blend in."

"This is as far as I go," I told him. "The horns and tail stay in this form."

His eyes widened. "All the time?"

"Yes."

"Well that doesn't help us at all." He rubbed his jaw nervously. "You're gonna stick out like a sore thumb."

Ariadne stepped forward. "I'm sorry, what's your name?"

"I'm Badge Number B3N155."

She smiled gently. "I'm Ariadne. Is there something you prefer to be called?"

He seemed taken aback by the question. "Oh. Um, Ben. No human has asked me that before."

"Ben, maybe there's a spare MSP uniform lying around that would fit Zeruhn?" Ariadne suggested. "It won't hide the horns but might help him blend in a little."

"Sure. You can use one of mine." He started down the tunnel. "Follow me." Stepping in line behind him, Ariadne and I both looked at the door we'd come through, which was now quiet on the other side. "They're probably regrouping," Ben explained, noticing our glances. "They'll want to seal off the tunnels next, but I have an override. We have to move fast, though."

"Can I ask why you're doing this?" Ariadne had to jog to keep up with the shifter's stride, and I lagged behind him to stay next to her. "Helping people out of MinoTek, that is."

"We shifters aren't as dumb as we present ourselves to be," Ben said, his tone a touch defensive. "We might act like well-trained animals for the State, but we know they use us as slave labor. And for humans, it's not much better. So some of us have been coordinating in secret."

"That's really brave of you," Ariadne said. "To do something so dangerous."

Ben shrugged. "Since our lifespans aren't long, we make the most of it while we're alive. The previous generation taught us when we were cubs. Now we're doing what we can before passing the torch on to the next generation." He turned sharply down another corridor and opened a small, metal door in the wall. From inside, he pulled out pants and a shirt identical to the MSP uniform he was wearing and held them out to me. "Here, put these on."

I remembered my manners. "Thank you." I shucked off my pants, the only pair I ever wore, and quickly pulled on the new, strange clothing.

"First time I've seen you in a shirt." Ariadne smiled while curling her finger at me. "Come here, let me help. You're missing buttons."

"Do these tunnels connect to the MinoTek capitol building?" I asked Ben while she fixed the shirt.

"Yes. The labyrinth is sort of positioned at the center of the government buildings. The MSP headquarters is further down this hall. Courthouse is up the main tunnel we were just in. Parliament chambers are that way."

"What about the prime minister's chambers?"

Ben took a long pause before answering me. "Yes, his offices are adjacent to the parliament chambers. Why?"

"I'm going there first." I straightened once Ariadne finished with my buttons. "Thank you, doe eyes."

"Wait, what?" Her hands remained on the stiff fabric of my shirt. "You're going to the prime minister's office? Why?"

"Because I'm going to kill him."

"*What*?" Ben jumped in. "I thought you wanted to escape."

"We do, but I'm going to kill him first."

"Zeruhn." Ariadne's small fists closed in my shirt, and I covered her hands with mine. "You don't have to do this. We can just get my mom and go."

"Yes, I do, sweet prey." I released one of her hands to hold her cheek, loving the fierceness in her stormy eyes. "For you. For your mother *and* mine. For everyone he has hurt in this city, I have to do this."

"You'll never make it," Ben said. "There are multiple levels of secure doors, armed guards, cameras, infrared sensors. They'll spot you coming a mile away."

"Then help me." I lifted my eyes to him. "You can override these tunnels being locked down. Any other areas?"

Ben sighed heavily, stabbing his fingers through his hair. "I mean, I can do basic shit like turn off camera feeds for the connecting corridors. But not his offices or the parliament building, which you'll have to go through to reach him."

"Do what you can. I'll figure out the rest."

The shifter shook his head. "It's a suicide mission, I hope you know that."

"The State has been trying to kill me for twenty years," I said. "I'm not about to let them be successful today."

"Zeruhn, please..."

Ariadne was on tiptoes, leaning against my chest, so I picked her up so that we could talk at the same eye level. Her arms went around my neck, and Ben looked away to give us privacy, another concept I'd recently learned from her.

"Zeruhn, I want us all to live through this," she whispered. "You, me, my mom, and Lago. Our chances are already slim as it is. Please don't risk your life because of what he's done."

"It will be my last kill," I told her. "I won't get another chance. He has to pay for what he's done."

"Let someone else make him pay!"

"You know that might not happen, my love." I rubbed my knuckle against her cheek. "He sentenced you to death. He attacked your mother and countless others. I'm the only one who *can* do this, Ariadne."

"But I can't lose *you*!"

"You won't." I wiped the tear from her eyelashes before it had a chance to touch her cheek. "I'll join you again when I'm done."

"Promise me, Zeruhn. And don't fucking lie to me." In all her fear and worry, that storm in her eyes kept brewing. That strength she carried, the power underneath her delicate surface, that was what captured me. And it was the reason I would succeed.

I set her down on the floor, then bent until I was kneeling, taking her hands in mine.

"I will kill one last time, for you," I said. "I will succeed, and I will return to you. I promise, Ariadne. I'm incapable of lying to you because I belong to you."

Ben cleared his throat. "I really hate to interrupt, but we need to get moving. They've already sealed tunnels and are probably waiting for us at multiple points, so..."

Ariadne threw her arms around me in a tight, desperate embrace, catching my mouth in an equally desperate kiss. "I wish I could stop you."

"After this, you can," I said, crushing her to my chest. "When this is over, you can do whatever you want with me." I grinned, trying to make her feel a little more at ease. "When we're gone, I want to hear all about what you'll have me do to you."

She forced out a laugh, holding on to me even as she stepped away. "That's the Zeruhn I know."

I returned to my feet as we separated reluctantly, our fingers the last to untangle from each other. "Where should I meet you?" I asked Ben.

"There's a fire escape under the bay window of the PM's office," he said. "That will be your best chance of getting out. We'll meet you at the bottom."

"Good. And you'll open the corridors and take out the cameras?"

"Only in the hallways connecting the buildings," he reminded me. "Not in the buildings themselves. We'll go to the control room first, that's where I'm supposed to be right now anyway. I can get you to the parliament building, but then you'll be on your own."

"Thank you. I'll figure it out from there." I had no other choice.

Lago thumped a foot on the floor, the sound strange and metallic, before Ariadne scooped him up into her arms again.

"You know what to do," I said, scratching the base of his ears one more time. "Guard them with your life. Stab anyone who tries to mess with you."

His nose twitched, and he flicked an ear in understanding.

I looked at Ariadne again, and she met my gaze with a mixture of fear and determination. My beautiful, brave woman. I leaned down to kiss her one more time. "I'll be with you again soon. I promise."

"You'd better." The steel in her voice made me smile.

"Good luck," Ben said, not sounding particularly hopeful.

"You too," I returned. With those parting words, we turned and headed in opposite directions.

I strode through the corridor that led to the parliament building, trying to act like a shifter police officer who had a reason for being there and knew exactly where he belonged. I didn't know what the surface typography looked like, but this tunnel system had to be underground. There were no windows, just lights on the ceiling and floors that illuminated the path. Air circulated from somewhere, but it felt stale in my lungs. Nothing like the open air of the labyrinth.

Discomfort itched under my skin. I didn't like enclosed spaces. They reminded me too much of the lab where I'd been kept. A small part of me yearned to return to the labyrinth, to run back to my mundane life of surviving and killing. It was where I'd grown comfortable but also endlessly bored.

Then a human woman changed everything for me, and here I was. A future with Ariadne was within my reach, and no claustrophobic tunnel would make me give that up. To go through this, knowing she would be safe with me at the end? It was easy.

The tunnel seemed to reach a dead-end, with a smooth metal wall blocking the way. Within seconds, it slid open with a gentle hiss. Before walking through, I noticed the camera lens in the top-right corner of the ceiling. The blinking red light from it shut off moments after the door opened.

"Thanks, Ben," I muttered, continuing on my way.

I was alone, and the corridor was silent except for my boots on the floor. But still, I remained alert, knowing that at any moment I could run into the shifter unit who'd tried to stampede us in the labyrinth. They were waiting at various exits, surely. I hoped they wouldn't be alerted to Ben overriding the doors and shutting off cameras.

He and Ariadne would be better defended if I had stayed with them. But I couldn't *not* kill the prime minister, not after all he'd done. Should I have brought them with me? No, because then Ben couldn't control the doors.

It was a small comfort knowing this was the best possible

plan, even though the human side of me ached to stay near Ariadne. She would be safest with me, always.

But the predator in me would not be sated until the one responsible for her suffering was dead. If we had left the city immediately, I would be on the first boat back to MinoTek to carry out this task. I would not be able to sleep, eat, or focus on a peaceful, loving future with my Ariadne until this was done.

Ben slid open two more sets of doors for me until I reached one that had MINOTEK PARLIAMENTARY CHAMBERS engraved on the surface. I examined the walls next to the door, wondering if there was an electronic panel that I could manually override. When I found nothing, I ran my fingers along the slim gap between the door and wall. If nothing else, I could just pry this thing open. It wouldn't make for the stealthiest way inside, but I had few other options.

Without any prompting from me, the door slid open quickly and revealed four shifted police on the other side, armed with guns, batons, and shields.

"Minotaur!" one of them hissed before chaos broke out.

They closed in on me and I went for the guns first, knowing those were the most important to take out. I was able to wrestle one away on sheer luck—he didn't expect me to go for his weapon. Little did he know that I once read an entire firearm instruction manual that had been tossed in the labyrinth and could recall every word of it.

I turned the weapon around, pointing it back at them and swung wide, firing a few wild shots. I hit the one I took it from in the shoulder. He must have been wearing body armor because he only jerked back once with a growl, gripping his shoulder.

They still surrounded me, but more cautiously now because of the weapon in my hand. My mind raced through possible options and outcomes. I didn't want to kill these shifters. I had told Ariadne there would be only one more kill. But if they tried to stop me from reaching my ultimate goal, I'd do what I must.

I also wasn't sure how this fight would go. These were trained officers in their prime, a fresh, young generation. The ones I'd fought in the labyrinth had been at the end of their life-span, their bodies and minds already breaking down beyond repair.

"Do not resist arrest, minotaur," the other one with a gun said. "Come with us quietly."

Was it more important to buy myself time or get this over with quickly? Probably the second option, but they didn't need to know that.

I lowered my gun barrel a few inches, then spotted movement in the corner of my eye. I spun around just as a shifter with a baton swung at my legs. The hit connected as I fired at his head, and he dropped dead to the ground. My knee throbbed with pain, but I could still stand on that leg as I spun, shooting at the rest of the shifters. That hit would've shattered the kneecap of a human, but it wasn't nearly enough to take me down.

These shifters had to have been armored because they took multiple shots to the torso without going down. I tried to aim for their heads and took another baton wielder out that way, but then my gun clicked empty.

My opponent with a gun smirked cruelly as he aimed at my chest, and I was forced to make a split-second decision. *Sorry about your clothes, Ben.*

I shifted as quickly as I could, closing the distance between me and the shifter in a single, massive stride. He fired one shot, and I felt burning pain near my hip. I roared in his face and knocked the weapon away. He roared back and shifted into a fully-formed bull.

Never before had I had another bull swing its horns at me, and he narrowly missed when I dodged out of the way. On his next swing, I was ready. I grabbed those horns and twisted his head away, but the bastard was stronger than I expected. He shook his head back and forth, but I held on, planting my feet wide.

A heavy strike fell to my back, and I roared in pain. There was still one more asshole with a baton to deal with. Using every bit of strength and leverage I had, I tightened my grip on the bull's horns and twisted my whole body, throwing the bull into the other shifter. They collided and slid across the floor, a tangle of arms, legs, horns, and hooves. I picked up the gun the bull-shifter had dropped when he changed and fired at them without a moment's hesitation. I shot until the gun emptied and they were motionless except for the blood slowly pooling around them.

They were most likely victims of the State too, created and trained for a specific purpose with no choice in the matter. I always tried to kill fellow shifters quickly. Their deaths didn't roll off my back as easily as my human kills. It was because of humans that they were like this. A rare few were like Ben, it seemed. But most didn't know better.

As much as I wanted to catch my breath and examine my injuries, there was no time to waste. I turned, holding my bleeding side as I examined my new surroundings. This was no longer a corridor but a single, massive, open room with a high, domed ceiling. The floors were a smooth, polished stone that reflected the many overhead lights. This room felt almost as big as the main valley of the labyrinth but more closed in.

There were signs above the doorways, and I quickly scanned them for clues on where to go next. PARLIAMENTARY HALL. PARLIAMENT OFFICES. MSP HEADQUARTERS.

COURTHOUSE CORRIDOR. OFFICE OF THE PRIME MINISTER.

I headed immediately for that last doorway, so singularly focused on my task that I didn't notice the MSP headquarters door open until the wave of shifters started pouring out of it.

"Block all the exits! Seal the prime minister's door!" their leader called.

The uniformed officers fanned out to surround me on all sides. I spun in a circle, snarling like the trapped animal I was. Every one of them carried a long shield, which I assumed was bulletproof. Not that I had ammo left, but I still carried the gun.

My eyes darted around as the shifters closed in on me. Blood ran down my leg from the graze on my side, and I saw some of them eying it hungrily. Every second, the space between me and the shifters grew smaller. Still, I held the gun across my body, turning to see who would try to fuck with me first.

"Surrender, minotaur," one of them said.

That would never happen. Not even if there were a hundred of them and one of me. If they broke all my limbs, I would still find a way to crawl to the prime minister and end him. Ariadne deserved no less.

Someone lunged, and I swung the gun, cracking the butt against their skull. Several shifters jumped on my back, and I threw at least one off with my free hand. Another jumped and I angled my head to spear them with my horns. Dozens of hands equally as strong as mine clasped at my arms, my waist, and my neck.

I thought of Ariadne, the love and worry on her face as she made me promise to come back, and roared out my fury. My arms and head swung, fighting to get free, but for every shifter I shook off, three more replaced them.

A blow crashed down on my head, either by a fist or a baton,

I didn't know. But my vision darkened, and I felt consciousness slipping away.

No! I promised her...

Another strike came down, and then darkness swallowed me.

29

ZERUHN

I roused slowly, my head pounding with a terrible ache. My body felt weighed down like I was made of cement. Why couldn't I move?

My eyes blinked open to a single blinding light in the ceiling. I was in human form, I knew that much. But when the shifters attacked, I'd been in bull form. I never shifted while unconscious, so that was definitely strange.

I was in a world of pain, disoriented, and confused. But I was alive, which meant I could still complete my task and see Ariadne.

The thought rallied my determination, and I moved my limbs and extremities, trying to figure out why I felt so weighed down. It became clearer when I heard the clinking of metal. Chains.

All I could tell so far was that metal cuffs wrapped around my neck, wrists, elbows, waist, and ankles. Links of chain connected them all together, draping me in this cold, heavy weight. All the various points of restraint were annoying but not unbreakable.

Which way was up? That was important to know.

I found the ground beneath my feet and something solid under my ass. *Sitting in a chair. Okay, got it.*

"Getting your bearings, Zero-Nine?"

My head snapped toward the voice, my adrenaline rising. How did I not sense someone else being here?

An elderly man sat across from me, though his chair looked far more comfortable than mine felt. It looked to be made of leather and had a high back, nearly a foot over the man's head. This human man was either particularly small or the chair was especially large.

He wore a tailored suit similar to Simon Gibbs, down to the MT pin on his crisp lapel.

"Who are you?" I demanded, pulling on my restraints.

The man chuckled with an ease that was unnerving to see. "I was told you wanted to see me." He spread his hands out to the side. "So here I am. What would you like to discuss, Prototype Zero-Nine?"

"*You're* Prime Minister Minos?" I didn't know what I was expecting but it certainly wasn't a man likely shorter than Ariadne, dwarfed by a *chair*.

"I am. Sadly, I haven't had the chance to visit the labyrinth since it became your domain." Minos raised a pale eyebrow. "I take it by the circumstances of your arrest that you're no longer happy with your situation there?"

I ignored him to keep testing and pulling at my restraints. It was only the two of us in the room, which was foolish of him. The moment I got free, he would wish his corpse looked as nice as his friend's in the labyrinth.

"Don't bother," he told me in a bored tone. "You won't be getting out of those."

I couldn't resist scoffing at that and yanked my right arm

against the chains as hard as I could. The cuffs dug painfully into my skin and the chains went taut, but they did not break.

"What?" I muttered in disbelief.

"You've been drugged," Minos informed me. "So your strength is roughly sixty percent of what it should be. Oh, and I know you're stronger in your second form, so for the time being, you can't shift either." He shot me a mocking grin. "So, shall we talk?"

I focused on the change, willing my animal side to take over, sinking deep into those instincts, but they simply didn't respond. That side of me was quiet, if even eerily silent. It was like I was telling my body to wiggle my fingers, but they did nothing.

This cowardly little man. I snapped my gaze to him, furious and snarling. Oh, he would pay. I would wipe that smug look off his face and enjoy his screams soon enough. I just needed to figure out a way.

"What do you want?" I said.

He shrugged and gestured a hand to me. "It was you fighting tooth and claw to reach my chambers, so why don't you tell me?"

"I wanted to kill you." There was no point in lying. It would happen one way or another.

Minos didn't seem fazed. "You're one of many," he said with a scoff. "But it's usually those slum rats from the lower parts that have the gall to make attempts on my life. I thought you were comfortable in the labyrinth. Has something changed, Zero-Nine?"

"Yes," I admitted. "You sent one of your henchmen to make sure I killed Ariadne Saavas. Your daughter."

"And you seemed hellbent on refusing to do the one task you're made for." He shifted in his chair, completely at ease. The arrogance was astounding to me. He seemed completely unaffected by what I said. "We could simply dispose of you, but you are not easy to replicate, Zero-Nine. Your genetic blueprint was deleted by an incompetent lab technician. We've tried cloning you, but your tissue samples aren't responding to the growth hormones." He chuckled again. "Stubborn as a bull, just like you are."

I let him keep talking, my wrists pulling at the cuffs and chains behind my back. Fuck. No matter which direction I pulled, another length of chain halted my range of motion. I also kept trying to shift, trying to see if any part of my bull would wake up, but I hardly even felt him there.

"You may have been a failed prototype but you have proven yourself useful after all," Minos went on. "You can still be useful to the State. How old are you now, in your thirties? Unheard of for a shifter! I bet there's a wealth of information in those genes of yours. Several labs have put forth requests to study your brain, you know."

"I would rather meet my death in the labyrinth than be experimented on again," I hissed, leaning toward him as far as I could. I shouldn't have reacted, but it was a sore spot for me. He must have known that because he smiled even wider.

"It's not up to you," he said eerily. "No one thought you would last this long, so there must be plenty to study in that horned head of yours."

"You don't want knowledge," I spat. "You want control. That's what this city runs on. ID chips in all infants? Experimenting on pregnant women to create shifter soldiers? Sweeping your scandals under the rug with bullshit crimes and sentencing innocent people to death over it?" I shook my head in utter disgust. "You humans are so pathetic. You're not satisfied until you've gone to all lengths to make yourselves superior to everyone else."

The prime minister clicked his tongue. "So intelligent for a shifter and yet, so short-sighted. The goal is innovation, son.

Every day we're expanding on what humanity is capable of. Before my father was prime minister, his company discovered the cure for cancer! No one but MinoTek has been able to do this. Now our citizens can live cancer-free!"

"If they can afford it," I shot back. "I've been ostracized from your 'perfect' society my whole life, and even I can see that it's rotten to the core. Only those closest to you have access to those treatments, while others are left to struggle with more treatable conditions, like arthritis."

My life experience was limited to that of the lab and isolation in the labyrinth. I had some idea of the class divides among the humans from what I'd read, but Ariadne had opened my eyes to how truly terrible it was.

Minos waved his hand dismissively. "Nothing in life comes free, son. Those who choose not to better themselves aren't entitled to the finer things."

"They can't do better when you send their parents, sons, and daughters to the labyrinth for made-up crimes! Not when you and your henchmen assault women for sport!"

He sighed as if disappointed in me. "I was going to offer you a position as a representative of the shifters, but it seems you're aligned with those that would rebel against me. All citizens of MinoTek must be kept in line in order for the State to thrive. Those who don't stay in line must be eliminated."

He reached into his coat pocket and produced a syringe. It was filled with the same thick, dark substance as the one Ariadne had shown me. I pulled in a deep breath through my nostrils. I couldn't afford to panic now. I had to think clearly, had to find a way back to her.

The despair was hard to ignore, though. I could barely move and couldn't shift. This cowardly man made sure he would be as safe as possible when alone with me. *Come on, Zeruhn. Use your big fucking brain for once.*

"I'm not usually a hands-on type of guy," the prime minister was saying as he uncapped the long needle. "But I really wanted to do this myself." He chuckled as he rose from the chair, indeed proving himself to be shorter than Ariadne. "I'll be known as the minotaur slayer."

He rolled up his sleeve with his free hand, the syringe pointing straight up in the air. His thumb rested on the end of the plunger. All I could think of was Ariadne and being awash with such trust and gratitude when she held out the syringe to me in the palm of her hand.

I promised her. What would my clever doe eyes do in this situation?

My mind turned to the memory of her cutting the ID chip out of her own arm. Her teeth biting down on her lip against the pain, her stormy eyes fierce and determined to see it through.

An idea struck me, and I rolled my left wrist to test the theory. Yes, it was possible. It would hurt like hell, but I could do it.

"I'll be seen as a hero," the prime minister continued as he approached. He circled me slowly, as if to savor the moment. "Even those degenerates down in the slums will rethink their complaints about me and realize they're grateful for such a generous, benevolent leader such as myself. *I'm* the one keeping them safe."

He paused at my back. The coward couldn't even look me in the eye when he intended to execute me.

A dry, brittle hand came to rest at the back of my neck, and then I acted.

I leaned into the left cuff, embraced the pain and the cutting of the metal through my skin until the bones snapped. The pain's sharpness gave me clarity, precision, and focus as I slid my broken wrist from the cuff and drove my elbow up and back to connect with the prime minister's face.

"Ahh!" He fell to the ground, dropping the syringe in his surprise. I might not have been at full strength, but I was still stronger than an old man.

With my left arm now free, broken wrist aside, I had the leverage to maneuver out of the remaining chains. Blood coated my left hand, and the pain throbbed up my arm. It fueled my adrenaline, my rage, while I used my shoulder and forearm to snap the rest of the chains from where they were bolted to the chair and the floor. I still had cuffs around my legs and waist, but it didn't matter. I was free.

I kicked the syringe away from the prime minister's trembling, outstretched hand, then promptly stepped on his hand. My shift still wasn't responding, so I sadly couldn't fully crush his hand under one of my hooves. His screams were satisfying, although they didn't reverberate around the room like I'd hoped.

"Soundproof walls?" I noted, looking around. "Interesting. So this is a dedicated torture room then?"

Minos continued to babble and wail until I lifted my foot from his hand, which he then cradled to his chest. He curled up like a fetus on the floor, pathetic and helpless. I picked up the syringe from where it had rolled away, studying it in my good hand while he scrambled to a far corner of the room.

"A shame I can't shift," I mused, my eyes on the toxin within the syringe, rolling back and forth as I tilted it in my hand. "I would've loved to tear you apart and feel your blood drip down my horns. I was hoping to see the holes in your body and the pain on your face."

"You're fucking insane!" the prime minister spat from his corner.

"Maybe, but what did you expect?" I asked. "I've been your killing machine for twenty years."

He was pale, trembling, and terrified, working to make himself as small as possible in the far corner. The weakest of prey, not even worth hunting.

"I suppose my last kill should be different." I rested my thumb against the plunger. "It should be a taste of your own medicine."

That sent the prime minister of MinoTek scurrying toward the door, but I beat him there. I pinned him against the wall with my arm against his chest and then plunged the needle into his neck.

I could see the neurotoxin taking effect before I depressed the plunger completely, the veins bulging in his cheek and jaw as the toxin flooded the main artery in his neck. Blood vessels burst in his eyes, and he convulsed with uncontrolled tremors.

When the syringe emptied, I released him and stood. The long needle remained in his neck, and I left it there. Let his people find out what happened. He was likely dead before I got up, assuming the dosage was for someone of my size and ability.

I tried the door with my good hand and broke the rusted deadbolt easily. Interesting. Where was this place where security was so lax?

A single shifter guard whipped around as I opened the door, and I popped him with a single punch to the face. In his stunned moment right after, I slammed his head against the outside wall. He went out like a light and crumpled to the ground while I quickly rifled through his pockets.

"Yes." I whispered the small victory when I found cuff keys, and I hurriedly removed the remainder of my restraints.

My left wrist was fucked, but I didn't have time to wrap it. I held it close to my body, grinding my teeth against the pain as I tried to figure where I was.

The building I'd been in was a small shack, and now I was outside. The night air was humid, and there wasn't much around. Another shack stood a few hundred yards away, and beyond it was some kind of brick wall. Over the wall, I saw electrical towers and the blurry lights of the city through the smog. Distantly, I could hear sirens, likely searching for Ariadne.

That was, if she and Ben hadn't gotten caught yet.

Fuck, I didn't even know how long it had been, or if it was even the same day as our escape.

I hurried over to the wall, trying to gauge how well I could climb it. It was no taller than the usual short cliffs I scaled in the labyrinth, so I figured the climb should be easy. Tucking my injured arm against my body, I jumped, reaching for the edge with my good hand, and tried to not scream when my wrist scraped the worn brick.

I pulled myself up, feeling a bit of my old strength returning, although I still couldn't shift. Crouching on the wall, my eyes darted all over the city, trying to figure out my location. I didn't know the outside, and I needed to meet Ariadne and Ben outside the prime minister's office.

Skyscrapers lined the horizon, and I squinted, trying to remember the buildings I'd read about and seen pictures of. Of all the random facts, figures, and theories I'd crammed into my brain, what I needed to know most right now seemed to escape me.

The courthouse! The recognition of those tall, white columns hit me like a kick to the chest, jumpstarting my heart and the urgency to return to my doe eyes.

The main corridor out of the labyrinth led directly to the courthouse, which faced north to south, which meant...

I smiled once I triangulated the location of the prime minister's office. He might have brought me to his torture shack in the middle of nowhere, but like all humans, he underestimated me.

I had performed my last kill. And I wasn't lost.

I'm coming for you, doe eyes.

With a sharp breath and holding my injured arm close, I leaped off the other side of the wall, landing nimbly on my feet. Not wasting another second, I took off running through the city.

30

ARIADNE

Ben gave me a look that was equally pleading and apologetic. "Ariadne, I'm sorry. But it's been hours."

"He'll be here," I insisted. *He promised.*

My worry and grief only worsened as we continued to sit in silence, watching the fire escape just outside of the prime minister's office.

All on-duty shifter units were called to the parliamentary building once Zeruhn made it through the corridors, which allowed Ben, Lago, and me to get out undetected. I knew Zeruhn expected to run into shifters at some point, but I had a terrible feeling about that call. There had to be what, forty, fifty MSP officers patrolling just the government buildings alone? Did they all figure out where he was?

"Come on. Where are you?" I muttered, peering up at the long series of ladders affixed to the building. The row of windows at the top were dark and had been since we got here. There had been zero activity, not a curtain flutter, nothing. The entire time we'd been here, it looked like no one was home.

Ben tried again to reason with me. "Ariadne, it's getting late.

The boat's gonna leave soon." He was sitting in the driver's seat of the squad car while Lago and I stayed hidden in the back seat. We were parked halfway hidden in a rear driveway meant for deliveries. If anyone came around, it looked almost like he was just on his regular patrol.

"We're not going without him," I insisted. "He'll keep his word. He'll be here."

"I'm really sorry, but something must have happened—"

"Obviously!" I snapped. "But he'll find his way out."

"Ariadne, you need to listen," Ben said more firmly. "If we miss this boat, I'm going to be hunted down by the MSP. They're already looking for me. I know you want to keep waiting, but we're all fucked if we—"

"Wait, what's that?" I pointed at a shadowy figure running up the road we were on. It seemed to be staying out of the street lights, but the silhouette was huge and coming straight toward us. And...did I catch the outline of horns?

Lago jumped up, his front feet batting at the window like he was trying to dig through the glass. That was when all doubt left my mind and relief flooded my system like a drug.

"It's Zeruhn!" I cried out.

"Nice of him to show up," Ben grumbled, turning on the engine and headlights. He reached over and opened his passenger door. The entire car rocked as my minotaur dove into the seat.

"Ariadne," he panted, twisting to face me. He was breathing heavily and covered in a thin layer of sweat, like he'd run across the city.

"You're okay," I whimpered, unable to hold the tears back. I went to embrace him over the seat but froze when I saw his grimace of pain. "What's wrong?"

"I'm fine." He gave me a strained smile, but I saw how he

braced his left arm against his body, his wrist encrusted with dried blood and bent at an odd angle. "Just had to wiggle out of a situation. I take it, I'm late?"

"Uh, yeah. By a few hours." Ben looked around and checked all his mirrors before turning the car out onto the main road.

"Sorry." Zeruhn reached with his good arm and scratched the base of Lago's ears. "You didn't have to wait."

"Yes, we did." I wrapped an arm around his neck, just needing to feel that he was really there. "We wouldn't have left without you."

"Doe eyes," he breathed, leaning his forehead against mine. "I did it. The prime minister won't hurt anyone else again."

I squeezed his shoulder, knowing that the task was important to him to carry out. He did it for me, but him being here and alive was all that mattered.

"Ariadne, want to direct me to your mom's place?" Ben called once we entered the lower side of the city, the slums.

"Keep going down this road, then hang a left at the second stop sign," I said.

He made the turn, then immediately cursed. "Shit."

The road was barricaded by two MSP squad cars and two shifters looking directly at us. I didn't have a moment to open my mouth to suggest side roads or anything before Ben said, "Hold on."

He threw the car in reverse, tires squealing as I got slammed against the back of my seat. I grabbed Lago and cradled the jackalope so that he wouldn't get thrashed around. Within seconds, Ben whipped the car around and sped down a side street to the sounds of shouts and sirens behind us.

"Do you know where to go from here?" Ben yelled.

"Left, then a right!" I shrieked, holding onto Lago and Zeruhn's seat in front of me. "It's two blocks down."

"You're gonna have to grab your mom quickly and make a break for the port. Just keep heading south, you'll find it."

The gravity of what he was saying hit me like a ton of bricks. "Wait, aren't you coming?"

He shook his head, sending me a regretful glance in the mirror. "I'll hold them off, it's the only way you'll make it."

"Ben—" Zeruhn protested, but the other shifter shook his head again, insistent.

"I'll only live for about three more years anyway. You're the fifth group I've helped get out of the city. Don't let me fail you."

"I can help you take them," Zeruhn argued. "You don't have to—"

"You're down one arm," Ben replied. "Seriously, I've made peace with this. Just get yourself to the port. Tell the outside world what's really happening here."

The conviction was clear in his voice. "Thank you, Ben. We won't forget this." My words felt shallow, but what else could I say?

I refocused on the apartments zipping outside the car just in time. "There, the nectarine tree in the front yard. My house is the next one."

Ben turned the car so that it was parked across the middle of the street. He left it running as he got out, loosening his shirt collar. "Get your mother out as soon as you can. I can only buy you a few minutes."

I wanted to thank him again, to plead with him in hopes of changing his mind, but every second ticking by was a wasted one. I spared him one last glance over my shoulder as I ran up to the front door, Zeruhn and Lago right on my heels. I thought I saw brown fur over Zeruhn's shoulder but had to focus on what was in front of me.

When I tried the door knob, it didn't budge. So I brought my fist to the door and pounded like our lives depended on it.

"Mom, it's me, Ariadne!" I yelled. "Mom, you have to open the door! We have to run now!"

"Let me, doe eyes." Zeruhn moved in front of me and grasped the knob. With a simple jerk of his shoulder, he not only opened the door, but pulled it off the hinges.

Any other time, I would have teased him, but right then, I could only rush inside and frantically look around our small apartment. "Mom? Mom! Where are you?" I spun around, my hope sinking like an anchor.

She wasn't here.

It was late at night, where could she be? Possibilities ran through my head. She could be staying at a friend's house or at the emergency clinic if she had a fall or something. Shit, could she even travel if she was unwell?

Growls and roars filled the air, stabbing through my frantic thoughts. Zeruhn stood in the doorway and looked toward the street, tension on his features. I couldn't see from here but knew it could only be Ben fighting off the shifters.

"My love, we can't stay," he warned, muscles tensing.

"I know, I just—she's not here!" My mind was racing so frantically I could hardly speak. "I don't know where to look for her."

"If you have any idea, we need to go there *now*." Zeruhn's eyes remained on the shifter fight, his whole body tensing.

"I...fuck, I don't know!"

Just then, I saw the light turn on in the apartment across the street and movement on the other side.

I bolted, sliding past Zeruhn and darting across the street to the sound of him calling my name. Mere feet away from my neighbor's door, a wolf barked and jumped over Ben's car toward me. I had no cover and froze in fear, not knowing how far Zeruhn was behind me.

The wolf stopped abruptly in midair, its scruff caught in the massive jaws of a grizzly bear. The bear shook the wolf like a ragdoll and tossed it in the opposite direction, lumbering after the wolf with a limp in its hind leg.

Ben, our 'thank yous' are not enough.

My neighbor's front door was cracked open when I reached it, and I recognized the eye peering behind it almost as well as my own.

"Mom!" I sobbed with relief. "It's me!"

"Ari!" She opened the door wider, urging me inside with a quick glance at the carnage on the street. "Hurry, get inside!"

"No, mom! We have to get out of here!"

"Are you crazy, girl? Those shifters will kill you!"

"No, you don't understand!" I grabbed her upper arms, careful not to squeeze too hard but also needing the confirmation that she was still here. "Mom, we escaped the labyrinth and now the authorities are after us. We have to leave the city *now*."

"Us?" she repeated. "Who's us?" Her gaze moved from my face to slowly tilt up at the massive, horned figure at my back.

"Mom, this is Zeruhn," I said. "The minotaur. We escaped together. We...*are* together."

Her eyes snapped back to me, and I braced myself for it—the shock and horror at her daughter not only falling in love with the elusive monster no living person had ever seen but also breaking him out of the prison he'd lived in for twenty years.

Instead, she calmly said, "Hello, Zeruhn. I'm Delia. Ariadne's mother."

Zeruhn lowered his gaze and inclined his head respectfully. "It's a pleasure to meet you, Delia. Ariadne has told me much about you."

Mom's gaze then went to the ground where Lago sat in front of my legs. "And who is this?"

"This is Lago," I said. "He's a jackalope."

The sounds of thrashing, battling shifters in the street interrupted the sweet introductions. The grizzly bear, Ben, rose to his hind legs and roared in the face of a hissing jaguar. Ben was bleeding in several places and stumbled forward. Sirens in the distance alerted us to more cops heading our way.

I turned back to face my mother. "Mom, I know this out of nowhere, and I'm so happy to see you, but this is our *one* chance to escape. I'm sorry, there's no time to grab anything. We have to go *now*."

"Go where?" she asked, taking in the scene on the street like she wasn't able to look away.

"I dunno! We're going to the port, there's a boat. Just out of the city, that's all that matters."

She gave me a look that was both loving and exasperated. "You're thoughtful, my sweet daughter, but you shouldn't have come for me. I'll just slow you down."

Zeruhn took that as his cue to wedge his way forward. "I'll carry you, Delia. If you'll allow me."

"Carry me?" Mom squawked. "What am I, a doll?"

"Mom, please!" I was ready to toss her to Zeruhn like a sack of potatoes so that we could get the hell out of here.

"I'll be careful with you. I understand you have some joint pain," Zeruhn said. "I'm much stronger than a human man. You won't slow us down at all." He stole a tense glance at the fight in the street. "But we have to go. Right now."

Mom looked at me again. "Ari, do you trust this guy?"

"Yes!" She'd barely finished asking the question when I answered. "With my life, mom. I love him. There's so much I have to tell you, but," I waved my hands around frantically, "later!"

"Well, alright then." She turned to Zeruhn, holding her arms out. "You better not drop me, young man."

"I would never," he said solemnly, then crouched to scoop under her legs with one arm.

Mom was shorter than me and already snug against his chest by the time she noticed his other arm. "What happened there?" she asked, nodding at his wrist.

"I broke it to escape capture." He flashed her a smile. "Don't worry. I can still carry you with one arm."

"You better set that, or it's gonna heal crooked," she warned him in a motherly tone.

"Again, later!" I ushered them off the front porch. "Should we take the car?"

No sooner had I voiced the question than Ben and another shifter crashed down onto the car's hood in a blur of fur, teeth, claws, and roars. They rolled into the windshield and shattered it on impact.

A footrace it was, then.

I scooped up Lago, then Zeruhn and I turned and bolted down the street together, heading roughly south and leaving the carnage of fighting shifters behind us. *We'll never forget you, Ben.*

I ran at full speed while Zeruhn kept an easy pace slightly ahead of me. He could go plenty faster, but I knew he wanted to be careful with my mother in his arms.

We ran a few blocks south without incident, although sirens wailed constantly and sounded like they were coming from everywhere. When Zeruhn skidded to a stop and cut a hard left through someone's backyard, I thought my heart would stop as well.

"They've headed us off," he growled. "There's a whole line of cars up the next block."

It hit me suddenly, and I cursed under my breath for not

remembering sooner. "Mom, it's your ID chip. They're using it to track us."

"Oh." Her eyes fell to the bandage wrapped around my forearm. "Well, let's get rid of it."

I released Lago to pat my pockets, my heart sinking even though I already knew. "Do you have your knife?" I asked Zeruhn.

He shook his head with a grim expression. Of course he wouldn't still be armed after being captured.

"Silly girl," Mom huffed and pulled out the multitool she always kept on her. It was one of those things that had a screwdriver, can opener, tiny scissors, corkscrew, and a million little other things that folded out.

Including a knife blade.

"Should be pretty sharp, I don't use the knife part often," she said, handing it to me.

I took it from her and held her forearm in my other hand, running my thumb from her wrist to her elbow until I found the small, hard bump under her skin where the chip sat. "Sorry," I told her. "This is gonna hurt, but I'll make it quick."

Mom sat like a rock, not making a sound as I made two small incisions in an X-shape like I had for myself. Then I pinched the edges of the cut and popped the chip out. It fell to the ground and Zeruhn immediately crushed it under his boot.

"We have to go around the blockade," he whispered while I applied pressure to my mom's bleeding arm. "Can we keep cutting through these yards?"

"We're gonna have to," I said. "Careful with her while you jump fences, okay?"

"Of course, doe eyes."

"Hm, doe eyes." Mom chuckled at the pet name, her eyes shining.

She seemed relaxed, which was a relief. Even a little happy. I guess when you've lived a long life under tyranny, a dashing escape was more exciting than terrifying. She'd lived through things I couldn't imagine. Even if we utterly failed, would it be anything worse than what she'd already been through?

Her mood sobered once we got moving again and started cutting through people's yards. "Ari, are you sure there's a boat waiting?"

"Not really," I admitted.

"It'll be there," Zeruhn said grimly, determined despite not knowing any better than me.

We stayed low under the fence lines—well, Zeruhn tried his best with his horns. Lago was able to jump fences or squeeze through gaps in the boards with ease. Some people gave us strange looks, but honestly, people cutting through yards as shortcuts wasn't unusual in the slums.

Once we reached a street corner, we all crouched low behind a retaining wall.

"Was this where the line of cars blocked us?" I asked, peeking around the edge.

"Yes. I don't know how long of a line they made," Zeruhn answered.

I looked down the direction we came, leaning over to get a clearer view of the street until my mom yanked me back by my shirt.

"They're down a couple blocks," I reported. "Not too close but they can still get after us if they spot us."

Zeruhn met my gaze steadily. "We just have to make a break for it then."

I chewed the inside of my cheek. The port was still a good six blocks away, and who knew if a boat was even docked in this area? Maybe it was better to keep waiting and lie low?

"We have to, doe eyes." Zeruhn seemed to sense my hesitation. "If they can't track us anymore, they'll split up and start searching."

"Car coming!" Mom hissed.

We sprung into action, diving behind some dumpsters so that we were out of view of the street. Poor Zeruhn had to curl up into a small ball to keep all his body parts from being visible.

The flashing red and blue lights and matching siren rolled by moments later, turning the corner we were just peeking around. All three of us held a breath and released it when the car drove on.

"They're already searching for us." Zeruhn's breath heated my ear. "It's now or never."

His fingers threaded through mine, and I gathered courage from that warm, steadying grip. "Now, then."

We waited until we could be as certain as possible that no cop cars were in sight, then made a break for it. I scooped up Lago and carried him like a football against my chest. No bunny was becoming roadkill on my watch.

"Don't slow down for me!" I told Zeruhn as he ran by my side. "Just go! Find a ship, and get her on it."

"I'm not leaving you behind," he snarled.

"You better not leave my daughter!" Mom hollered, her arms clinging to his neck.

We crossed two blocks. Then three. Then four. I heard water sloshing and could smell the salt in the air when I heard screeching of tires and a wailing siren like it was right next to my ear.

"Go, keep going!" Zeruhn darted behind me, I realized it was so that he could shield my back. I wanted to yell at him for going even slower, but every microsecond counted now.

Find a boat. Escape. That was all that mattered.

The terrain changed underneath my feet. I was at the port now, running along the shore and scanning the docks under the murky lights for something that resembled a boat. What did Aaron say? That it looked like a party yacht? I didn't even know what that was.

I heard popping sounds, like gunshots, and pumped my burning legs harder. As long as I could still hear Zeruhn running behind me, I wouldn't stop.

Then Lago started squirming like mad in my hold.

"Stop! I'm gonna drop you!" I doubled over, trying to contain him, and promptly got several sharp antler points jabbing in my stomach. "Ow! No, fuck!" He didn't break the skin, but it hurt like a motherfucker and forced me to loosen my hold just enough for him to slip out. "Lago, stop!"

"Follow him!" Zeruhn called from behind me.

I was already on it, chasing our antlered rabbit onto a dock stretching out toward the water. This dock was shrouded in darkness with no lamppost at either end. All the other lights from the shore had blinded me, and it felt like I was running into endless darkness.

But I wasn't.

Lago stopped at the end of the dock and thumped his foot hurriedly on the rotted wood. Back here, hidden in plain sight and yet near-total darkness, was a boat.

I didn't know a thing about boats, but it was massive, sleek like an arrowhead, and painted entirely black. There were no lights on inside that I could see. It just floated, silent and ominous next to the dock like a sea monster patiently awaiting its prey.

Well, I took my chances with one monster. What was one more?

I couldn't see a door or even a window, so I pounded my fist on the boat's hull next to the dock just as Zeruhn ran up with my mom.

"Is this the one?" he asked, looking behind him at the mass of cop cars converging onto the harbor.

"I dunno, but it's the one we've got." I pounded again, my pulse thumping in my ears to the sirens. "Help! Is anyone in there?"

A door slid open, much like the pressurized one in the labyrinth, and I squinted, trying to make out the figure on the side.

"You leaving the city?" a voice asked from within.

"Yes!" Did I have a choice? It was either board this sea monster boat or die at the hands of police. "Please! The cops are after us!"

"Get in." An arm stretched out from the darkness and I grabbed it without a second thought. Lago hopped in after me, and then Zeruhn carefully handed my mother over to the sounds of more gunshots filling the air. Once he stepped inside and I heard the door hiss closed, only then did I take a breath.

A light flicked on, and I blinked to adjust my sight. We were in a cozy but high-ceilinged room with wood-paneled walls and plush couches. A man stood across from us, handsome and middle-aged with salt and pepper hair and deep lines around his eyes, which were a golden-orange color. He also had the height and build of a shifter, but what really gave it away was the two long, canine teeth that descended past his upper lip.

"Welcome aboard the *Lorenza*," he said softly. The fangs didn't seem to impede his speech at all. "You're all safe now. I'm Taj, your captain."

"They...they have guns." My brain continued to process danger, unable to accept safety as the reality.

"Her hull is bulletproof," Taj said with a patience that

suggested he'd said that many times before. "And the *Lorenza* is fast. The crew will sail at any moment." He regarded each of us with a mild curiosity, gaze lingering on my mother. "We expected passengers hours ago. We had started to think you wouldn't make it."

"Where are we going?" Mom asked.

"The Dominican Republic. Or if you prefer, Puerto Rico. Both islands have set up refuge bases for those escaping Mino-Tek." At our blank stares, he asked, "Have you heard of either of those places?" When we all shook our heads, he smiled and chuckled softly. "Ah, well. It's a long journey across the gulf. There will be plenty of time to learn about the outside world. Now, please, relax. Make yourselves comfortable. My chef will bring you some food, and another crew member will show you to your rooms. Oh, and I'll get a doctor to look at those injuries."

"Can I ask you something?" Zeruhn spoke up for the first time since we came aboard.

"Yes, of course," Taj answered.

Zeruhn hesitated, swallowing before asking. "Are you a prototype?"

Taj's smile only widened, his fangs on full display. "Yes, I lived the first half of my life as Prototype 0-2. My other form was a tiger, but I actually haven't been able to shift in the last decade or so. My old bones can't handle the change these days."

Tension bled out of Zeruhn's shoulders as he returned Taj's smile. "I didn't think there were any others still alive. I was Proto-type 0-9. I go by Zeruhn."

The captain gave my minotaur an understanding nod. "I think you and I are the last ones, friend."

"Well, at least two of us have been able to hang on."

"Yes," Taj said. "That is something to be proud of."

31

ARIADNE

We spent about a week at sea, during which we got to know more about Taj, his crew, and the group's secret efforts to get people, shifters included, out of MinoTek.

It turned out that MinoTek was severely isolated from the rest of the world, something the founders, Prime Minister Minos and his father, did intentionally. At first, it was under the guise of becoming completely self-sufficient and to not depend on trade or imports with any other countries or states. The mega-conglomerate MinoTek Industries became so entwined with providing tech and innovation for the government's self-sufficiency plan that the two eventually became one and the same. The CEO of MinoTek Industries became the first prime minister of the MinoTek city-state, and then his son followed after him.

And that was just the tip of the iceberg. The massive class divides, mandatory ID chips for all, and the creation of shifters were all side effects of a powerful tech company cementing its powers over people's lives.

The second prime minister had no known children when

Zeruhn killed him, but that didn't mean the city-state would topple from that assassination alone. No one really knew how to dismantle their power, but Taj and his crew members assured us that other governments were working on plans to liberate the people of MinoTek.

Mexico, Canada, the United New England States, and the Pacific Republic were all in alliance to help refugees and reduce MinoTek's power. These countries were just beyond our borders and I'd never known about them. I felt like I'd lived in a cardboard box my whole life and the lid had just opened for the first time.

It was, frankly, overwhelming. I still couldn't wrap my head around the most basic concepts, like being allowed to leave the country or state if I wanted to just to visit somewhere new. No one would stop me? The cops wouldn't care if I left?

I could watch almost any movie or TV show I wanted, and Taj repeatedly assured me that the authorities in the Dominican Republic would not care. They didn't even monitor what people were watching. I could even read books that criticized the government or contained explicit sex scenes.

I could go to school and study almost anything that interested me. In some places, depending on what was available, I could even pick and choose what kind of job I wanted to have.

All the choices were exciting but, in a way, also paralyzing. I spent a lot of time on the *Lorenza* holed up in my room. The subtle patterns in the wallpaper weren't as overstimulating as all the information the crew members threw at me.

Plus, I had a big sexy minotaur wrapped around me most of the time. And as my stint in the labyrinth had taught me, that was all I really needed.

"Your mom is spending a lot of time with the captain," Zeruhn mused, tracing his fingertips over my hip.

"Mmhm, she's totally banging him." I snuggled deeper into his chest, my lips brushing his sternum.

He laughed and the deep, delightful sound rumbled over my lips. "She's like her daughter, I see."

"Inhuman men are just better."

"I'm glad you think so." His voice carried a note of sadness, obvious enough to make me look up.

"Something wrong?" I nudged a kiss along his jaw.

"No, doe eyes. Everything is better than I ever could have imagined."

He caught my mouth in a deep, sensual kiss, but I was determined not to be distracted. "Talk to me, my love. What's on your mind?"

Zeruhn sighed, flopping to his back on the king-sized bed, which was still too small for him somehow. "I'm glad to not be a human man in many ways, but there is one thing I wish was different."

"And that is?" I draped myself over him, unable to keep myself from the expanse of muscle and scar tissue.

"I can't...start a family with you." He frowned. "If you want children, I can't provide them. That's the only thing I wish I could change."

My heart ached something fierce at the regret on his face. "Zeruhn." I took one of his hands and laced our fingers together, placing a kiss on his knuckles. "That doesn't bother me at all. You're enough for me." I let out a snort. "And anyway, we have Lago."

His face lit up with a grin. "I don't know about that. He's barely left the kitchen since Chef Manny's been spoiling him with those hydroponic greens. I think the *Lorenza's* just taken on her first jackalope crew member."

We laughed together, and I allowed a few quiet moments to pass before asking, "You really want children, don't you?"

Zeruhn lifted a shoulder in a shrug. "I don't know if it's that I really want them or just the chance to have them. I was never given the choice."

"Well, once we're settled and if we ever feel ready to take that step," I placed another kiss on the back of his hand, "maybe we could adopt?"

"Adopt?" He lifted an eyebrow.

I nodded. "Taj was telling mom and me about his kids when you went fishing this morning. He's adopted two children, a human girl and a shifter boy. Apparently, they take a lot of human orphans out of MinoTek because the state doesn't keep tabs on them as much. And I guess a lot of young shifters don't meet certain criteria when they're created, so his people try to smuggle them out of the labs too, before...you know. They get disposed of."

I scooted down Zeruhn's body and threw a leg over his thighs. "So, there are a number of children who will need parents."

"I see," he mused, running his free hand up my back. His wrist was still in a splint, but he expected to have it off any day now. "I like this idea. I think we would be good parents to an adopted child. Shifter or human."

"I do too," I said, smiling as I rested my cheek on his chest. "But we don't have to rush. I want some time to enjoy ourselves too."

With a growl, he slid out from under me at lightning speed, pinning my wrists above my head while his knees spread my thighs apart. "I will absolutely enjoy stalking my prey on new hunting ground."

I wiggled in his grasp and lifted my hips, making sure to

brush my pelvis against his cock. "Don't forget to give your prey a head start sometimes. It's only fair."

"Oh, I will. Sometimes." Those beautiful golden eyes heated. "As long as you remember that you are mine and I will always catch you, doe eyes."

"Promise?" I grinned, anticipation unfurling in me already.

My gorgeous monster leaned down with a predatory smile and gave his answer in a whispered kiss against my lips.

"For as long as I draw breath, you are mine to hunt. Mine to please. Mine to protect. I promise you, Ariadne."

"You're mine to love," I whispered back. "Mine to keep. Forever. I promise you, Zeruhn."

He deepened the kiss, pressing me into the mattress. I let myself sink into the bed, into his kiss, his love, and the protection of his body all around me.

And I couldn't wait to fall headfirst into our new life together.

EPILOGUE
ZERUHN

ONE YEAR LATER

"You're quiet," Ariadne observed, threading her fingers through mine. "What's on your mind?"

I pulled in a breath, the salty breeze sharpening my senses. Even a full year later, I still couldn't get used to this feeling of real freedom—the ability to just leave home and walk with my love to the beach or down the street. The ability to order food from a restaurant and buy things from a store.

To hopefully start a family, which was where we were headed now.

"What if I scare the kids?" I tightened my fingers around hers. Shifters were more commonplace here on the island, but with my horns and tail in human form, I still stood out like a sore thumb.

Ariadne leaned against my arm. "You won't," she insisted. "You're really not as frightening as you think you are."

I leaned down next to her ear and made sure to growl. "Is that so?"

She laughed and squirmed when I tickled her waist. "You can't fool me. I'm your wife, I know how much of a softie you really are."

"But will a child feel the same way?" I asked, returning to seriousness once again. "I haven't been around children much, and they're so much smaller. Even more fragile than you. What if I—"

"Stop." Ariadne swatted my stomach with her other hand. "Children are also observant and very instinctual. Shifter children are probably more so. Just meet them at their level, don't force anything, and you'll be fine."

"Hm, I'll try."

"That's all I'm asking for." She brought our hands to her lips and kissed the back of my palm. "I have a good feeling about today."

"Why's that?"

"Well, because I got you to put a shirt on, for once." She laughed. "We're already starting the day off with miracles."

"I actually like this one." I plucked at the fabric of the short-sleeved, buttoned shirt. "I think I'll get more from her."

"Really?" Ariadne's eyes widened, and she smiled as she wrapped a hand around my forearm. "It looks good on you."

"It actually fits."

Finding clothing was a nightmare, since most of it was made for humans. But Ariadne's mother, Delia, recently became friends with a seamstress who specialized in clothes made for shifter proportions. My wife and mother-in-law took my measurements a few weeks ago and gave them to the seamstress, who made this shirt as a test run. It was the most comfortable thing I'd ever worn.

"I'm glad. She'll appreciate the business."

Ariadne's hand slipped into mine again as we paused next to

the bronze grizzly bear statue on the main street. It was the first public art piece we commissioned as MinoTek refugees. Ariadne and I had planned to fund most of it ourselves, but the community came out in full force wanting to contribute to its creation. The bear stood on its hind legs, nearly nine feet tall. Instead of open jaws in a roar, we opted for a calm, curious expression. The plaque at the bottom read, *Ben, an exceptional friend and a saver of lives. Our thanks are not enough.*

Ariadne and I said nothing, but as she always did, she placed her hand in one of the bear's paws, holding it for a few seconds. When she was ready, we kept walking.

She squeezed my hand as we turned a corner and a red brick building came into view. "This is it. Are you ready?"

My heart began a fierce drum beat as I stopped abruptly, prompting Ariadne to turn and look at me. "Are you?" I asked her softly. "Do you really want this...with me?"

Her arms went around my waist, her torso pressing against my stomach as she gazed up at me. "I want everything with you, Zeruhn. You know this."

I brushed a lock of hair from her face, staring into the large doe eyes that had captivated me from the first moment I saw them. "I love you. I just wonder if everything with me is enough."

"I love you too. And it's more than I ever could have imagined." She leaned away, grinning playfully. "And you haven't killed anyone in a year, which has done wonders for my stress levels."

I huffed out a laugh. "The things I do to make you happy."

Ariadne walked a few steps backward, pulling me by the hands toward the brick building. "Come on. Let's see if we'll meet our son or daughter today."

The nerves in my stomach started up again as I followed her.

Behind a fence in the play yard of the orphanage, children of various ages chased each other and climbed playground equipment. A small group of girls hopped on one leg over chalk squares on the pavement. A couple of boys pored over a book together.

They all looked human, at first glance. But every child in this orphanage had been smuggled out of MinoTek bioengineering facilities. Some were registered shifters and would have become the next generation of shifter police had they not been rescued. Others had no documentation and had been founded in closed-off, hidden areas of the lab. It was speculated that they were created for the purpose of so-called "exotic" adoptions. Essentially, they would be privately sold off to the highest bidder on a black market, and who knew what would happen to them after that.

Ariadne and I also discussed at length what would happen if we adopted a child with the same short lifespan as the police officers in MinoTek. After many emotional conversations over several nights, we ultimately decided to cross that bridge when we came to it. If we could raise a child with love and happiness, it would be worth the pain in the end when we had to let them go.

Once we felt prepared to take that step, Ariadne contacted the local adoption agency. We went through many rounds of interviews over several weeks before today, when we could finally meet adoptable children.

"Hello!" Ariadne cheerfully greeted the human staff member at the front as she walked up to inform them of our appointment.

I hung back and looked at the posters on the walls. Even now, Ariadne was better at talking to people than me.

That was another thing I worried about. What if a child loved her like a mother but didn't like me?

"Right this way, please." The staff member rose from the front desk, and Ariadne took my hand again as we followed. "We can start with the indoor playroom and then move outside if you'd like."

We were led through a door into a brightly colored room. Whimsical music played while the children did various activities at low tables. Many were coloring and drawing, some played board games or read books. A few of them talked softly, but many were silent in their activities.

"Many of them were ordered to stay silent at their previous locations or they would be punished," the staff member muttered to us. "They're not comfortable expressing childlike exuberance yet. It'll take time and the right family before some of their personalities will shine."

"Are they getting any help for...what happened before?" Ariadne asked.

"Yes, we have an excellent child psychologist on hand who will continue to work with the children after they're matched with compatible families. It's one of our terms for adopting."

"Oh, good." Ariadne shot me a nervous smile, and I gave her one back. What were we supposed to do from here?

"I'll be with Miss Sandler while you two introduce yourselves." The staff member smiled encouragingly as she crossed toward the teacher on the other side of the room. "Let me know if you have any questions."

Ariadne glanced up at me. "Should we split up?"

"What? No, don't leave me."

Too late. She had already let go of my hand to visit a group of children playing some board game. "Hi, can I see what you guys are playing?"

I didn't want to loom over them, so I stood in place for some time before wandering to the reading nook. Some children had their noses buried in books, others openly stared as I walked past. It didn't bother me. My horns made lots of people look.

I made sure to look down every time I placed a step, knowing I would never be allowed to adopt a child if I stepped on one. The bookshelf was low, so I had to bend nearly in half to crouch. Eventually, I decided to just sit on the ground. Meet them at their level, Ariadne had said.

The carpet was soft and colorful underneath me as I scanned the book titles on the shelves. It wasn't like I was trying to ignore the children, I just didn't know how to approach them. Reading things was calming and allowed my brain to process information in a way that was familiar.

I pulled one book from the shelf and read the title. *Horns, Antlers, and Tusks, Oh My!* The subtitle went on to say, *Which animals have these and what are they for?*

A snort left my mouth as I flipped through it. I'd bet my new shirt they wouldn't have minotaurs or jackalopes in the book.

"That book is stupid," a small voice at my side said.

I looked up and did everything in my power to keep my jaw firmly shut.

A little girl had spoken, one with short, rounded horns peeking through waves of brown hair. I'd seen some people with tails or animal ears in their human forms but never horns like me.

"Because they don't have anyone that looks like us." I gestured to my own horns. "Right?"

The girl nodded. Her large eyes were a warm brown, and freckles dusted her nose and cheekbones.

"We'll just have to write our own book then," I said, returning the stupid one to the shelf. "Do you like to read?"

She nodded again, going quiet after I turned my attention to her. But she wasn't afraid, which was a good sign.

"I do too. What's your favorite book?"

"I'll show you!" She flopped onto the floor next to me and proceeded to dig through a stack. "This one." She shoved a book into my hands titled, *Where the Wild Things Are.*

"This looks interesting." I noted the large, horned creature on the cover. "What's it about?"

"It's about a boy who goes to a jungle and he finds the wild things, and they try to scare him, but he's not scared! Then he becomes king of the wild things!"

The girl's voice brightened, her eyes flashing excitedly as she told me the story. Clearly it was what did the trick to connect with her.

"That sounds like a really fun adventure," I said to her. "My name is Zeruhn. What's yours?"

"Cathy," she said softly.

"It's nice to meet you, Cathy. My wife over there is Ariadne." I pointed over my shoulder. "I think she'd like to hear the story too. Could you read it for both of us?"

"Yeah!" Cathy hugged the book to her chest, smiling widely. "Right now?"

"Sure. I'll be right back. Let me bring her over." I got up from the floor and realized as I went to Ariadne that the nerves fluttering in my chest were new, different. This wasn't anxiety but elation. Something about this just felt *right*. As right as they felt when I decided Ariadne was mine.

"Doe eyes," I said with a hand on her shoulder. "There's someone I'd like you to meet."

Ariadne's brows went up in surprise. "Oh? Who?"

I slid my fingers through hers and led her to the reading area. "Her name is Cathy, and she wants to read us a story."

Thank you so much for reading The Minotaur!

If you'd like more time with Ariadne and Zeruhn, maybe some monstery lovin' (wink), click here to sign up for my newsletter and receive a bonus scene!

* * *

THE HORNED GOD
COMING FALL 2023

He's a king of beasts, a god of wilderness.
I'm a queen of...spreadsheets?

The Horned God will be available for pre-order soon!

Sign up for the newsletter to get updates and more news!

A NOTE FROM THE AUTHOR

Hi! Thank you so much for reading The Minotaur, my first full-length novel as Sophie Ash. If this is the first book you've ever read by me, I appreciate you taking a chance on a new author and hope you enjoyed the story!

If you've read me as Crystal Ash (my reverse harem name), it's probably no surprise to you that I not only wrote a story based in mythology, but also a dystopian society. I can't seem to help myself these days, but I promise there will be some not-so-bleak worlds in upcoming books. The Horned God will (probably) be a more light-hearted read.

Also thank you for your continued support while I now straddle two pen names and genres!

If you'd like to discuss my books with fellow readers, plus get updates and sneak peaks to what's coming next, join my reader group, The Ash Coven on Facebook.

See you all in the next book! Until next time,

-Sophie

ALSO BY SOPHIE ASH

<u>**Gods and Myths**</u>

The Minotaur

The Horned God

<u>**Howling Death MC**</u>

Traitor Wolf (coming Spring 2023)

Interested in my reverse harem books?

Check out my catalog as Crystal Ash

www.ingramcontent.com/pod-product-compliance
Lightning Source LLC
Chambersburg PA
CBHW061220310726
48971CB00007B/1883